# O Eve

L T SAUNDERS

*For Mum*

First published in Great Britain in 2015
by L T Saunders

Copyright © 2015 L T Saunders

The moral right of L T Saunders to be identified as the
author of this work has been asserted in accordance with the
Copyright, Designs and Patents Act of 1988.

All rights reserved. No part of this work may be reproduced,
stored in an information retrieval system (other than for purposes
of review) or transmitted in any form or by any means, electronic,
mechanical, photocopying, recording or otherwise, without the
express permission of the publisher. Any person who does any
unauthorised act in relation to this publication may be liable to
criminal prosecution and civil claims for damages.

This book is sold subject to the condition that it shall not, by
way of trade or otherwise, be lent, resold, hired out, or otherwise
circulated without the publisher's prior consent in any form
of binding or cover other than that in which it is published
and without a similar condition including this condition being
imposed on the subsequent purchaser.

*O Eve* is a work of fiction. All incidents, dialogue and characters
are products of the author's imagination. Any resemblances to
persons living or dead are entirely coincidental.

A CIP catalogue record for this book is available
from the British Library.

Paperback ISBN 978-0-9934132-2-3

Also available as an ebook
mobi ISBN 978-0-9934132-3-0
epub ISBN 978-0-9934132-5-4

Cover design and typeset by
www.chandlerbookdesign.co.uk

Front cover images sourced through royalty free photo libraries:
© Davidevison | Dreamstime.com, © Valuavitaly | Dreamstime.com
© Pixattitude | Dreamstime.com

Printed in Great Britain by
4edge Limited

*I would like to thank John Chandler for yet another fantastic cover design and for his overall artistic input. I thank Frances Chandler for his excellent organisation, efficiency and guidance. Again, both have done first-class work in helping me get O Eve to print. I would like to thank Averill Buchanan for her editorial help. I would also like to thank Paula Charles at YPS for her invaluable help regarding publication minutiae.*

# 1

'YOU REALLY MUST PUT A SMILE on that not-half-bad face of yours,' I say to my reflection as I put my hair up in a ponytail. 'But how does one do that? How do you actually do that unless you're truly content?'

'What's that, love?' asks Mum, who has obviously just got out of bed and is waiting to use the bathroom.

'Nothing. Sorry, was just muttering to myself.'

'First sign of madness,' she says predictably.

'Isn't it just,' I say with a sigh opening the door. I have to edge around her such is the limited space on the landing. I also have the trial of avoiding the sight of her partially exposed breast peaking out of granny nightie. Resentment rises as I squeeze past my dishevelled mother and spills over into disgust when I get a whiff of her sweet-smelling night sweats.

I close my bedroom door filled full of guilt at having such emotions, but I'm powerless to free myself from their tenacious grip. I'm alas one of those unfortunate creatures who used to have better, and fight it as I might I can't help feeling hard done to when I remember the spacious house we once lived in. I can picture the rolling green hills and flowery embankments that surrounded our village in Shropshire where I used to live in what, of course, seemed like perpetual summer. Now we live in a cramped terraced house in a rundown part of Liverpool that seems to sink more every year by miserable year.

Sorry, I'm worse than usual today—it's not that bad. Perhaps it's because I didn't sleep too well. A police helicopter woke me up at midnight and kept me awake— more scallies being pursued in the BMW they robbed, I bet, and don't 'the bizzies' just love it.

I'm in telesales by the way. I work for Harrison's Office Supplies. It's a prestigious company keeping most of the North West in printing cartridges, but Lord knows, I should have done better. Trouble is, I went to a shiny comprehensive with a high turnover of staff, all of whom had diplomas you wouldn't wipe your bum on. They were woefully ill-equipped to tackle the large unruly classes I sat in. I practically had to educate myself. Thankfully Mum is a voracious reader and there were plenty of 'improving' books around at home. Of course it was poor compensation for the grammar school I was cheated out of. But then my mother had too much on her house-being-repossessed plate to bother about which shitty comp she was sending her only daughter to. And there was the not-so-small matter of my dad disappearing. But arrrrgh—enough!

I suppose I'm blessed not to be vegetating behind the checkout at Sainsbury's listening to *bip, bip, bip* all day, asking people if they want help with their packing while they dozily roll three items towards the till.

I know, too, that really I only have myself to blame *vis-à-vis* not doing better. I lack drive. I'd like to be something remarkable, like a hard-hitting documentary reporter- presenter for the BBC or Channel 4, lifting the lid on crap schooling and the under-funding of—of whatever, or a hawk-eyed journalist working on a critically acclaimed newspaper (*The Independent* maybe, or *The Observer*); or—I don't know, a PhD zoologist in charge of rare collections at Tonga Wildlife Park in whatever part of the sub-tropical world that is. But since I do absolutely nothing about it, apart from chasing dead-end links on the internet, I languish in telesales. I haven't found the get-up-and-go to leave Harrison's. I was meant to be promoted to sales rep with a car after a six-month review. How many years ago was that?

I stare inside my wardrobe feeling uninspired. I'm sure it must be a sign that things are getting worse with me. Lethargically I close its doors and turn to the chest of drawers. I open the deep drawer and pull out the usual stretchy woollen wear. Within a few minutes I'm ready.

Anyway, why don't you come with me to work? Hold on—I just need to say *ta raa to me ma*, as they say in this part of Liverpool (I'm terribly au fait with the lingo now). I must just avoid tripping over the boxes on the landing. Mum has a shopping problem and we're running out of space to put the 'bargains' she's snapped up. One box contains a barbecue set, which she bought because it was half price. She doesn't even like barbecued food. I'm pretty sure it will never make it to the patio. For God's sake, we never make it to the patio.

I think the barbecue was part of her muddled fantasy that we'd rent a holiday cottage in the Lake District (with her anticipated lottery winnings—another bad habit she's picked up). She also shelled out on walking boots and waterproofs in preparation for this venture, and more stuff besides. We did actually hire a car and spent a wet weekend—a day and a half really—in Cumbria. We got as far as walking the Claife Heights at Windermere, whereupon she declared that between the mud and exertion, rain and wind, all pleasure in such activity was 'quite destroyed'. We drove home without keeping our appointment with the letting agent, Mum declaring that she detested the sight of sheep and couldn't possibly holiday in a place 'strewn with wet, bleating mutton'. My mother doesn't make a lot of sense.

'Bye Mum. See you later,' I call out, having made it to the front door safely without injury to digit or limb (it's quite an obstacle course down here too).

'Oh, that you already? Bye love.'

I open the front door tentatively and peep outside. Good, the coast is clear. As I'm closing it, I hear a small voice say 'All right?' I turn and see little Tommy from next door. He's just coming out too. He's a pint-sized rough-arse but a real charmer. His mum's a peach—three kids to three different men and never worked a day in her puff. Oh, not that I'm judging. No, no, no. But let's just say she's no Erin Brockovich. Talk about idle! It wouldn't surprise me if she had bedsores on that fat arse of hers. She is what polite

BBC journalists laughingly call 'working class'—she is if sitting on your neighbour's wall all day can be counted as employment. Okay, now I'm judging.

'I'm going to breakfast club,' says Tommy enthusiastically. He smiles, showing a comical gap where his front teeth are missing. I'm about to ask if he got anything for his two teeth but stop myself—if there's no breakfast to be had what chance of a visit from the tooth fairy?

'You going to work?' he asks, sounding like he actually cares. I could weep at his earnest little face and the way he's blissfully unaware of the stains on his cheeks and tie. And that coat he's wearing—it can't possibly keep him warm. God, he's so pale and small, probably from undernourishment. From what I see, he lives on cola, cheap white bread, chicken nuggets and sausage rolls (I've seen what the Iceland van delivers).

'I'm off to work—yes,' I say, forcing myself to match him in cheerfulness.

The slam of a door and some loud swearing makes us turn. It's one of Tommy's brothers—half-brothers—I forget his name (he's the middle one; the eldest is hardly ever around). He's a few years older than Tommy, about thirteen I'd say. They look nothing alike. Tommy is fair, with a mass of dark-blond curls framing his dimple-cheeked face. His brother has black hair and, though good-looking, is already getting fat. Junk food, it would appear, has different effects on different people. Or perhaps it's the a mount you eat of it. He grunts disapprovingly at the sight of Tommy and me and passes by sullenly, swinging his arms in what I assume he thinks is a 'hard' manner. Tommy's smile disappears and he quickly follows his brother and doesn't say 'Bye', although there is a perceptible look of apology. Tommy's at that age where life hasn't knocked the hopefulness or niceness out of him. If only it could remain so, but his family, his schooling, his environment—everything—will work against him. Perhaps I'm wrong. It's certainly too depressing a thought to go to work on. Let's hope for better things for 'r' Tommy.

So, yes, come on. Come and queue with me at the smashed-in, canary-yellow bus shelter, which stands next to the smashed-in, buckling-in-the-middle silver phone box (which looks like it's made of tin foil). Come and furtively stare at the jumpy heroin addicts hanging about in wait for their morning fix—some on crutches because of contaminated 'gear'. I would say come look at the alcoholics too, but they seem to have moved on. What a macabre diversion they used to make: red-faced horrors thirstily glugging brandy at eight in the morning. But do come jostle with the darling school children. Let's not forget them. Such language one hears flowing from their cherubic gobs. Just watch the dog shit there. Yep, you're fine.

# 2

ON ENTERING MY PLACE OF WORK I see the usual slew of reps gathered around the coffee machine. Notice how most of the other girls ignore me, telesales being beneath their notice (a chronic case of the politics of minor difference). Then again, most of them do get to drive a big company car, swing a flash briefcase and rent an apartment in the heart of the swanky Liverpool docklands with The Three Graces, or the rolling hills of Wales across the Mersey, for a view. I grant that many of them manage whole areas of the North West while the likes of me sit on their backsides and cold-call for most of the day, each week, every month, all FUCKING YEAR. But do I care that they ignore me? *Nooooooo.* It is utter Yawnsville around them. Besides, I have Adam to talk to. He hasn't seen me come in yet.

I nod hello to the table of new telesales recruits. They're all keen as mustard. Give them a few weeks and they'll soon look as crushed and forlorn as me and Adam. For now they're all thrilled to be working for Harrison's because of its name.

But, oh now look who it is! I must tell you that one particular rep, practically management and something of a veteran in the firm, is just this moment particularly earnest in his salutation to moi. His name is Egremont. Naturally enough, he comes in for a great deal of stick thanks to his somewhat old-fashioned name. You could imagine him having a Victorian father called Obadiah or some such nonsense. In fact almost no one calls him Egremont; he invariably gets some silly play on it, like Eggy-bread or Egg-on-toast or something equally unfunny. Not that Egremont cares one straw for their ribbing; he acts as if they were using his proper name, which is something that stands in his favour as far as I'm concerned. He's a bookish, thoughtful individual with an air of understated superiority, and he's reverential towards me in a touching way, and everything the others aren't. Oh, and he was going to be a priest. For some reason I find that a turn on, that and his limousine-sized, dark-green, top-of-the-range Mercedes—ha!

Seriously—I like him.

See how pleased he is with my wave back? See how he keeps his eyes on me as I take off my coat? There—he's just dropped his head to end the greeting. The gesture is peculiarly chivalrous. Oh, I do like Egremont!

'Okay, okay everyone. Let's get this show on the road!' That's Mitchell, the BIG BOSS (top tosser) clapping his soft little hands together in order to get the reps' attention. He's monumentally bad tempered, not very bright and, unsurprisingly, a terrible manager, but he married into the firm—Mr Harrison's daughter no less—so there's no getting rid of him. And since the last male Harrison died off, Mitchell Harrison (yes, he took the name) rules the roost.

He's behind the recent push for new publicity. He's just opened a hotel on the docks too: The Harrison Plaza. It has a huge H stuck on the top like some sort of cross or Christmas fairy (except this H rotates). Mitchell's face and voice hasn't been off the TV and radio publicising it—only local stuff, but the hicks in here think it's a big deal, and needless to say so does he. He never stops going on about 'me hotel'. He's originally from somewhere down south; the Pearly King is never too far away when he pronounces some words, especially ones beginning with 'h'. 'Hotel' becomes *ohtel* and Harrison's *Aaarrison's*. Adam and I find it highly amusing and mimic him regularly when we dare. Oh, there's Egremont's last little smile for me before he's herded into the brightly lit torture chamber—sorry, meeting room.

'Ready to go kill 'em kiddo?' asks my immediate boss, Laetitia (telesales manager) as I sit down opposite her. She's apparently named after her grandmother who was French Lebanese, Hawaiian—or some bloody thing.

'Sure am,' I say, all gung-ho, trying to look neither amused nor horrified at Laetitia's headgear. She's wearing something that resembles a tiara-cum-fan smack on the top of her head. It's supporting a hillock of jet-black hair and is not very well done. I guess it's meant to complement the off-the-shoulder red gipsy top. She's got a garish Spanish theme going on today (she's invariably some kind of fashion explosion), and at the risk of sounding bitchy (okay, bitch*ier*), the cat-scratched raw-sausage arms bursting out of the comely frills are doing nothing to soften the effect.

She winks and beams a fat-toothed lipstick-stained smile at me (she's got terrible piano-key veneers). Throughout the day I'll catch her glistening tongue doing a full lickity-lick of her mouth Scooby style—DISGUSTING! Why can't she keep that organ in her face?

'You out at the weekend, kiddo?' she asks with raised eyebrows and a saucy smile.

'Nope, just stayed in,' I say, switching on my computer.

'Can't take the pace, eh?' she replies, shaking her head slowly and sucking in her mouth, pitying me for the lamentable state of my social life.

I don't want to ask about hers, but as she'll only volunteer the information piecemeal throughout the course of the morning, I might as well get it over with. It's the same scenario every morning.

'You out then?' I ask with fake enthusiasm.

'Sure was,' she says brightening. 'Me and some kiddos hit Garlands on Saturday. We had a …'

I watch my antiquated computer flicker into life, letting Laetitia's version of events evaporate in the ether (she probably didn't go out at all). As long as I just smile and nod now and then she's satisfied.

Laetitia, by the way, has been in television—or so she says. Adam and I can't find any evidence of this, leading us to the conclusion that the woman is a total fantasist. Her tweets suggest that she's nothing but a celebrity stalker. So I guess I should rephrase that and say, Laetitia HAS NOT BEEN in television. But this is no use. I had better get some work done.

God, the tedium of it all. Everyone dreads being called by sales. They're happy with their current suppliers.

They have enough shit to deal with without being pestered by someone flogging paperclips. It's ignoble, humiliating, *pointless*. Harrison's loses as many customers as it gains. But such is the exhausting choppy tide I swim against, and the sooner I'm dragged to the dry, calm shore the better. Jesus, that was an appalling analogy.

'*Eeeve!*'

'Adam. Sorry, I was miles away,' I say, throwing him a warm smile.

'Too right you was.' He slides his chair next to mine and leans in. After casting a look at Laetitia, he says, 'What's with Jennifer fucking Lopez?' I laugh, but only a little.

'Wassup?'

'Oh the usual life-isn't-worth-living-might-as-well-stick-my-head-in-a-gas-oven feeling,' I say, staring at him with jokey mad eyes.

He laughs and tuts at me, sliding his chair back to his desk to answer his phone. I suddenly notice that Laetitia is regarding me with particular interest. I raise my eyebrows in a *yes-what-is-it?* expression. She smiles displaying her worse-than-ever stained gnashers. She's forever reapplying her lipstick, which she pulls out of a drawer bursting with make-up smudged junk. I imagine her just having eaten something small and alive.

'What's up? Tired kiddo?' she asks.

'A little,' I reply in a brighter voice, scolding myself for being so transparent.

'Shall I get you a coffee?' she asks in a concerned voice. I raise my eyebrows again—Laetitia offering to fetch coffee, for me? Adam looks at me and we exchange baffled glances.

I have to say, at this point, that I do wish people would stop with all this '*a* coffee'. A cup of coffee, yes, or some coffee, but not *a* coffee. Pedantic perhaps, but it really gets on my tits. People are even saying 'a tea' these days! Jesus, it has to be the linguistic equivalent of holding your knife like a pen.

'Hey Laetitia, that smacks of favouritism,' says Adam sounding more annoyed than he can possibly be.

'Cool it, Adam. I'll make for you too,' she says, getting to her feet (with some effort). A few of the close-sitting telesales look hopefully at Laetitia but she ignores them.

'Thanks Laetitia. I'd love some coffee,' I reply, taking out my first calling-card. We're supposed to make an average of fifty cold-calls a day. I'm lucky if I make twenty. Sometimes it's ten. On Friday it was five! We haven't gone digital with regard to how we monitor our cold-calls and follow-up calls, and so we keep each client's info on a card in a box. Harrison's is rather stuck in the past—so much so that it's frowned upon for women to wear trousers here!

I don't dare look at Adam right now. He'd only give me the eye about Laetitia's teeth. Adam's been getting increasingly reckless with his contempt for her. Once or twice it's been a close call—she's eye-balled the two of us with knitted brow on several occasions. I do actually like her, despite my mean mouth. And if Adam knew what I thought about Egremont (Eggers, Egg-salted) no doubt I too would cop a good share of his derision.

'No probs,' says Laetitia struggling to release the hem of her skirt from under the wheel of her chair. I notice she's covered in cat hairs. Lucky none of us in her immediate vicinity has an allergy to them.

'Have you seen the fucking mouth on Senorita?' whispers Adam when she's gone. As I turn his face is practically touching mine. This is quite a common occurrence—our faces being in close proximity because of whispering—but this time he seems to pull back a little. Nah, it's probably me. I mean, I don't think he pulled away.

'I know. I fancied she'd been nibbling on a hamster,' I say, smiling.

Adam grins broadly. 'More like some poor bastard's scrotum.'

'Errrrh, Adam.'

'Can't you just see it—her with Mitchell in her gob?' He presses his tongue against the inside of his mouth.

By the way, as well as being a bullying tosser and married, Mitchell is also a male slut. You should have seen him on the opening night of The *Aaarrison* Plaza. He had a bevy of beauties around him like he was Hugh Hefner (okay not so old). They were all over him like he was some sort of sex god. But get this; he's reputed to be terrible in bed. Our source is Laetitia who's a female slut and proud of it. She once told Adam and me that she likes to use male escorts. Adam and I sat open-mouthed for a good ten minutes after she'd said matter-of-factly, 'When I'm asking for a "long black" I'm not always ordering coffee, kiddos.' I found the comment funny, but Adam was quite disgusted, which surprised me. Interestingly, Mrs Harrison wasn't at the opening night of The *Aaarrison* Plaza; nor is she ever here. She's something of a mystery woman. She's reputed to be a hot-shot wheeler-dealer running companies out in Malaysia. I reckon she can't be that business savvy if she's left the Artful Dodger in charge of the family assets—husband or not. But anyway…

'But probably even Mitchell wouldn't touch it.' 'Touch what?' I ask, confused.

'*Hir*,' he says with exasperation, nodding in Laetitia's direction.

'Mitchell would touch anything that would let him,' I say, wondering at Adam's increased abhorrence of Laetitia. It can't be because of her apparent like of gigolos because we both agreed, on reflection, that she had to be joking. Perhaps she's just part of Adam's growing intolerance for everything connected with Harrison's. I'm thinking again about when our faces almost touched just then and his momentary pulling back. Could he be getting tired of our friendship too? No, now I'm being ridiculous, or paranoid or—I don't know what. Adam's cool with me, but there *is* something on his mind today—I can tell.

I should point out, if you haven't already noticed, that political correctness has bypassed Harrison's. Mitchell acts like The Wolf of Wall Street around this place, dick or no dick, or whatever his problem is in the bedroom. I swear, no one would raise an eyebrow if he had a naked hooker over his desk while another felched his arse through a golden straw. In fact, if you walked in on that he'd probably pass you the figures you were after without even looking up.

'That's true,' says Adam, sucking in air. I look at him, having forgotten for a moment what we were talking about. Oh yes, Laetitia gobbling off Mitchell. We need to change the subject.

'We shouldn't be so mean about her, especially when

she's making the coffee.' I'm trying to strike the right balance between sincerity and persuasion here.

'Yeah, and what's all that about? It's about as strange as that garb she's wearing, which even by her standards is pretty fucking skanky.' He leans back and stretches. A moment later he runs both hands through his hair. When he catches me looking at him, he holds my stare and provocatively wets his lips, lowering his eyelids at the same time. He's going to have one of his joke porno moments, which he does whenever he gets the chance because of the reaction it gets from me.

And perhaps you're wondering whether there's any attraction between me and Adam. There's none whatsoever. He thinks as little of me in that way as I do of him. From the moment we sussed we were two like-minded losers thrown together in this disgrace of a place, we were all the happier for knowing that our comradery existed without the messy business of lust. When our eyes meet the only thing that registers is respect, which is a great thing if you can find it.

He's subtly caressing his nipples now. Oh! He's adding sound to this one.

'Arrrrrrrh,' he groans.

I'm starting to laugh already.

'Harrrrrrrrrrh,' he moans, cranking it up. It is very funny.

'Hey, stop all that cackling and yacketee-yacking, and get back to bloody work. How many calls have you made this morning, Evelyn? As for you Adam, you look like a fucking gay boy. Now knock it off the both of you or I'll dock your pay.'

That's Mitchell again—he's doing his signature menacing walk-through-the-office, disposable glass water bottle in hand (he's rarely without one, and it's always Evian – they do quite a range). He's obviously stepped out of the meeting. Perhaps he forgot some instrument of torture. It amazes me that he notices us at all. The reps continually look over with surprise when Mitchell 'interacts' with telesales. I'm sure they feel we should be shut up out of sight in some closet somewhere instead of occupying centre stage in front of the managers' offices. Actually, our close proximity is probably so he can exercise nine-to-five control over telesales. He can watch us all day long from the comfort of his executive chair, which he does do. I've often looked up to see him staring darkly our way. Consequently we've adapted the art of looking busy while really just gossiping. The calling cards are one of our props.

'Mincing little wanker,' sneers Adam, pulling his calling-card box toward him. I throw him a sly smile. 'Calling me gay! If anyone wants to take it up the shit shoot it's him.'

'Adam!' I say, astonished. He shrugs. 'How long have we known each other?—how long have we known him?' I nod toward Mitchell.

'Two years? Maybe three?' he says vaguely, looking like he couldn't care less.

'Five years. It's been five long fucking years in this dead-end. We were sent here out of the same job centre—remember?—on the same frigging day.' Adam looks at me with an intense expression I can't interpret. 'And now you've decided that Mitchell's gay?'

'Well, look at that walk. He's got more wiggle on than Marilyn Monroe.'

Now he mentions it, Mitchell's walk is rather effeminate. But no, I'm not having this. 'It's an impossibility. Gay men are typically sharp, intelligent, funny, fun to be around and *nice*—remarkably human on the whole.'

'He'll be an exception to the rule,' says Adam with a smile playing about his lips.

'I'll grant you the walk, but Mitchell's not gay,' I whisper. 'Hmmmm,' is all I get by way of reply. A moment later, he mouths, 'Pub for lunch?' (I'm pretty good at lip-reading him now). I nod eagerly, instantly pushing Mitchell's 'sweet cheeks' to the back of my mind. 'Nice one,' he mouths back and takes out another calling-card.

Before either of us has a chance to make a call our phones ring simultaneously. With matching expressions of here-we-go exasperation, we both pick up.

'Morning—Harrison's—Telesales—Eve speaking—How may I help you?' I sing in an efficient and enthusiastic voice. Whatever else, I have to avoid the brain-dead automated variety of greeting. I hate that we have to say so much on picking up but Mitchell decreed the script. 'Morning—Harrison's' used to be enough before he took over. Honestly, the noise from the telesales desks because of our verbose 'hello' makes our area sound like an overcrowded aviary for particularly squawky birds.

'Yes, hello. I'm calling on behalf of Geoff Barry—of Barry, Semple and Moore,' drones a familiar female voice down the line. This account is a recent convert of mine and she's been ordering more and more since switching to our company.

'Hi, Sharon,' I chirrup, hoping to impress her by having remembered her name. I also nod thanks to Laetitia who has just placed a mug of good-smelling coffee on my desk. She wrinkles her nose at me affectionately, admiringly. My eyes widen. What can it all mean? Haven't time to dwell—Sharon ...

'And how can I help you this morning, Sharon?' I tap into the Barry, Semple and Moore account on the computer.

'Well, the thing is'—I sense trouble—'Mr Barry isn't happy with his order.'

Shit.

'Oh no? What's the problem?' I scan the account.

'Well, one thing—we ordered ten bottles of Tipp-Ex, and ten boxes have come.' I see the obviously wrong order plain enough on the screen.

'Sorry about that, Sharon. I'll have them picked up today, and I'm refunding you as I speak'. I must have mistakenly added a nought to the order!

'It's not just the Tipp-Ex.'

'Oh?'

'Mr Barry ordered some stencils, but the ones that came were the wrong size. They don't fit the screens.'

Okay, I'm puzzled. I don't remember Sharon ordering any stencils. Oh shit—Oh no—Mitchell! There they are—his initials on the screen in front of me. Mitchell took the order. The fucking moron has gone and done it again.

He has this thing for taking our calls when we're at lunch and Laetitia can't pick up. He probably does it to make sure it's not a personal call but then he goes and takes a half-assed order. And just try to complain—he'll rocket-launch a sarcastic bomb at you.

'Sharon, I'm really sorry about this. A colleague of mine took the order.' We're not allowed to discuss Herr Mitchell with customers.

'But we should be able to trust all of you to take the orders.'

I sneer. Shazza is beginning to enjoy this—I can hear it in her voice. 'Yes, you're absolutely right, of course, but it would be better if you dealt with me—'

'What if you're not there? If I'm at me most busiest then I can't keep on ringing *you.*'

God, how unpleasant she's becoming. 'I'm generally around. But if Adam or Laetitia don't pick up the phone, it might be best just to call back.'

'How should I know who I'm talking to?'

'They usually say their name,' I say encouragingly.

'I haven't got time for all that.'

'Okay, I hear you. Now let's get your stencils sorted,' I say breezily, trying to disguise my annoyance. 'Now, what size are the screens?' I flick through the catalogue on my desk as Sharon, in her most fed-up tone, gives the details. Eventually, coffee completely cold, I get to put down the phone on Shazza. It rings on contact. 'Morning—Harrison's—Telesales—Eve speaking—How may I help you?' I'm straining to keep the irritation out of my voice (dear God, it's only my second call of the day). I notice Laetitia regarding me again with great interest. Normally she's totally absorbed in making her own calls or going round monitoring the newbies. But for some reason she's studying me. Odd! I smile and turn my attention back to my call.

'Oh, good morning,' says a posh croaky voice. Ah no, it's the old timewaster. He gets on for hours and orders jack shit. 'I'd like some information about certain products we spoke about last week …'

Jesus. We're supposed to be selling, not trawling through the catalogue and getting cross-eyed staring at the products on the screen. 'Do you have the catalogue in front of you, dear?' he asks. I catch Adam's eye momentarily; he blows a teasing kiss.

Oh, oh, there's Egremont. He's heading out of the office. And what a look he shot me! It's common knowledge, by the way—perhaps I should have said before—that 'Eggy-bread' fancies me. It's the other 'great' joke of the office besides his nicknames. It's also widely believed that I wouldn't touch 'Egg-regious' with a twenty-foot barge pole, me being young and gorgeous an' all. Ha—if only they knew!

The other reason they think it's impossible that I could be interested in 'Egg-salted' is because he's considered an oddity. They think he's deeply religious (which he isn't), and they believe that because he's heavily involved in charitable works (hospital visiting and the like) he must be a do-gooding creepy Jesus freak. The creepy bit probably has something to do with the fact the Egremont exudes a kind of beatific piety that makes their hard hearts recoil. To the reps, his quiet shy demeanour when they make fun of his name, and his passive acceptance of Mitchell's assaults on his competence make him a loser. I see nothing but gentle strength and selfless kindness. He doesn't drink either, which is probably reason enough on its own to be considered strange round here.

Mitchell's attacks on Egremont can be brutal though, and sadly, Egremont cops more than his fair share of them because of his mild nature. It's stomach-churning to watch and listen to—at least for me; the reps look on with glee at the entertainment. Yet Egremont doesn't even say, 'Do you think we could take this somewhere else?' when Mitchell starts on him. At times I half expect Mitchell to swipe 'Eggers' across the face with the back of his hand. Seriously, the guy's a sadistic psycho. He's reason alone to get out of this place. You know, one day I hope Egremont does snap and knock Mitchell's ugly head off.

Egremont doesn't cower at Mitchell's feet, however. He merely takes the tongue-lashing in the biblical cheek-turning fashion, and then goes on his way—a little troubled, yes, but, well, there's dignity in his actions. So where some see a spineless coward, I see the bigger man. Others have walked out or been sacked after letting fly at Mitchell. Still, one day, like I said, I'd love Egremont to lose it and floor that mouth-on-a-stick to the ground. Physically Egremont is strong enough. That's another thing I love about him—his body. It's lean and muscly. He has large hands too, which means he's probably well-endowed!

As you can see, I'm really into Egremont. Lately it's given way to something more—it's made me—never mind. I have my own private pun on his name—it's *Eg*stasy. Okay, not original, but believe me, it's apt. These days when he comes close to me I feel something stirring inside, something I haven't felt in years—desire.

I like to imagine Egremont's home life. He lives alone, I know. I picture him sitting in front of a log fire, a kettle singing on the stove. He has a large paper unfolded in front of him, probably *The Telegraph*, as he's a tad conservative—in a nice old-fashioned way: more interested in the test-match results than how many immigrants are taking up hospital beds. Perhaps he even takes a nip of single malt before climbing the wooden hill at night—I can't quite accept that he's totally teetotal.

What's more, I know that Egremont knows I like him even though others—not even Adam—have a clue. Now that's intelligence. Oh yes, more and more I want to know that man.

There's something magical between us too (sorry, I can't stop thinking about him just now). When our eyes meet in the office I find myself brightening, and it's as if he's pouring strength into me. It's pure phototropism. Do you know it? *The movement of an organism in response to the stimulus of light.* I respond to some heliotropic stimulus from Egremont. I'm the flower and he's the sun.

You know what? I'm going to make him ... marry me.

# 3

Adam and I descend the stairs of Harrison's on light feet, that glorious hour once again upon us—the sweet release from bondage. And it's only Monday! Adam links his arm in mine.

It crosses my mind to tell Adam about Mitchell's cock-up with my order, but his reaction would probably be explosive and I want a relaxing drink. Mitchell seriously messed up a printing order of Adam's a few weeks ago; I think he's lost the account altogether now. Better not risk taking him back there.

I've mentioned it to Laetitia and asked her to try to put a stop to Mitchell picking up our phones. By the look on her face she's been a victim too. But as he's the head honcho, all hopes are slim. It's most definitely Mitchell's way or the highway.

A convoy of large white trailers, with 'BBC' in gigantic print on them pass by. Adam looks on with envy. This area of the city centre is a popular spot for filming because of the architecture, regardless of where the film is supposed to be set. Georgian-pillared houses, granite-stone court-houses, cobbled streets, old-world pubs and churches abound. The majestic Liver Buildings are just across the way too. When you think Sherlock Holmes is walking to an opium den in Soho, chances are it's a place around here. It's a world away from where Mum and I live, though it isn't twenty minutes by bus. It's funny because street and place names around here ape those of London. Covent Garden, Cheapside, Whitechapel and Islington are all within a stone's throw and where a lot of the filming is done. It must have tried to be a mini-me capital at one time.

'I'll have to see if there's any extras work going,' Adam says, craning his head to see where the vans park up. The convoy disappears into Water Street. 'Actually, maybe I won't ask because I'll be alright for a while.'

'Why alright?'

'I'll tell you in a minute. After you, girl,' he says, pushing open the old saloon door of Vern's pub. 'What you drinking, babe?'

'Glass of red, please.' I look around with satisfaction at the animated clientele. As always, the place is busy—or as Adam would say, *buzzun*. It has a courtyard, so mercifully the smoking ban hasn't diminished its popularity, or atmosphere—the smoke wafts in, maintaining the familiar warm smoky haze.

The regulars are mostly smart legal professionals and journalists, some politicians too; the type of men Mum wishes I'd go out with. Some of them are not so smart—greasy hair and suit to match. But what's the betting that if I brought one of those home Mum would say, 'He'll clean up.' Occasionally we get some famous (or semi-famous) actors frequenting the place, such as those who'll be utilising the BBC trailers and hanging around in period costume. I think this is why Adam particularly likes this pub, or is that a *no shit, Sherlock* observation?

At least there's no one in here from Harrison's. Mitchell makes no secret of his disapproval of lunchtime indulgence (he disapproves of alcohol full stop, and although he likes to party and be seen out, he's usually on designer Evian). Adam and I have escaped his radar so far, no doubt because we're not sales reps getting behind the wheel of one of his precious company cars.

'Grab them seats, Eve,' shouts Adam from the bar, gesturing toward a table at the back that is just being vacated. I quickly make for it. Vern's is one of those places that maintains its old-fashioned air, like some of the London pubs (the ones that aren't chains). It has leather House of Commons seats, ancient dark-wood tables, semi-frosted embossed windows and old photographs of the city before it became crawling with sameness. It has plants too, which I love.

'Thanks,' I say, squeezing past the couple leaving in a bid to head off the competition. They smile and nod, perfectly understanding my gratitude and pushiness. I sit down with a triumphal smile and take off my coat, avoiding the disappointed looks of the thwarted bystanders.

I can whiff steak. I look to my left. Yes, there are two—barristers, I'd say, tucking into rib-eyes. That's another thing about Vern's: it has a chef who cooks food from scratch, as opposed to heating up frozen rot. Also, the general smell of the place appeals, and I don't mean stale booze and fags. It's kind of musty, almost like a church, because it's fitted out with natural materials. The floor isn't carpeted, it's slate; the bar's real marble too. I love to run my palm over its chilly surface. And sometimes—

I can't go on because—is that them? A suit in front of me moves aside and I see it *is* them. Oh, what terrible admissions I will have to make to you now, for 'tis the ski-resort couple. She's clocked me already. And her look! Her eyes darted, as if she was saying, 'You staring at us again?' Not that she dislikes it; she's not of the prickly Liverpudlian *Ooh-the-fucka-you-luckun-a'?* species. Not at all.

I call them the ski-resort couple because I can never look at them without imagining snowboards and alpine scenery, and my suspicions were confirmed a month ago when I saw them, loaded down with skiing paraphernalia, getting into the back of a Land Rover not five yards from here. I was walking to the bus stop from work. It was dark and snowing hard, that wonderfully fat snow you see falling in Russian films. Their little scene was lit by one of the Victorian lamps that line the boulevard here. Observing them was like looking into a snow-globe, so happy and idyllic were they. I think it was the end of my first day back to work after Christmas. I was doubly depressed by knowing they must have been going somewhere for New Year. My New Year's celebration highlight was watching The Graham Norton Show. As good as it was, it was no compensation for fireworks and glühwein around an inglenook fireplace with a town clock striking in the New Year.

But where was I? Oh yes, still talking about them! I see they've been reading together again, but their books are now lying idle on the low table in front of them (this place is a bit of a library-cum-reading room too).

She looks at me again across the pub without any embarrassment (she's one of these people who can comfortably look through you as if you don't exist, all the while eyeing you intimately). Her look of 'I hope you're drooling with jealousy at this cosy scene' is just perceptible. She and her ridiculously handsome man are a love-struck couple who seem independently wealthy—tall, handsome, rich, and in love. Yes, to an extent, I am drooling with jealousy at the sight of them cosying up on the Chesterfield. She has a deluxe accent too—we've sat in close proximity before—and every word uttered seems to be boastful. He has too, but it doesn't have the same degree of listen-to-me about it. Oh, how to describe the way she talks—it's smiley and fruity and y-wordy: 'tricky' instead of 'difficult', 'beastly' instead of 'shit', that kind of thing—and 'masses' instead of 'loads' (slightly different, not being y-wordy, but you get what I mean).

Her voice says: 'I'm so comfortable, and unlike you, I have happy wealthy parents who are still together. And I have a great big home in Bigbuckshire that has a back garden the size of Wales. I sleep in the bedroom I've known all my life, which is still decorated with the hand-painted Beatrix Potter wallpaper. I look in your direction now because you look unhappy and pathetic.'

She's a first-class chick-lit protagonist—legs like a giraffe and thick, wavy blonde hair down her back, when it's not swept back from the requisite low forehead into a fat bouncy pony tail. Yes, I see her a lot.

Seeing him run a hand down her leg I suddenly see them in bed together. He would be playful, pulling her to him when she's half asleep (he's been watching her for hours in between reading his book). He would say, 'Little piggy, little piggy, let me in'; she would stir and give him an irresistible sleepy smile, and say, 'Not by the hair of my chinny chin chin.' Then he would envelop her, whispering. 'Then I'll have to huff and puff and blow my way in', and he'd growl, and she'd squeal with delight, and they'd—

'Fucking hell, it's a bastard trying to get served in here today,' says Adam sitting down next to me in a huff.

I sigh at his bathetic interruption (yes with a 'b'). He places the drinks on the table and I continue to stare furtively at the ski-resort couple. I put me and Egremont in their place, not here, but tucked away in some exclusive country pub. We're in the snug in front of a fire, our cheeks rosy from its heat. Egremont is playfully whispering sweet nothings in my ear while looking at me longingly. We're laughing together just like the ski-resort over the little idiocies of our day.

'You're not listening to me.'

'Sorry, Adam, what were you saying?' I wrench my gaze away from them.

He doesn't answer and instead stares at the place where I've been engrossed. This time I decide to come clean. 'You know, I have the unhealthiest envy of those two.'

'What? You fancy *him*?' Adam explodes. '*Che-Gue-fuckin-vara*? You are fucking shitting me. There should be a sign on the door: No Mancs, no Southerners and definitely no fucking students.'

I stare at him, wondering if he heard me right.

'Fancy him?' I repeat. 'Who said anything about fancying him?' When Adam doesn't respond, I carry on: 'No Mancs, no Southerners and no students? What, dear boy, are you talking about?'

'Those two students.' He nods in the direction of the ski-resort couple. 'If you mean those posh gits playing footsie with each other.'

'What makes you say they're students?'

'Oh please.'

'Adam,' I laugh, astonished. 'What are you getting upset about?'

'You envying students. Thought you had more sense.'

'Jee. It was a passing remark. Wish I'd kept my mouth shut,' I say taking a drink and beginning to wish we hadn't come out. But it's bugging me too much. I ask him again why he thinks they're students.

'They're always reading; they wear stupid clothes and they have no fucking job,' he growls. 'Like I say, should be a sign on the door saying, No Mancs, no Southerners and definitely no fucking students.

'Complete with the word fucking?'

He doesn't answer but merely sneers, although there is a trace of a smile now. He lifts his pint, shaking his head. 'Come on, Eve, you're not serious. I mean *him*. He looks like he changes his clothes as often as Noddy. And the greasy head on it—middle-class tosser. Yeah, I can just see you and him reading out loud for all the fucking world to have to listen to. *Call me fucking Ishmael* and all that bollocks.'

'Me and him? Adam, I think you've—'

'Can it, they're looking over.' I pick up my wine hiding a smile (clearly he's as envious as I am). What he says is true. They do read out loud to each other sometimes, and there is a look of the Che Guevara about him. But come to think of it, Adam sometimes reads aloud and he looks more like Che than that guy.

'Reading out loud in a public place? That's rich coming from you.' I'm remembering the many times he has when he wanted me to appreciate some line or other from a play or novel he was into.

'Yeah well, that's different. I'm not showing off.' He blows out a contemptuous snort and looks in the opposite direction of the ski-resort couple.

'You said you had something to tell me,' I remind him.

We need a change of subject.

'I had an audition for that play,' he says with a smile that almost overtakes his face.

'You *didn't*.' I actually don't have a clue which play he's talking about but I'll wing it.

'Oh, I did babe, and what's more, I GOT THE PART.'

'You've got a part in a play?'

He nods vigorously.

'Wow, well done. Finally, Adam, finally.'

'I know, girl. It's been a long time coming. We start rehearsals Monday.'

'Monday? You mean in the evening?'

'No, honey. I mean Monday morning.'

I feel my cheeks getting hot. I want to say, 'But what

about *us*, what about—' How stupid of me. I take a deep breath and with my brightest smile I say, "Well, this calls for a celebration. A large brandy, *mate*?'

'Don't mind if I do, *babe*.'

But it's with heavy heart and heavy legs that I make for the bar. The office without Adam—unthinkable.

In my distracted state, I'm failing to catch a barman's eye. And if one more person pushes in I'll karate chop the bastard in the neck. I know they say the English are a nation of alcoholics, but this rugby scrum is taking the piss. Here's another one trying to get in; I can feel myself being edged aside.

'Excu—,' but I don't finish. It's the male half of the ski-resort couple.

He smiles apologetically and moves aside. Then he turns. For the briefest of moments I think he's going to address me.

'Tilly, do you want water?' he says across the top of my head.

Evidently *Tilly* does because he's mouthing 'Sparkling or still?' Naturally she would balance her wine with water. One needs a clear head TO DO NOTHING. Tilly? *Tilly*? What's that short for? Til—Tilla—Atilla the Hun. No wait. I know it—it's Matilda. Yes, it has to be. Oh, now I hate you even more. Oh, a pox on your perfect little world and your cutesy, babyfied, y-wordy name. I need a cigarette.

'I was beginning to think you'd died,' says Adam, setting his empty pint down.

'Only metaphorically,' I reply, placing the two large brandies on the table.

'What?' he asks, frowning.

'Never mind.' I sit down and pick up my glass. 'A toast to your bright future. My friend, the thespian.' I raise my drink to him. Adam does the same and then we both take a gulp. Seconds later we're both wincing. 'So, you finally did it!' I say, once I get my voice back.

'I finally did it,' he replies and sighs with immense satisfaction.

'You must be really thrilled. What's the name of the play again?'

'*Jill's House*. I play the role of Jack, Jill's handsome and droll—though socially inept—boyfriend.'

'Playing yourself then?—bar the wit and the looks.' I smile. He puts his hand to his chest as if wounded. 'Jack and Jill. How cute. Where's it on?'

'The Everyman,' he says casually without looking at me.

'You're playing a lead role in a play at the *Everyman*?'

Adam looks at me, grinning broadly. 'I can't quite believe it myself, but so it is.'

'You've told Laetitia, I take it?'

His smile disappears. 'No. What makes you say that?'

'Because she seems to have been laughing at me all morning. As soon as you told me it made sense—she's been *ha, ha haaring* at me.'

'Don't talk soft. She wouldn't do that—even if she did know, which she doesn't.'

'So you haven't told her?' 'No!'

'Will you tell her this afternoon?' I ask, trying unsuccessfully to keep the sadness out of my voice.

'No, I'll just turn up late and throw sickies till they fire me.'

'So, you're still coming to work?' I say, brightening.

'Too right. I need the money, babe.'

I raise my glass to him again.

'Drinking brandy at lunch time,' he says, chinking my glass. 'What a couple of lushes we are, girl.'

'I know! Good isn't it?'

'Not bad, I have to say, although Christ only knows how we'll get through the afternoon.'

'What does it matter? All we do is answer complaints and trawl through the catalogue. We should have somebody keying in our orders, like the reps have. How are we supposed to drum up new business when—' I stop myself. 'Like you could care anymore.'

'Indubitably,' he says with mock seriousness. 'Yes, we *ac-tors* care naught for the work-a-day minutiae of plebeian thraldom.'

I stare at him in astonishment. He sounded like Sir John Gielgud. 'And I thought you could only do Scouse mouse,' I say before I can think better of it.

'Me *liddle see-cress*, honey.' He's doing an exaggerated Scouse accent.

'Come on, let's go outside for a fag.' I get up and put my coat on the table to mark our territory.

'Right, and we need to order some scran,' he says, following me.

'You know, you should do more of the RP accent. It suits you. It would probably open up a hell of a lot more doors too.'

'Would it now?' he replies sarcastically.

'Don't say it like that—it *indubitably* would.'

'Just get outside.' He pushes me playfully.

The ski-resort couple, or rather Tilly, gives me more cause for disquiet as I'm heading for the courtyard. She looks straight at me but this time she smirks. Her expression seems to say, 'Off you go, little wage-slave. Have one last taste of freedom and leave me in peace with my delicious boyfriend. We shall fall asleep in front of a fire this afternoon while you're gazing out of the office thinking of the life you'll never have.' As I have no proof that these are indeed her thoughts I refrain from thumping her.

\* \* \*

When we get back to the office telesales is in full flow. Adam gives a boozy belch and heads to the lav. Laetitia is cooing down the phone, doubtless conning some gullible wretch into replacing his perfectly good office chairs with ours. She'll be seducing the sucker into believing her pseudo-scientific rot about the dangers of back injury due to non-ergonomically designed seating. The unique selling point of our chairs, you must understand, is that they come with a guarantee (a ropey one) claiming all but everlasting life. She winks at me when I sit down, giving me the thumbs up after she's pointed at her phone. Yep, she's got the deal. A few seats to my right I hear Colin *not* closing on yet another cold-call. Colin, despite being with Harrison's for as long as Adam and I have, is an utterly useless salesman. He hasn't been fired because there's enough business to keep him busy taking orders. Plus he grovels to Mitchell like you wouldn't believe. I smile when I hear Colin saying to a newbie, 'Got blown out again.' There are quite a few new faces now in telesales (we have a high turnover of staff). The guy who Colin's currently complaining to lifts his eyebrows with overstrained sympathy. He's probably wondering how he can wangle a seat somewhere else.

'Didn't win the lottery again,' says another telesales.

The only conversation that animates anyone around our desks is the Lotto, that and scratch cards. Someone comes in selling them and everyone says, '*Givvus one 'o them, mace*'. And the price of them! I can see some know themselves to be sucked-in fools, but others seem oblivious. How I hate the place when there's a Lotto rollover: '*See ya Mon-dee*', '*Norrif me number's come up!*' Then all the bantering starts about who would still bother coming in to work, and who would make straight for Las Vegas.

A similar conversation is now taking place with Colin taking centre stage. His choice of destination is Jamaica. It must be because he's so cool. Not. Adam rolls his eyes as he sits down. We sit together at the head of the telesales desks. There's only room for three of us because Laetitia takes up two desks with all her files and junk. I wish we were in our old spot by the vast windows. I miss the view of the skyline and the Mersey. I could lose myself in thought for hours watching the boats coming in and out of the channel. Adam often said 'Penny for them?' while I was dreaming of where those boats were going and wishing I was on one.

Now Colin's back on the phone trying to sell and he's already asking all the wrong lead-in questions. For some reason, at every training session given by Laetitia, Colin never ceases to make a fool of himself by not being able to get his head around the difference between a 'selling point' and a 'feature'. Laetitia and I—even Adam—have tried and tried to instil in him that a 'selling point' means what the product will do for the customer, like save them time or money, while a 'feature' is merely concerned with appearance, but it's no use. His head implodes every time the two concepts are mentioned. With the distinction between 'open' and 'closed' questions he's equally at sea.

Many times I have sat him down and explained: 'Colin, the golden rule in sales is that you NEVER ask a closed question. When you cold-call you don't say, "Would you like to see if Harrison's can beat your current supplier on price?" because the person on the end of the phone can just say "NO". What you have to ask is an open question: "Why are you so sure you're getting the best deal from your current supplier?", and "Go on, impress me. How do you go about sussing out the competition?"'

Incredibly, Colin always shakes his head at us in a don't-tell-your-grandmother-how-to-suck-eggs manner as if he knows it all, and then gets back on the phone only to be blown out of the water again. It's painful to listen to him within minutes of my counsel: 'Would you like me to send you a Harrison's catalogue? Are you sure?' The poor sod is already being laughed at by the latest recruits.

Funnier still is when Mitchell cocks a thumb at Colin when Colin's midway through one of his calls merely taking orders. The thumb says, 'You're the man, Colin. Keep up the good work.' And other times when Colin's dying on his arse, he often gets some other gesture of encouragement from Mitchell, which is noisily delivered to bring our attention to this spectacle of valiant persistence from the only true

Harrison's crusader. Adam nearly explodes with incredulity and scorn at it all. No one else is ever singled out for such praise. We get nothing but grunts of disapproval or outright criticism from Mitchell. You can imagine the confusion it creates among the telesales team, which is why, like I said, we have a high turnover of staff.

Talk of the devil. Mitchell's coming our way—Evian bottle in hand—with Egremont and a striking-looking tall guy who has to be a good head above Egremont, so we've got to be talking six-foot-six at least. And what's this? Mitchell's laughing and joking with Egremont as if they're best mates. Did Mitchell just pat my Egstasy on the arm? He did, and he's doing it again! Who must this giant stranger be to bring on such a bogus display of buddyship? I smile because Adam too has clocked the unusual scene being played out before us. He's staring at them, hardly paying attention to his call. Egremont, good man, isn't fooled. He's being cool in his responses. Ah! My man just shot me a look saying as much. *God* I love how subtle he is. Frustratingly my phone rings as the three come to a halt near my desk. I jump slightly when Mitchell slams his empty water bottle next to me (he's always dispensing of them in this way. I push it out of sight immediately lest he reclaim it later. With their pretty flower designs they make for excellent flower vases).

Laetitia, having just put down her phone, is watching the unfolding drama with interest too. My call is for the renewal of a routine order, so as I'm getting the client's account up on the screen, I tune in to the conversation among the men.

'My idea is to have a line of pictures all along here,' Mitchell is saying. 'Each one almost the same as the one next to it but for one little difference. I don't want anyone to notice the difference until I point it out to them. Think your artist can do that?' He's asking the tall guy.

'Ya, ya—absolutely. It's your call, and I love the concept. The branch motif will work really well in this space.' The guy splays his fingers out in front of the wall and opens his arms wide as if trying to measure up. 'How many walls are we talking about?' he asks, suddenly slapping his hands together and spinning on his heel to look around. It makes Mitchell jump.

I'm laughing a little at the guy's accent. He's one of the *How the hell are you?* brigade. His accent is Prince William southern, but with a lion's roar of volume and confidence. Mitchell sounds like an oik next to him, and doubtless the guy thinks he is one.

'I want the art—the sculpture paintings—to make a line around every room, on all floors,' says Mitchell biting his bottom lip furiously and pointing around with waggling index fingers like he's play-shooting guns. 'Put them between the offices and make the walls that garlicky pinkish white, like you said. I'm going to launch Harrison's into the twenty-first century. We're moving up and on, and this snot-green wallpaper has to go. I want that cool minimum look.'

'Ya, absolutely. Go minimalist. That will work well in here. You have such a cool spot in the city. And this building—it's art-deco-chic plus.'

I try not to look at Adam, who I know is eyeing me with surprised/amused brow at what we've just heard.

'You're not going with the light red background?' asks Egremont sounding alarmed. He gets shaking heads from both men. 'But don't you think we'll need some more colour—some warmth?' he adds bravely.

'*What?*' snaps Mitchell as if he's talking to an imbecile (killing off his role as Egremont's best pal). The tall guy slaps Egremont on the back—hard. Egremont staggers back a little but quickly recovers himself. He doesn't say any more, however. No doubt he knows it's pointless.

'Trust in the artist, Eggers,' says tall guy, beaming a satisfied smile. Before Egremont has a chance to answer him, the guy turns to Mitchell with his hand outstretched. 'So we have a deal then, Mr Harrison?'

'We have the beginnings of a deal, Chaz,' says Mitchell shaking the guy's hand. 'Now we need to talk figures and if I like the price, you have the job. Then I'll meet Picasso in person to talk details.'

The client on the phone has to repeat her order for an alternative colour of copy paper. I don't apologise for not listening properly in case Mitchell gets wind of my inattention. Thankfully the rest of the order is identical to the last time she ordered so I can put the phone down and key it in without further instruction.

'Oh you'll like the price, Mr Harrison.'

'It's now Mitchell to you.'

'Mitchell—yes, thank you. Look, there's no doubt you'll like the price. And you'll be making an investment too—art appreciates. Come on, let's strike while the iron's hot.' They begin to move off in the direction of Mitchell's office.

'Slow down there, Chaz,' says Mitchell thrusting his hands in his pockets and staying where he is. 'You can put the quote in writing. Go size up the joint first. I've got a few other people to see. It's not just you who wants this commission, you know.'

Long-limbed Chaz seems a little taken aback by Mitchell's unwillingness to be rushed. He stops in his tracks. 'Oh—of course,' he says unconvincingly. 'But I'm sure you'll go with us,' he adds and gives a snooty sort of sniff raising his nose in the air.

'No one gets a free ride with me. Not even you, me new China plate.' Mitchell leans back on his heels and grins broadly at the guy. 'But I like your confidence, and don't get me wrong, thanks to your strife, and yeah I saw her in that posh Cheshire rag covered in lah-di-dahs. More celebrities in there than *OK!* Magazine, and looks like who she don't know ain't worth knowing. I can see she'll pull the big names in and all the do-ray-me that comes with it. Well, she'd better.'

'To be sure,' says Chaz, looking uncertain of himself for the first time.

Adam and I exchange puzzled looks at this baffling conversation.

'But that portfolio—those designs,' Mitchell continues, 'I really like that branch mo—mo—what was it?'

'Branch motif,' says the guy, smiling once again with what looks like relief.

'Yeah, that's it.' Mitchell nods vigorously. 'I like the branch motif. That's what I'm doing here with *Aaarrison's*—branching out. The new shoots of—whatever.'

'The green shoots of renewal and growth,' says Chaz whimsically.

'I used to think all that stuff was soppy shit, but I'm different now. Eggers has done good introducing me to you and yours.' I look at Egremont—he's bristling with pride. 'So go and have a look around and send me the quote by the end of the week. Eggers will show you around.' And with that, Mitchell marches off in the direction of his office.

Adam throws me another look of amused surprise at what's being proposed for our walls. 'Looks like we're in for a radical makeover,' says Laetitia, nodding thoughtfully and raising her eyebrows signalling that she's impressed.

I turn to Egremont and I'm delighted that he's looking my way. He smiles and makes big eyes at me before following his tall friend out of the room. A feeling of satisfaction fills me at the idea of Egremont having such contacts in the art world, and not only that, with people who appear in *Cheshire Life*! I want in.

'What's the dopey look for?' asks Adam, snapping me out of my reverie.

'Nothing.' I shake my head and smile.

He looks down the room at Egremont then stares at me suspiciously. Is he on to me? Adam picks up his ringing phone, though not before having another glance at me with a scowl. Shoot. I need to be more discreet.

# 4

It's Friday again and I'm bubbling with excitement and anticipation—and anything else that means 'wild with delight'. Egremont has upped the intensity of his looks at me from across the office. He's positively lustful! He can't keep his eyes off me now. I've actually seen him bump into people, so distracted is he by me; although, there was a moment when his preoccupation led to mortification—he collided with Mitchell, who promptly spilt coffee all down his Amani (the one time he wasn't carrying water!) Mitchell, nearly busting an artery with rage, called Egremont a 'dopey fucking Muppet' and 'a blind bastard bat', among other things. In fact, Mitchell lost it like I've never seen him lose it before. But the detail about the incident that made me secretly swoon was that even through this very public dressing-down, Egremont couldn't stop staring my way. It was as if he'd put Mitchell's venomous outburst on silent. I tell you, it's on my friends—it's sooooo on between me and Egstasy.

It couldn't come at a better time either because I have to get out of my mother's house. She's getting too ridiculous with her shopping. The hallway looks like bag collection at John Lewis. I swear there won't be room for me in that place before long. Do you remember when I told you about our Lakeland excursion? The aborted weekend looking for a holiday home—after our muddy, windswept walk up Claife Heights? Well, I saw just this morning that the boots she wore that day are now in my wardrobe in the same muddied state they were brought back in (in a bag of course). These great encrusted hiking boots, worn once, are now filling up the little space I have in my wardrobe, along with the other crap she purchased for that trip. There are several waterproofs (one light/one heavyweight), a rucksack, a portable canvas seat and a wax picnic throw. All of it has been squeezed into my wardrobe without so much as a sorry-but-could-you-find-room-for-these-please?

I've also had enough of the noise from next door. It feels like I'm in their horror-show home with them. In addition to the angry yelling of the eldest boy, who seems to compete with his mother in spewing out foul language and tantrums, they've acquired a dog. Naturally it's one of those pit bull terrier things. It barks when they row, which is to say it barks constantly. I could weep for poor Tommy who tries to be the peacekeeper and invariably gets shot down with 'Shut it, you little fucker.' 'Little fucker' seems to be their favourite name for him. It makes me hate the mother because she doesn't use that kind of language with the elder boy, who is indeed a little fucker, and getting to be a bigger one by the day. To make things worse, no one takes the dog out for a walk; he merely gets to crap on the pavement outside. I nearly stepped in its 'do' this morning, deposited right in our pathway. The fat mother gave me a sorry-about-that simpering smile but no actual apology and it hasn't been cleared up, which means I'll have to do it. As Lloyd Christmas says, 'I've had it with this dump.'

But back to happier thoughts—Egremont. Like I said, he's been giving me penetrating, almost brooding looks all week. It's making me wild to get him alone, in private—to have intimate conversations and really get to explore the man. Oh what am I saying? It's making me wild to fuck him. You know, I can actually sense his frustration when he's in my presence. It's making his closeness thrilling, and he's been getting *a lot* closer physically. Adam was absent twice this week attending rehearsals and Egremont took the opportunity to commandeer his desk on the flimsiest of pretexts. It won't be long now before he asks me out.

I know Laetitia has noticed the subtle sexual tension between us (I'm taking it this is the reason she's been fetching me coffee and keeping an eye on me). She's given me discreet little nods of encouragement and approval. I'm so grateful she knows not to breathe a word. Eggers and I would be teased mercilessly by the reps if anyone knew, and Mitchell (thankfully absent a lot this week) would disapprove and spend his entire time calling us idling lovesick puppies or whatever that is in cockney rhyming slang. What Laetitia doesn't know, of course, or suspect, is how far gone I am on Egremont, and she certainly won't guess that I'm planning to get the man to the altar.

I turn over the calling-card in my hand again. I've made only ten cold-calls this morning without any success and yet I can't be bothered to make any more. I look at my watch. It's almost lunch time. Adam has hardly been off his phone and seems to be making up for lost time. He's been exceptionally successful too. I've heard him say, 'Sound, I'll put you down for two cases of cartridges' (or whatever it is), several times, and he's finished those calls with 'Welcome onboard'. Maddening!

The return of the telesales team from their twelve o'clock lunch break signals that it's our turn. Adam and I are both on one o'clock. It's a perk of having been here the longest—we get to choose our lunch time. Laetitia does as she pleases.

When Adam puts his phone down, I ask if he's up for the pub. I know Egremont's out for the day, so there's nothing to stick around for, and it is Friday.

'Why not?' he says, but without much enthusiasm. 'I'll just finish keying in these orders. Then I'm all yours, girl.' I look round for Laetitia to see if she wants to come too. She'll probably say no because she's dressed down today, but I should ask because she likes a Friday drink now and again and her ever-tuned radar will know where we've been. I see she's in Mitchell's office (didn't notice his return). How odd that she's in there. That almost never happens. The door is closed. *Hmmmmm*, curious. Guess we're off the hook about inviting her to the pub at least.

'Come on,' says Adam grabbing his jacket. 'Let's get out of here.'

I don't need telling twice and do the same.

When Adam and I cross the road and get clear of Harrison's he doesn't link my arm in the usual fashion. I look at him and see his hands are firmly thrust in his trouser pockets. He looks rather glum.

'What's up?'

'Nothing,' he says, looking down.

'Are rehearsals going okay?'

'Yeah, not bad.' He frowns and looks anything but excited.

'When's it on again?'

'About a month.' He frowns more and looks anxious.

'That's not much time.'

'It'll have to be enough time,' he says pushing open the door of Vern's. As we walk in I see the Chesterfield is free of the ski-resort couple. I chuckle to myself when I see Adam looking at the same spot. No doubt he's relieved Che-Gue-fucking-vara isn't there, although, actually, they could be somewhere else—the place is packed.

'What you drinking?' asks Adam.

'White wine, thanks.'

'A bottle of Chardonnay, barman, thanks,' shouts Adam over a cluster of people trying to get served. They turn with faces full of protest at this pushing in. Adam waves a twenty pound note in the air and ignores them. When he sees my expression of surprise at his asking for a full bottle, he says, 'I'm thirsty' and gives me the trace of a smile.

'Good,' I say, returning his transforming smile—how it changes his face into something wonderful.

To my delight a bottle and two glasses are being handed over immediately.

'What do you want for lunch?' he asks, taking the wine.

'I'll have a cheese toastie.'

'And take for two cheese toasties, mate. Thanks.'

The barman nods, snatching the note from Adam's hand. 'Look, we can squeeze on the end of that table there,' says Adam taking his change and motioning with his chin to a free spot. We move to the vacant corner and as luck would have it two people are freeing up bar stools in front of a window sill.

When we've sat down and offloaded our coats I go to take out the money for my lunch.

'Leave that in your purse,' he says firmly.

'You're buying lunch?'

'Yep.'

'Thanks.'

'You're welcome.' He unscrews the top of the bottle while looking at me. I can see a question is coming—he's gone all serious again. Here it comes: 'I notice Egg-salted has been eye-balling you like you were the winning lottery numbers,' he says finally, pouring our drinks.

'What?' I laugh. 'God Adam, that's an appalling simile.'

'Best I got, babe.' He lifts his filled glass in a silent toast and takes a sip still looking at me intensely. 'Is he getting some encouragement?' He asks with eyes narrowed.

'No!' I surprise myself with the force of indignation I've pulled out the bag. I should have been an actress—he relaxes at this news. Wow, he really does believe me.

'But what would it matter if I were—though I'm not?' Sod it—I feel like a little mischief.

'Behave. As if.'

'Oh leave him alone! He's not that bad.'

'Old men chasing young tail makes me sick, that's all.'

'Tail, he calls me.' I have more wine and congratulate myself on the deception.

'You know what I mean.' He looks at me with his friendliest eyes. 'So who are you going out with these days? Do you have a liking for any of the newbies? Some of those recruits aren't half bad looking. Now I'd give my approval to one of *them*.' He smiles broadly.

'Urrgh, there isn't one of them that's datable. And most of them look about twelve.'

'Ah, they do have too much youth, 'tis true. You like old but not young.' He puts his tongue out a little and squeezes my knee playfully.

'Shut up, you fool.' I'm laughing but I see I'm going to need all my powers of persuasion to bring him round to the idea that Eggers/Egg-salted/Egg-regious and I will one day be a couple. But until that day comes, I'll just enjoy the wine.

'I wonder what foolery Mitchell is planning for the office décor.' I'm changing the subject again.

'Looks like whatever it is it's going to be expensive. I think it's time we asked for a raise—he seems to have money to burn.'

'Yeah, it's true—what with the hotel and everything.'

'Or maybe his missus is sending the profits of her sweatshops back.' Adam laughs cynically.

'That's probably it.' I wonder again why it is I can never find a trace of Mitchell's wife on the internet, not that I share my thoughts with Adam on that subject—he's long since got bored with the Harrisons, particularly the mysterious wife.

\* \* \*

When I get back to the office almost half an hour earlier than usual, I see Laetitia is still in Mitchell's office. Has she finally summoned the courage to challenge him about interfering with our orders? Unlikely—she still has her head on! And if that's why she was in there, it wouldn't take this long. So what's going on?

I hang up my coat and hear Laetitia shout my name. It appears I'm to join her in Mitchell's office. Oh dear, perhaps it's my head that'll be lopped off. I don't have time to tell Adam where I'm off to because he's gone to the loo. Nor do I have time to search for a mint in my desk as both Laetitia and Mitchell are looking at me expectantly.

'Evelyn, come in,' Mitchell says in a friendly enough manner, but then that's no indication of what's about to happen. I step past Laetitia who's eyeing me nervously.

'Hi! What's up?' I'm trying to sound unconcerned and praying my breath doesn't smell like I live in a bus shelter.

'Pull up a chair, love,' Mitchell says as he takes a seat behind his desk. He isn't being sarcastic and it makes me tense. I sit down. 'I'll come straight to the point,' he begins, cupping the back of his head with both hands. This action threatens to make me break out in a fit of giggles. His arms are so disproportionately short that it looks like it's a real effort for him to keep his hands there. They constantly slip forward towards his ears and he pushes them back around his head. I force myself to keep my eyes fixed on his nose.

'There's an opening for a rep,' he says, staring at me.

*A rep? A rep? Did he just say there's an opening for a rep?*

'We want to try for the floating Birkenhead and Wallasey business.' I try hard not to picture turds in the Mersey. Mitchell continues: 'We figure you'd be the right person to spread our good name.'

*You'd be the right person to spread our good name.* Does he really mean me? Mitchell is complementing *me*? Is he offering me a job? I wish I hadn't had a drink.

'As you know,' he goes on, 'we've just gone in for the printing game, and we reckon we can beat what's currently out there on price *and* quality. You up for the challenge, Evelyn?' Before I can reply, he adds, 'There's a Ford Focus in it, which you can pick up tomorrow.'

'Saturday?'

'You can pick it up from our car lot across the road. It'll be there from nine in the morning. Here.' He releases his head and rummages through a drawer under his desk. 'Them's the keys.' He throws me a set of keys.

I can hardly believe what's happening. I look at Laetitia with incredulity. She grins lipstick-stained encouragement at me. 'Thanks,' I say in disbelief, staring at the shiny alien object in my hand.

'Let's see what you can do when you're not distracted by lover boy, eh?'

'Yes, let's see.' But is he alluding to Adam or Egremont? And why did I agree to being distracted?

He gets to his feet. 'You'll come out on the road with me for the next two weeks, give or take, and then you're on your own. I'll get you started Monday. Well, that's it. And don't look so worried, Evelyn. But do lay off the liquid lunches because if I catch you smelling like a winery again during office hours it's all off. If it wasn't for that drink you'd have the car today.'

Before I have time to respond, he says, 'Okay, she's all yours, Laetitia. No, one more thing.' He pauses, putting his hands on his hips. I stand up. 'You'll be with us for the *Aaarrison's* dinner now. It's in a month or so. Hmmmmmm. If you do well you could give a talk on what it's like moving up from telesales—something like that. Yeah, I like it. We'll see. Okay, you're free to go.' He indicates the door with a swift point of the finger.

Once we're outside the office and the door is closed, Laetitia turns to me. 'Sorry, kiddo, I should have told you, but Mitchell swore me to secrecy. You're pleased, though?'

'Yes, of course. Does this mean I'll be getting a pay rise?'

'Oh, *yeah*—a clear five thou a year. Plus all the commission you'll be making. Congratulations, Eve. You deserve it, kiddo. You've been working really hard.' She says this with insincerity. She's right—I don't quite deserve it. I've been slacking. Plus, if anyone should be getting promotion right now it's Adam, at least based on his performance. But then Adam's attitude alone is enough to debar him, and it's clear by his lateness and absences that he doesn't want anything more from the firm. So—hey, yes, that means I deserve it!

'I've got off to a bad start though, haven't I—the wine breath?' I dearly wish I hadn't had that pub lunch.

'Nah, it's all right. We saw you coming out of Vern's and he joked about giving you a hard time about it.'

'Actually joked?' I say sceptically.

'Yes,' she laughs. 'It seems he can be human.' I blow out a puff of surprise.

Laetitia pats my hand. 'Believe me, you don't smell like a brewery, kid. And you know Mitchell—he was happy to have something to tick you off about. Seriously, forget it.'

I smile with relief. 'And I won't be doing any more telesales?' I ask with growing euphoria.

'Nope.'

'Will I have someone to key in my orders?'

'Ah, probably not at first, kiddo, but yeah, once you've proved yourself.' She puts an arm around me and I'm almost suffocated by her bosom. 'I'll miss ya, kiddo.' I'm touched, but trying hard not to breathe—there's an aroma of cat's piss. 'Come on,' she says, 'let's go wind up your calling cards.'

I follow, sneezing out cat hairs on the way.

'*Well*?' demands Adam as I approach. 'What were you in there for, babe?'

'Mitchell's made me a rep.'

'Right,' he laughs.

'He has! I'm going out on the road with him from Monday. Look I've already got the keys to the car.' I dangle them in front of him. Adam raises his eyebrows, grimaces, and nods that he's impressed, although I can see that he's a little troubled. Is he hurt that he's been overlooked for promotion? Having a car and being out of the office would suit him right now.

'Come on, kiddo, let's get your calling cards wrapped up. I need to divvy them up for the rest of telesales,' says Laetitia, probably sensing Adam's tension and doubtless feeling awkward herself because she can't offer him something similar. I suddenly feel bad about it all. But what can I do?

'Yes, I'll get the boxes out.' I inwardly shrug the awkwardness off. Adam's getting out; he'll be fine.

'I'll need you to clear out your desk too,' says Laetitia. Adam looks at her then at me.

'Where will I sit?'

'With the reps.' She nods at the other end of the office. 'Mitchell will set you up either later today or on Monday.'

Adam looks away, shaking his head a little.

'Eve! Over here. Follow me,' shouts Mitchell. 'I'll show you where your new desk is now.' Talk about efficient!

Laetitia signals for me to leave the calling cards for now and follow Mitchell.

When we're at the other end of the office, Mitchell points to a dark windowless corner. 'Take that one.' I stare at what looks like a plank stuck to the wall. 'Just move the boxes to one side. There's a chair in there somewhere,' he says, eyeing the cluttered space.

'Thanks.' I just manage to keep the sarcasm out of my voice.

When I've finished setting up my new desk, I go back and finish clearing my old one. I offload what I can to Laetitia and try to talk to Adam, but he's deliberately avoiding my gaze. Once I'm relocated to my lonely corner of the office, Mitchell calls me back to his office and gives me a catalogue for the new printing range we're offering. 'Study that over the weekend. It's what you'll be flogging next week. And make sure you can know the deal-breakers off pat.'

'Right-o.' I take the weighty tome from his desk. 'You all done moving? he asks.

'Not quite. Just tidying up around the desk.'

'When you've finished you can go.'

'Home?' I ask, confused.

'Yes, home. Where else?'

'Oh! Of course. Errrr, thanks.'

'And over the weekend, go into town and get yourself some of those feminine business suits. You know how the reps dress. They do *Aaarrison's* proud. Want you looking good out there next week.'

I look to see if there's a wad of notes on the desk to assist me in this power-dressing venture, but nothing is forthcoming. Mitchell points at his door.

'Right.' I realise it's my cue to leave.

I walk past the noisy telesales area feeling a little sad. It's deathly quiet down where Mitchell's put me, and there's no view. But then I'll be out on the road. I shake my head inwardly; there's no point worrying. Now, do I have money for clothes? No! Mum will have to help me out with the shopping—she'll be happy to do it. I hope.

'Did I see you clearing out your desk?' asks a familiar voice. I turn to face Egremont. He looks the picture of sadness.

'I've been promoted to rep—just now. Got the keys and everything, although I can't pick up the car till tomorrow.'

'Really?' He's looking and sounding both startled and excited.

'Yes, Mitchell's going to take me out on the road next week. Think Birkenhead and Wallasey are my areas.'

'Congratulations.' He offers me his hand to shake. 'Really, you're a rep—one of us—that's fantastic. Congratulations, seriously, congratulations.'

I take his hand, which dwarfs mine. The feel of its slight roughness is thrilling. 'This is great news, really,' he says finally letting go.

'I know. I'm excited.'

'You said you're not picking up the car today?'

'No, it'll be ready tomorrow.'

'Can I give you a lift home then?'

'Er—yes, thanks. That would be great. Oh, but Mitchell said I could leave when I'm done and I'm almost finished.'

'Well I'm done here too—almost. I just have to make a call and then I'm going over to Cheshire. I can drop you on the way. So that works out, right?' I nod eagerly. 'I'll meet you downstairs in ten minutes?' He looks like he'll burst with happiness.

'Sure.' I break into a broad smile that matches his.

He nods vigorously, looking even more delighted. As he's walking away, I notice Mitchell standing at the door of his office looking over at us. I smile at him, but he doesn't respond and instead twitches with annoyance. He turns away moodily. No matter—Egremont.

As I'm going to pick up my coat from my desk, Adam finally looks at me but says nothing.

'Well, this is me,' I say with forced cheeriness. Laetitia blows me a kiss (she's on the phone).

'On the job already?' he says flatly.

'No, I'm going home, but I've got plenty to—'

'The perks have started already.'

'I was about to say, I have lots of research to do.'

'Ah, well good luck with it all.'

'We'll still go out for lunch now and again—right?'

'We'll see, eh?' Wow, he sounds so sad. Then he is upset about this break-up of our working duet (for want of a better phrase). Then again, it could be the just fact that I'm no longer allowed a 'liquid lunch' and therefore lunches won't be the same. But perhaps this is just as well.

'Keep me updated about the play,' I say, leaving.

'Yeah, sure.' His tone seems to imply I won't be interested any more. I go to protest but leave it—like I said, it's probably best we cool things now.

I turn back and plant a kiss on his cheek—but his face—I'm astonished to see it's tearful. It makes me emotional too and I head out of the office with my head down.

When I get to reception Egremont is standing looking out of the doorway. 'Ready when you are,' I say passing him and walking outside. I'm praying my eyes have cleared up without leaving mascara smudges.

We cross the road to his car practically in silence. I sneak a look at his face now and again. He looks tense, or is that shyness? Or perhaps he's embarrassed. I hope it's not going to be awkward in the car, which I see is parked on the kerb and not in the car park. Something tells me Mitchell is probably watching us from the windows above. When we reach the car I go to the passenger side and furtively glance up; yep, he's looking down on us. I get in the car quickly.

When Egremont has turned the corner I thank him again for offering to give me a lift.

'You'll have to tell me where you live.'

'I live off West Derby Road.'

'That's easy. I know that way.' He turns to me smiling.

I wonder if it will fade when he actually sees my road. 'And you get your car tomorrow?'

'Yes, I had some wine with lunch today and Mitchell didn't want me to drink-drive. It was only a glass and a half though.'

'Of—of course it was. I can give you a lift to fetch the car if you like—tomorrow—tomorrow morning. I mean I'll come and pick you up at your house—in the morning.' He nods uncertainly but encouragingly as if he really wants me to accept the offer.

'But don't you live out near Ormskirk?'

'Yes, but it's no trouble.'

'Then no—thanks. There's no need. I can get the bus like I usually do. Seriously, I wouldn't have you come all that way to give me a lift into town.'

He finally nods in acceptance. We're silent for the next few minutes. I break it: 'I hope I'll be all right out there on the road.'

'I can give you coaching lessons if you want,' he says, laughing a little.

'I wouldn't say no to that.'

'Since you have to start on Monday, would you like to come to dinner tonight at my place? I'm not a bad cook.'

'Tonight?'

'Sorry—it doesn't have to be. I was only thinking—no, you're right. Tonight's too soon.'

'Tonight's fine,' I reassure him speedily (and I'm having to suppress the squeal of delight that's bubbling up inside me).

'Really?'

'Yes, really. I'd love to come for dinner.'

'Then I'll pick you up at seven. Ah, we're coming into West Derby Road. Which is your turn off?'

It's with mixed emotions that I direct him to the street where I live. I burn with frustration at my snobbery and shame, but I swear if I could I'd sell my soul right now to be asking him to turn into a sweeping driveway.

'It's very nice,' he says, looking around at the scruffy tired-looking houses with overflowing bins outside them. He pulls up in front of mine, which is rather like a good tooth in a row of rotten ones. Thankfully no one's out.

'No, it's not nice, Egremont. But thanks for saying so.' He laughs. 'I'll see you at seven.' I release my seatbelt.

'Yes, at seven.' He says 'bye' in a whisper as I get out.

I fumble with the front door key. When inside I lean against the closed door and compose myself. Instinct tells me to drop these displays of embarrassment and humiliation, or whatever I'm feeling about my home. He probably sees nothing and if I continue I may convince him that there is disgrace in my 'situation'. My only focus must be on me and what I have to offer.

I dash upstairs with renewed energy, scarcely able to breathe. My mouth is gaping open in wonder at all that's happened today. I honestly think I'm going to wake up from a dream. But it's not a dream because I'm really going for dinner at Egremont's tonight and I'm getting a free car tomorrow and I have a pay rise and I'll be out of the office. Why, it seems I have a life!

I fling open my wardrobe doors and stare at the sorry array of clothes hanging there. I won't pretend I can talk about them being 'last season'. I can't claim to be one iota fashionable, but perhaps it's time for a change. Mitchell's right. Underneath my clothes is Mother's abandoned Lake District kit. 'You have to go,' I say to them. 'She'll never wear any of you again and you're all too large for me'. With determination I grab the bags and fling them out onto the floor. I'll take them to the Oxfam shop by the post office; I'll be doing the community a favour. The weather is terrible now and someone could use this stuff. Come to think of it, half my wardrobe could probably go with them. It's time for a clear-out.

When I get the bundles for the charity shop downstairs and into the hallway, I have another idea. I look at the accumulation of bags, particularly the John Lewis and M&S ones. They contain clothes, bed linen, cushions, all sorts. They've been there for months, some for years. Mum won't remember these impulse buys. They always put the receipt in the bag, and even though Mum usually pays by credit card and so I can't get cash back, I can ask for credit vouchers, or exchange them for clothes. I could get myself an entirely new wardrobe.

It's dishonest certainly, but if I asked Mum she'd say no. Well of course she would. She'd growl at me like a dog guarding its feeding bowl. I've suggested she take things back before, or that I'd do it for her. Boy, did I cop a wrathful outburst of mind-your-own-bloody-business and don't-ever-touch-what-isn't-yours. She'll never admit she doesn't need the half of what she buys.

I look at my watch. It's two thirty. I need to get a move on. Egremont's picking me up at seven. I rifle through the bags under the stairs. It's mostly clothing—dozens of tops and pants that all look exactly the same. 'You'll do.' I haul several of the large bags out. I push the remaining ones back together so the missing ones are less likely be noticed. But what's this?

I'm staring at a collection of brand-new Tula leather bags and purses. I remember Mum saying she'd bought Tula purses as Christmas presents for her friends at work but she couldn't find them. She thought she'd left them in the taxi.

With a thank you on my lips, I drag out that booty as well and call a cab.

I blow out a breath of grateful release when I'm in the taxi, having just missed Next Door. She would have been agog at all the bags I was removing from the house into a taxi and wouldn't have failed to mention the odd sight to my mother. 'Never saw so many bags being taken *out* of the house. They're just like the ones you're always taking *in*.' Oh for sure the little minx would have had sport with us. But I foiled her—ha!

I tell the cab driver I've got to stop for a minute at the Oxfam shop. He gives me the thumbs up.

'I'm sorry but the boots are muddy. I didn't have time to clean them. They're good boots though,' I tell the Oxfam assistant who's looking pleased with the size of the bags I'm bringing in.

'It's not a problem, love. We're grateful for all donations,' she says, asking me to put them on the counter. I imagine when she sees the quality of the stuff she'll take it for herself or for her family. I would.

I leave the shop feeling cleansed, and I'm buoyed with excitement when I say to the taxi driver, 'Town!'

I waste no time getting to the clothes section of John Lewis and to my utter delight I see there are racks and racks of designer names at discount prices. There are big '50% OFF' signs, even '75% OFF'. Oh, oh, oh, praise be! It's the beginning of February but the January sales are on their last super-cheap legs. 'A credit note. You need to get a credit note', a voice tells me.

Yes, a credit note. I need customer services.

Minutes later I'm hauling my mother's shopping bags onto a counter and the woman with a half-suspicious, half curious eye is looking at all the purchases I'm bringing back. 'I got carried away at Christmas and bought too many wrong things.'

The sales assistant pulls out some receipts. 'You paid by credit. Do you want the items refunded to your card?'

'Oh, no. I don't have that card any more. They tore it up. Can't think why.' She smiles sympathetically. Phew I picked a good one.

'I can't give you cash back but what I can do is give you a credit note for all this.'

'Perfect! I'm in the mood to shop again.'

She laughs, pulling out the clothing and scanning each item for refund. Twenty minutes later I'm walking away with a credit note for £2,700 or thereabouts (it was the Tula bags that did it). It's certainly enough to get me some great suits and dresses in the sales here.

I'm between an eight and a ten and without time to try anything on, I use judgement to size up the clothing. In a frenzy, I flick through the rails and pull item after item off the racks. A hawk-eyed assistant steps in to help me.

It isn't too long before I'm at another counter and offloading little black velvet dresses and powder pink Chanel-type suits. Ghost silk evening dresses reduced to under £100; blouses, skirts and suits at a fraction of their price. Shoes too. I've hit the jackpot.

I'm back in a taxi by six and on my way home. When the cab pulls up at my house, Next Door is out, but I can relax. I'll tell Mum that Mitchell gave me an advance to buy clothes.

'You win the lottery?' asks one of Mum's friends as they all stare agog at the shopping bags the cab driver is helping me into the house with. As 'the girls' are here it must be Mum's turn to host their Friday-night in.

'It's all sales stuff,' I say breezily, struggling to get through the door with it all.

'What on earth is all this?' asks Mum coming out of the living room. I close the door on Next Door who is leaning over to stare into the hallway. 'You've been shopping, Eve— without me!'

'Mum'—I stop to catch my breath—'I've such a lot to tell you. I got promoted to sales rep today. I'm picking up a car tomorrow. Mitchell gave me an advance on my salary and told me to get suitable togs—*kit yourself out in some new whistle and flutes to show off ya clothes pegs*. I think they were his words.' I get a laugh from 'the girls' at this, but Mum is looking worried.

'I'm going to be giving a speech at the Annual Dinner. Mum, this is my break.' Mum's hands go up to her mouth and I can see that she's about to burst with relief and joy. 'Really?' she says hesitantly. I nod. 'Oh Evelyn! This is marvellous. Well done! Oh, come here and give your mum a kiss.' Her friends look at each other with noses wrinkled in *arrrrrrh* gestures.

When we've done hugging I tell her I've got to get ready because Egremont is picking me up in half an hour. 'Egremont—from the office? Why's he picking you up? Do you have a staff do on?'

'He's just going to show me the ropes sort of thing—prepare me for Monday.'

'I'm sure he is,' she says sourly. She's met Egremont a few times. It was way back when I first started and, alas, I told her all the jokes about his name and more unflattering things besides. Owing to his bashfulness, she saw immediately that he liked me. She called him ridiculous and seemed almost offended by his acting like a love-sick puppy around me.

'Sorry Mum, I've got to get ready.'

'Right,' she says hesitantly, watching me head up the stairs with as many bags as I can carry. She thankfully returns to her friends and in a buoyant mood—from what I can tell. How fortunate they're here!

I shut the door with my foot and throw everything on the bed. My heart starts to race and I begin to panic. I've done too much and I can't think straight. I have to get ready but what shall I wear—a dress? Yes, it needs to be a dress—easy access and all that.

A toothbrush—will I take an overnight bag? NO, of course not! I don't want to look like the hussy I am—ha! But it's bound to get heated later, and he'll remember that I've got to pick up the car in the morning. He'll probably say something like, 'You might as well stay and I can drop you at the car park tomorrow.' Naturally he'll insist on me staying in the spare room, only to end up carrying me into his, like in that scene from *An Officer and a Gentleman*. I'll take a large handbag and put some spare knickers in it.

Shower. I must take a shower.

Coming out of the bathroom I hear the doorbell. Shit—Egremont. Oh God—the girls! Mum will die. With relief I hear a door-to-door salesman trying to get her to change gas supplier.

Back in my bedroom I fly round getting ready, randomly stuffing make-up and toiletries into my bag. It's one of those massive leather ones with an oval cut-out handle. He'll never suspect what's inside. But I tell you, if I can make tonight happen, I will. We've waited years to get together—there's no need to play it cool now. I know he's nothing like the man he pretends to be at work and boy, am I gonna make him show me the real one! Wine—I must get a bottle of wine too.

Thankfully when the doorbell goes again I'm there to answer it. I give my Mum and company a rushed *bye* and hurry out.

# 5

As I emerge from Egremont's car, I'm disconcerted: his house is too small and too close to his neighbours, and his car takes up practically the entire driveway. Wasn't he supposed to be, well, wealthier? I curse my shallow thoughts before they're fully formed. What does it matter? It doesn't. I don't really think of him like that. I'm not so—why is he taking so long to get out of the car? My stomach's churning; I was hardly able to speak on the journey here. When he finally gets out of the car he apologises for having had to take a call. 'Won't you come in?' He opens the door wide. I go in, almost stepping on his foot. 'Welcome to my *humble abode*,' he says jokingly and does a funny head wobble thing.

I follow him through his—Jesus!—*empty* house.

'It's a little spartan,' he says awkwardly, taking my coat. Yikes, I was too transparent.

'No! It's elegant, homely, *nice*,' I gush. He smiles in confusion.

Stepping into the kitchen, I'm relieved to see a well-stocked wine rack. I rummage in my bag for the bottle I've brought. As I pull it out I see with horror my lace knickers have caught on the neck of it. I snatch them off not daring to look at him. Perhaps he didn't notice, or didn't see what they were, but I catch his eye, and yes, he's seen—he's gone red. He takes the bottle blinking with embarrassment as I stuff the offending panties back in my bag.

'They're for emergencies.' When he frowns, looking alarmed, I say quickly, 'I mean hospital emergencies, like in case I have an accident.' I shut up but a strange laugh escapes me. 'Yes,' he says vaguely as he puts the bottle on the side.

I shake my head. We must move on! I see he's begun preparing dinner already.

'This all looks good.' I nod at the little piles of leaf salad and vegetables scattered about. 'What are we having?'

'Linguine con aragosta, alla insalata di campo.'

'A Spanish dish—you like Spanish food?'

'I live for *Italian* cuisine.' He gives me a playful frown.

'Oh! I didn't catch what you said. That was Italian you were speaking? Sorry.'

'Sì,' he says, laughing kindly.

'I don't speak any languages. There were problems with our courses at school. I ended up dropping them. I was doing really well at German at the time, and before that I was excelling in French but ...' He's looking startled at my verbose explanation. 'Anyway, I don't speak any languages.'

'Would you like a glass of wine?'

'I would.' Good man! I relax instantly. He takes out two very large glasses from a cupboard. Things are looking up.

'I have a *Barolo*.' He says it like it has some significance. 'I've been saving a very particular one for a special occasion.'

'Sounds good.' I'm wondering if it's Champagne or the Italian equivalent. I soon see it's wine—red wine.

With some difficulty he begins to open the bottle. I try not to look at his bum as he twists and turns to get some purchase on the cork. When it eventually pops I have to conclude that he doesn't have much of a backside at all. The pockets of his jeans have nothing pressing against them—at least at the back! He hands me a glass with—I have to say—a disappointing amount of wine in it. But perhaps I'm to taste it first?

I take a sip. 'It's very nice.' I hesitantly offer the glass back to him for refilling. He ignores it, or doesn't notice, and carries on talking.

'The Nebbiolo grape is one of the best varieties in Italy, if not the world.' He puts his nose in his glass and inhales. I marvel at his air of—I'm not sure what to call it—his air of confidence I suppose. Actually, it's more than that. He has a distinct aura of superiority.

'I wouldn't argue with that.' I smile cradling my wine as if I'd never had any intention of asking for more.

'Right, now to grind *ze erbs*.' He puts his untouched wine down and claps his hands. 'I'll drink that when it's had a chance to breathe,' he adds.

'You must be a connoisseur, Egremont. It tastes great to me.'

'Leave it a while longer and you'll see the difference.' Without waiting for a response (and good because I don't have one) he busily begins gathering up bunches of herbs.

I put my glass down feeling a little plebeian. 'Can I help with anything?' I ask, watching him chop leaves like a TV chef. He looks at me and smiles hesitantly. 'Well, can I?' I repeat.

'You could wash the lettuce—and maybe peel the mushrooms—if you don't mind.'

'I don't mind at all.' I go to the sink. He smiles at me indulgently. 'So, tell me, Egremont, how come you speak Italian?' I release the lettuce from its string as I wait for his answer. Half a ton of soil falls out. I laugh. 'I take it these veg are organic.'

'I *only* buy organic.'

'Oh?' I turn on an overhanging tap and get soaked by the splash-back when the water hits the sink.

Egremont comes over and turns off the gushing tap. 'It's a bit keen,' he says, pulling a face by way of apology. He turns it on again, slowly.

'That's better, thanks.' I shove the lettuce underneath it, ignoring the fact that I'm a bit drenched. 'Did you learn at school or do you have Italian connections?'

His reply is an embarrassed smile, which I have no idea how to interpret.

'Do you speak Italian?' I ask hesitantly, wondering if I've got something wrong. Perhaps he doesn't speak the lingo after all—just knows a few phrases. He nods bashfully, biting his bottom lip. 'Oh, say something for me.' I try not to think how unattractive his coy look is right now (give me back the man with his confident nose in *Barolo*).

'I don't know what to say,' he simpers. Sorry, but he is simpering. Isn't he?

'Say anything. Ask me something about what we're doing now.'

He looks around and pulls a pestle and mortar down from a shelf, then says, 'Mi puo spiegare che cose-e questo?'

'What does that mean?' I ask when he offers no translation.

'It just means, "Can you tell me what this is"?'

'Well, I'm impressed.' I'm lying—his accent wasn't authentic; that's to say, it didn't sound like an Italian accent.

He nods and bites his lip again. I begin shaking the lettuce leaves dry over the sink.

'Oh, I have a salad spinner for that. It's just here.' He comes over.

Awkwardly, he reaches into a cupboard above me. The sensation of his closeness sends a thrill through me. He hands me a white plastic spinner and looks into my eyes. I forget to breathe for a moment. I tell you, something happens when he gets close to me. He smiles as if he can read my thoughts then moves back to his side of the kitchen. When I'm done spinning the lettuce, I turn to the mushrooms. I see there are just a few specks of dirt so I begin to rinse them.

'Don't do that!' he shouts in a panic.

'What?' I look at the mushrooms with confusion.

'You should never wash mushrooms.' He's sounding genuinely distressed. 'They have to be peeled or dusted. Washing releases toxins.'

'Oh—sorry.' I stand dead still holding the offending wet mushrooms in my fists.

'I did say to peel them. But here, it's okay. I'll take over. You're the guest. I shouldn't have asked you. You should be relaxing. Please—have a seat.' This is definitely a command

and not a suggestion. He stands aside for me to pass.

I pick up my wine and take a seat at the small kitchen table. He begins peeling the mushrooms with a look of consternation showing that he's still reeling from the shock of me washing the things. I have to look away from this slightly unmanly Egremont. I find myself face-to-face with a large photograph of somewhere in the countryside—it looks like olive groves.

'Was this picture taken in Spain?'

'Italy,' he says without turning around.

'It looks like a beautiful place.' I wonder at myself for not thinking of Italy first.

'It's Tuscany. My folks have a place there, not far from where that picture was taken.'

'Lucky you.' To this he nods, still without turning around. I look at another picture; it's of snow-capped mountains. I don't hazard a guess as to where it could be. Perhaps I should recognise them.

'We're all going there soon,' says Egremont finally looking in my direction.

'Where—here?' I point at the snowy scene, which could be a picture of Mount Everest for all I know.

'Yes. We're off skiing there.'

He skis! Do I like the idea? Not sure—no—I don't know. 'I didn't have you down as a skier,' I say, more to myself than to him.

'Why not?' he asks in a tone that suggests my assumption is a strange one to him.

'I'm not sure. It's just you seem …' God, I don't know what to say.

'The indoors type?'

'Perhaps.' I smile and take a sip of breathed wine. 'Ummm, I see what you mean. It tastes even richer now.'

'Told you it would.' He picks up his own glass, takes a sip and nods with approval. 'Do you ski, Eve?'

'Me? Err, no. Never tried it.'

'You should. It's great fun.' I wonder whether his next sentence will be an invitation to join him on the piste in the French Alps, but instead he tells me to take my wine through to the dining room. Guess it's just on the piss for now then—ha!

'Don't you want any more help in here?' I ask not sure if I want to be banished to another room.

'No, I'm nearly done. The water's almost boiling for the pasta. And don't worry, it'll be *al dente*—always to the tooth in my kitchen.'

I refrain from telling him that out of a tin would be fine by me.

'Please—go into the dining room,' he says firmly, indicating an adjoining door.

I go through into a small but earthy room. It has coarse wooden flooring and exposed brick walls. I like it! One wall is filled with summer-infused pictures of—I'm guessing— his place in Tuscany. I look closely at the ones featuring Egremont. He's beaming a big smile in most of them, standing among flowery green meadows or under a canopy of leafy grapevines. There are some more of him sitting at a table groaning with food. How different he looks! More handsome. I wonder who the other people are: family or friends? There are no alpine photos, I notice with relief. I don't want to see him in a ski suit.

I hear the door open. Egremont comes into the room bearing two dishes. 'Per questa sera, linguine con aragosta,' he sings, putting the bowls on the black wood table. 'We'll have our salad and cheese to follow. I like to mix things up. I know—call me a maverick!' He chuckles to himself and sits down, indicating for me to sit down too.

A fake laugh escapes me. But I'm not sure if he's serious. Was that a real joke? Was it funny? And what's he mixing up?

'Would you like more wine?' he asks, getting up.

'Please.' I look at my empty glass. I don't remember finishing it!

'Be right back.' He practically skips out of the room. Good boy! Seconds later he's topping me up, giving me a little more than before.

'Well'—I pull the dish toward me—'this looks and smells a-m*a*-zing.'

'It's one of my signature dishes. I hope it's not *too awful*.' He takes his seat again. I look at him, not quite sure how to respond. Should I say something about his use of the word 'signature'? He must be something of a cook. 'Please—begin.' He nods encouragingly.

'Right—yes!' I pick up my fork and take a spoon from the top of the plate.

I gather up the pasta hoping it won't spring out of control and deposit spatters of sauce all over my face. I manage all right. I look to see how Egremont is attacking his meal and am surprised to see that he hasn't begun yet.

Instead, he is sitting motionless and regarding me with great anxiety.

'What is it?' I ask, pausing with the fork in front of my mouth. He bites his lip and smiles weirdly. 'Egremont, what's the matter?'

'It's just that Italians don't use a spoon to eat their spaghetti.' He winces as if this news may be devastating to me.

'Oh, don't they?' I put the messy spoon on the bread plate and await further instruction but this doesn't seem to relieve Egremont's fretfulness on my behalf—he's still smiling in the same constrained manner.

'I'll get you a fresh spoon for your dessert,' he says getting up and taking the offending cutlery away.

I watch him leave and shake my head. But this is Egremont; he'll be all right soon. He's just not used to having women—me—in his house.

'It's an English affectation,' he says when he comes back, clearly relaxed again. 'I don't know how it started—probably with Delia Smith. You can always spot the English abroad just by their *spooning spaghetti*. The Italians think it's hysterical. And we do too, I have to admit. It's naughty of us, I know.'

Trying not to show my disdain for this nonsense, I say 'One shouldn't mock the afflicted.' He laughs as if it's a good joke. Still laughing, he wades into his food, deftly swirling pasta around his fork. What else to do? I follow his lead. Ha! I'm humbled to find that the spoon is indeed unnecessary, and perhaps in future I too will stare in stupefied horror, or superior amusement, at the ignoramuses who commit that gastronomic no-no—or perhaps I won't.

'This is really good,' I tell him enthusiastically. It's actually just okay. The pasta is underdone and the sauce is bland; but whether he can't cook or I have no taste I couldn't say.

'Thank you.' He shakes his head a little as if uncomfortable with praise.

'So tell me, Egremont, if you don't mind me being nosey'—he shakes his head vigorously —'I know that you were going to be a priest.' I pause, waiting for some kind of reaction, but he continues eating, his head down. 'What happened?—if that's not too impertinent a question.'

Now he looks up and I smile gently to encourage him. He nods his head from side to side. Perhaps he's contemplating how best to answer me, or maybe he doesn't want to speak with his mouth full. Either way, it's taking him a while to answer.

'When I got to sixteen,' he says finally, almost in a whisper, 'I knew it wasn't for me.' I suddenly have a vision of him kneeling before Christ on the cross. His eyes are streaming with tears as he begs forgiveness for not being able to sacrifice body and soul to the calling. And all the time he's tormented by scenes of the hellfire that may await him when he goes to the grave—or when he tells his parents. My heart bursts with respect for his bravery.

'Was it a terrible blow to your family?' I ask, feeling a lump in my throat. I can hardly swallow my wine.

'Not really.' He laughs. 'My family have always been incredibly supportive. And they could see I was more suited to Jesus boots than Jesus Christ.' He laughs at his joke and I wonder how many times he's told that anecdote over the years.

'Oh—that's nice,' I say deflated, though I laugh at myself a moment later—so much for the agonised martyrdom!

He continues to eat without offering more information. 'Have you any brothers or sisters?' I ask after some minutes of silence, which I spend looking at the pictures on the walls.

He nods and waits until he's swallowed his food before replying. He flaps a hand in front of his mouth as if to hurry it down. Eventually he says, 'I have two brothers, Robert and Rupert. One's a teacher and the other's a stockbroker.'

'A stockbroker!' I say it like I know what that is. Then I come clean. 'What does a stockbroker actually do?'

'He buys and sells securities and stocks—through the stock exchange.'

'I trust he's not a rogue trader?' I laugh.

'He's extremely ethical and takes his financial commitments very seriously.'

'I'm sure he does.' I cough and straighten my face. 'You said your other brother was a teacher? Where does he teach—what does he teach?' I hope this is a safer ground.

'He's a math's teacher—in Leeds.'

'They're very much in demand I know. He must be clever.'

Egremont nods and says, 'Oh, he is—very clever. Our family are gifted in that respect.' I refrain from coughing again, but perhaps he doesn't mean it how it sounds.

'What's the school like where he teaches?'

'It's at the top of the league tables.' He smiles with pride.

'He doesn't have to deal with any ASBO kids then?'

'No, no, no,' he replies and seems to laugh at the ridiculousness of the idea.

'Did he ever try a little inner-city philanthropy—the teachers' baptism of fire?' Why am I talking like I know anything about it?

'No,' he says with a frown as if such an idea is inappropriate. I wonder again if I'm misreading him. I pick up my wine glass; it's almost empty. I put it down immediately. I see Egremont is watching me closely. He's hardly touched his wine.

With relief I suddenly remember we have something else to talk about. I haven't asked him yet about what was happening on Monday with that mysterious tall guy and the office décor.

'So Harrison's is getting a make-over and I see you've helped Mitchell out again with your connections.'

'My *connections*?' His eyes twinkle mischievously and he finally has some wine. He's clearly enjoying this line of conversation.

'In the office on Monday—you, Mitchell and that tall guy—what was it all about? It sounded like you'd found some internationally renowned artist.'

Egremont just smiles at me.

'It's not Damian Hurst is it? Please tell me we're not going to be having our coffee over pickled foetuses.'

He shoots me a look of surprised disgust.

'Sorry, that was in bad taste. But tell me who it is. I won't breathe a word.'

'If I tell you, I'll have to kill you.' He makes large eyes at me. I love it—he's getting sporting! I think back to the knickers incident—is he also getting horny?

'Ooooh, I love a mystery. So it's top secret? But you'll

tell me?' I say flirtatiously picking up my glass and finishing the contents.

'I can't say anything about it yet.' He picks up the wine bottle and pours me a little more. Yes!

'Nothing?' I tease.

'Would you like more pasta?' he asks signalling that the subject is closed.

'No thanks, that was just a perfect amount. It was really delicious. You certainly know how to cook.' To this he tips his head to one side and smiles at me with lips firmly closed. His eyes seem to twinkle with pride and delight at what I've said. He has so many facial signals.

'Now for our *salad and cheese*,' he says with relish and a lift of his shoulders as he gets up and takes my plate. So I still haven't got to the bottom of his connection with the tall guy, the art make-over and all the rest of it. Later then.

Looking away from a stack of books on Italy I turn to another array of family pictures on the wall. I stop at one where they're all enjoying an *al fresco* meal. Will I be joining them at their chateau or villa, or whatever they call cutesy cottages in Italy? Will I want to? I suddenly have a conviction that Egremont would do better if it were just me and him. Maybe I'll persuade him to buy another villa, complete with a kidney-shaped swimming pool. Yes, and I'll live in it all year round. Ha! Sounds like a plan.

When Egremont returns I gasp at the sight. He's wheeling in a trolley covered with cheeses of all different shapes, sizes and colours. And the smell! I see on the shelf below there is a corresponding quantity of bread and crackers. There's enough for a wedding buffet.

'Told you you were in for a treat!' he says, bringing the trolley to a halt next to me. 'I'll be right back with our salads.' I push it away slightly to give myself some breathing space. When he comes back he's carrying bowls the size of satellite dishes.

'Salata verde proprietati.' He places a bowl in front of me. 'I hope you don't mind but I took the liberty of dressing the salad for you.'

'Not at all.' I look down at the very green meal in front of me.

'And with it you must have some cheese. Which would you like to try first?' He sweeps an upturned palm over the trolley like a dolly bird with an array of prizes in a TV game show.

'I'd like to try that one.' I point to one of the less scary-looking blocks.

'That's taleggio, Rupert's favourite.' He cuts into it then places a piece on a plate. I ask him who Rupert is.

'My brother—the *stockbroker*.'

'Oh yes, sorry. You just told me. He's the one who's not a rogue trader.' He smiles constrainedly and ducks down under the trolley. He soon emerges again handing me my plate now with the addition of crackers. 'Hope you enjoy. That cheese is produced in the Taleggio valley, north of Bergamo. The pasture there is particularly sweet and luscious.'

I take the plate thanking him.

'Also try this one.' He's cutting at another cheese. 'It's Robiola, made with unpasteurized full-cream cows' milk. Robert likes it because it's a little *spicy*.' He says the word 'spicy' with emphasis and lifts his eyebrows as if it's a little risqué. I offer my plate when he lifts up the slice of cheese.

'Robert would be the teacher?' I'm surprised by a trace of fatigue in my voice.

'Sorry, I can get carried away when discussing cheese. We're a family of *cheese lovers*.' I nod with a forced smile and go to taste some cheese. 'And you must try this one—Asiago, it's from …'

Egremont loses me as he reels off the background info on the cheese. He doesn't wait for me to lift my plate this time and just leans over dropping the cheese (and then another) where there's room. I pray they're not too strong. But at least he hasn't said the words 'Stinking Bishop' yet. 'I'm quite fond of that one myself,' he says as I put some cheese on a cracker. 'It's our mum's favourite—Castelmagno, made with both …'

He's off again, and the cheese knife is soon being put under my nose with other samples. I reach for the wine, telling him to sit down and enjoy his own cheese and salad. Mercifully he obeys. A good sign for marital harmony?

However, it isn't long before he's back on his feet telling me, 'You're going to try new kinds of bread. I'm going to give you an education in dough.' He laughs like it's a joke. I try to do the same, but it comes out as a groan. 'And when I'm through with you, I promise you'll know your farinata from your biovetta, and your bruschetta from your ciabatta.'

'Great.'

'Here.' He hands me a chunk of bread. 'Try this ciabatta. It's one of the most popular breads in Italy. It's made with type zero wheat flour.'

'Actually, Egremont, I'm a little full. I think I'll have to forgo the delights of your breads—on this occasion.'

'Really? But shouldn't you soak up your wine? Don't want you getting tipsy.'

He doesn't want me tipsy? Why? Because it will hinder sexual play, or promote it? He's right, sex is far better without alcohol—from what I can remember, anyway!

'I'm very full. There won't be a problem there.' I smile and make meaningful eyes at him.

'What about dessert?'

'I couldn't eat anything else. Sorry.'

'If you're sure then. Maybe later.' He starts picking up the plates.

'Here, let me help you clear away.' I get up.

'I can manage. Please—go through to the sitting room.' Shit, I think I've offended him. But how? Not wanting anymore? I'm prevented from dwelling on it by a sudden pressing feeling in my bladder.

'Can I use your bathroom?' For a few moments he looks at me and doesn't reply. Has he forgotten where his own bathroom is?

'It's upstairs at the end of the landing.' He says this without looking at me. It's making me slightly ashamed that I need to go.

On my way upstairs I have to admit that I'm conflicted in my feelings. No, conflicted is too strong a word. It suggests—well, I don't know exactly. Okay, he's not as shy or reserved as I thought he was. And the food thing, the family of cheese lovers—do I want to be part of a family of cheese lovers? Oh shut up. Poor Egremont! He's probably never had a woman in his house—not on a date, anyway—and doesn't know how to behave. He's trying to impress me, bless him. I need to make some allowances, that's all. Yes—that's all it is.

When I reach the landing I push open a door knowing it's not the bathroom. I'm going to peek at his bedroom, although this doesn't look like it. It's a spare room I'd say, judging by the stuff on the bed. Interesting that it's covered in clutter—not ready for a guest. The house is too small for another bedroom so if he has ideas of me staying, well, there's only one other place for me to sleep! Are those more books on Italy I see? I leave the room noiselessly without investigating further.

With all the stealth of a cat burglar I move on to the next room. I press down the handle slowly. When it's open enough for me to put my head round, I gasp. Unlike the spare room with its colourful queen-sized bed, before me is a single bed covered in a grey blanket with a large cross on the wall above it! The room looks like a monastic cell. On the side table there's nothing but a jug of water and a plain black bible.

'It's the door at the end,' says Egremont just behind me. Shit, caught out! I pull the door to and turn to face him. He's paused at the top of the stairs.

'Thanks,' I say cheerily as if I've done nothing wrong, but I go into the bathroom with my face the colour of a tomato.

Sitting on the loo I readjust my fantasy about him carrying me into his bedroom like that scene in *An Officer and a Gentleman*. Me dragging him to that spare bed like a femme fatale would be closer to the truth, because despite the monastic cell, or even because of it, I want this guy.

When I'm finished in the bathroom I see him heading downstairs with a large blue book in his hand. It looks like the book I saw lying on the spare bed. I join him on a small cottage suite in his sitting room and try to match his I-didn't-see-anything-untoward-just-then smile. The poky little armrest digs into my side as I sit down and turn to face Egremont. He puts the book between us.

'They're all scenes of Tuscany,' he says enthusiastically. I *ummm* and *ahhhh* at various pictures of ancient ruins, poppy fields and olive groves, and try to look interested as he points out cute little farmhouses where he and various members of his family have stayed at one time or another. But his closeness isn't boring; it's exciting. Physically he's in good shape, and those hands—I do love his manly hands. My flesh burns at the idea of them all over me. Eve!

'Have you got any plans for tomorrow?' he asks suddenly.

'None that I can't change—I mean, if you wanted to—'

He smiles and I stop speaking. 'I have two tickets for the opera, or rather my brother does. Rupert asked me if I wanted them. He had to return to London and now they're going begging.'

'The opera?' I'm looking into his eyes warmly.

'Yes.' I hardly heard that, and now he's smiling so shyly and awkwardly under my gaze. I love that I can take his confidence away.

'I've never been to the opera.'

'It's *Turandot*.'

'It's *what-n-dot?*' I say, taken aback. I immediately regret my scornful show of ignorance.

His face betrays a trace of irritation but it thankfully

passes and he says cheerfully, 'Oh, the usual saga of love, betrayal and *despotism*.'

'Then I'd love to go to the opera. Actually, I've always wanted the experience.' I suddenly see myself as Julia Roberts in *Pretty Woman*, the bit where she's mesmerised by the operatic performance and Richard Gere is thrilled by her reaction, and no doubt congratulating himself on giving her something else to do other than sucking cock for a living, although technically she still is. But I digress!

'I don't know why I haven't been before.'

'It's not very *Liverpool*. The city's more panto than Pagliacci.' He laughs at the thought.

The snobbery irks but he's probably right. 'Well, I'd love to go.' And I truly do.

'Then we'll go to the opera tomorrow.' His face breaks into a broad smile like he's the happiest man alive.

'Okay.' I laugh a little at how we're throwing ourselves together.

'I'll get the tickets first thing tomorrow.'

'Brilliant.'

'I'll put some coffee on and we can discuss it.' He closes the book and heads off to the kitchen.

'Would love some coffee, thanks.'

When he's gone I look around the room. There'll certainly be a number of changes when I'm installed as lady of the manner. This poky cottage suite will go, that's for sure, as will the orange-patterned wallpaper. I'll get some soft lighting too.

When he comes back in I see the coffee is accompanied by dessert. 'It's tiramisu,' he says excitedly. Right—what else! 'You don't mind having it on your lap? We left the table somewhat prematurely.'

'No, that's fine, thank you.' I take the small dish and scoop a spoonful into my mouth. 'Mmmmm, it's really good.' And it is.

'It's home-made, but not by me.'

'Oh? Who made it?'

'The owners of my favourite trattoria, Modigliani's. I'll take you there some day, if you don't mind.'

'Mind?' I laugh. 'I'd love to go.'

'Would you like more coffee?' he asks as I finish my tiramisu.

'No thanks.' I hand him the empty dish.

'There's more if you'd like,' he says encouragingly.

'No thanks.'

We become awkwardly quiet. 'Do you want to go now?'

'Go? Now? No!' I protest.

He smiles at my reaction. I move closer to him. His excited smile fades. He knows what I'm about. I'd move even closer but it's not possible. He has to seize the moment and kiss me. I look at him, making my eyes as big as I can. He drops his head a little. He's too shy. Am I putting him off? Another few moments pass and I can tell he's not going to make a move. That's okay—softly, softly, catchee monkey.

To ease the tension, I put some space between us and ask him again about his very public meeting by my desk (then desk) on Monday with the tall guy, Chaz. 'I know you can't tell me about the artist who may or may not be hired, but can you tell me what's going to happen with the décor at Harrison's? Sounds like a radical makeover whoever is chosen.' He pulls his face in a no-can-do expression.

'Well, Mitchell's pleased with you, that's clear.'

'Yes,' he says looking confused.

'But the way he treats you normally—I'm surprised you care for his—Sorry, what I'm trying to say is that I really admire the way you handle him.'

'Handle who?' The same confused smile makes his lips twitch. Surely he can't be oblivious to the bullying?

'*Who*?—Mitchell, you goose.' I can't help but laugh.

'I don't know that I *handle* him exactly.' He's looking at me as if I've suggested something awful.

My laughter disappears and I take a deep breath. 'So who was the tall posh guy?' I ask bluntly.

'I'm blessed to know him'—he closes his eyes and bows his head—'He comes from very grand stock.' He looks up and laughs. 'They're like royalty.'

'Really?'

'Yes, he's very *grand*,' he says again with a head wobble (he does this head wobble a lot when he emphasises words).

'He looks like a toff I have to say. But can you really not tell me who the mysterious artist is that he knows?

I suppose he mixes in the first circles, or whatever the expression is. Is it someone famous?'

'They will be one day I'm sure.'

'Ah, so it's an unknown.'

'I really can't say anything yet.' He shrugs his shoulders and bites his bottom lip as if it's all just too exciting. It has the effect of making me annoyed.

'I guess it's late,' I say, looking at my watch.

'Do you want me to call your cab now,' he asks, looking at me with concern.

'You're not taking me home?'

'Sorry, I've had too much wine.' Too much wine! I want to say, *you've barely had a glass*. A frustrated sigh escapes me. 'Don't worry, I know the firm. I have an account with them. It's all paid for too, so please don't think of the fare. Here, let me call them.' He reaches for the phone at the side of the couch.

'Thanks.' I can hardly keep the disappointment out of my voice.

'Ten minutes is fine,' he says into the receiver and hangs up. He looks at me, smiling. 'And we have the opera to look forward to tomorrow.' He seems to sense my disappointment.

'We do indeed.' I force an enthusiastic smile.

Ten minutes later a hooting horn indicates that the taxi has arrived. I've been sitting with my coat on and my bag on my knee for nine minutes.

'Well,' I start to get up. 'Thank you for a nice evening—no, a *wonderful* evening.'

He gets up too and we practically bump into each other. 'Yes, I've really enjoyed having you here.' He looks at me seriously. Is he going to kiss me now? But instead of leaning toward me he leans backwards. 'We'll *do it again* soon,' he says, wobbling his head and ruining the moment.

'Good, and of course I'll see you tomorrow night.'

'I'll pick you up at seven.' We're walking to the door.

'See you at seven then.' I give him a peck on the cheek. He squeezes my shoulder and the gesture makes my stomach flip. It's as if he's telling me that although nothing happened tonight, something will—soon.

I wave goodnight to him with renewed desire.

# 6

I LOOK AT THE CLOCK AND SEE it's gone eleven.

'Will you be getting up anytime today?' It's my mother.

'I'll be out soon.' I stretch and breathe deeply with satisfaction. I'll go and fetch my new car as soon as I'm dressed. I thought I'd leave it till midday to pick up. Mitchell wouldn't have been in any hurry to have it there for nine. My first port of call after that will be town to get some super sexy nightwear (don't want to spend the morning at his in a boring dressing gown). I have a feeling Egremont may forget himself tonight. I'll buy some sensual perfume too. Not one inch of me will be neglected!

'You're picking up the car now?' asks Mum as I enter the kitchen.

'I sure am.' I grab a banana from the fruit bowl.

'Shall we go shopping after you've got it?'

'Erm—not sure. I have a few things to do.' I peel the banana.

'Like what?' she asks, frowning.

I'm stumped for a reply. 'Where did you want to go?' I eventually ask, biting the top of the banana aggressively. 'We could go the Gemini. We need some food shopping. We could have a nice tea tonight and a bottle of wine—or two.' I smile to myself at her saying 'tea' when she used to say 'dinner'. She's forgotten she was once a middle-class snob.

'I'm going out tonight.' How much should I reveal?

'Oh?'

'With Egremont.'

'Again! But you were with him last night.'

'He's got tickets for the opera. There's a bunch of us going, or I think there might be. Can't remember what he said.'

'Well, we still need food,' Mum says somewhat dryly. 'Can you take me?'

'I suppose so.' I throw the banana skin in the bin and grab my bag.

'Don't you want some coffee?' she asks as I head out of the room.

'No thanks. I'm impatient to get the car.'

'Oooooh, a car. How grown up you'll be.' She hugs herself in excitement.

I nod, flash a smile and leave.

To my relief the car is where Mitchell said it would be. I throw my bag containing a super-sexy angels-lace babydoll nightdress (tasteful silver blue satin). Got perfume too. How would Laetitia put it? *It's time to knock 'em dead, kiddo.* I got off the bus a stop earlier to get the shops out of the way. I sigh with satisfaction at the new smell of the car.

Getting into the front seat is equally gratifying. Everything has a solid luxurious feel to it. It may not be a Merc but it's the next best thing. It's been about a year since I've driven. Mum and I shared a car before she sold it—or rather, failed to make the payments. I pull out on to the main road with a stupid smile on my face, waving at Harrison's and thanking Mitchell for giving me a promotion (yes, actually thanking Mitchell). I'm home within fifteen minutes.

'Can we stop at the post office first?' asks Mum who has opened the car door before I've had time to switch the engine off.

'I was going to have some coffee.' I look on with annoyance as she gets in.

'We'll have coffee out,' she says, rubbernecking over her seat to look at the car.

'Fine.' I drive on.

'This is lovely,' says Mum stroking the seat. 'And what have you been buying?' Before I can answer she's pulled the Victoria's Secret bag onto her lap.

'Mum, that's private. Leave it alone.'

'Private! What nonsense. Let me look.' She pulls out the nightie. 'Gosh, what or *who* is this for?'

'No one.' I snatch it out of her hand and throw it onto the backseat.

'No call for that. I was just—'

'You said you wanted to go to the post office?' 'I need to pay the TV licence,' she says curtly.

'Right, okay, the post office it is.' I turn into the high street. Thankfully there are plenty of spaces to park.

'I won't be a minute,' says Mum unclasping her seatbelt. As she's getting out my eyes are drawn to the Oxfam shop and I'm horrified. It's decked out with all Mum's Lakeland stuff.

'What's the matter?' asks Mum, putting her head back in the car.

'Nothing!' I frantically undo my seatbelt so I can get out and distract her. 'I'll come in with you and give you something toward the payment.'

'You can do it later,' she says, looking at me surprised.

'I need to get a card—for someone at work.'

'They'll have nicer cards in Marksies.'

'I want to have a look, Mum.'

'Okay, I'll meet you in there.'

To my relief, she walks into the post office without so much as a look at the Oxfam shop. I go closer to inspect the window display. I can't help but gawp when I see her Timberland boots and Hunter wellies all cleaned up and on sale for a fiver apiece. The Timberlands must have cost her near £200 and the others not far off. Everything I brought yesterday is on show—her wax coats, canvas seat, expensive weatherproof picnic blanket and so on—are all on sale for less than ten quid each. My mother will have a fit to end all fits if she sees this, and after the tongue-lashing about how I've betrayed her trust and gone against her word she'll take it all back. I rush into the post office. Mercifully, we're back in the car within ten minutes and she didn't see a thing. What she does see, however, is me laughing into my jumper. 'What's the joke?' she asks several times along the motorway.

'I saw a very funny sight while you were in the post office.' I fight back the laughter.

'I only saw some very depressing things.' She sighs. 'What happened to our high street, Evelyn? There used to be butcher's shops and banks—fresh groceries.'

'You never supported any of the high street shops,' I say, astonished at her indignation.

'Don't confuse me with the truth.' She laughs.

'I know what you mean, though. It's all pawn shops and takeaways now. That and scruffy bargain-booze shops. They serve you through a hatch.'

'Yes, it's grim,' says Mum with a shudder.

Mum continues her lament on the sorry state of the high street and as she's doing so I begin feeling guilty about having tricked her. That I felt I had little choice isn't any consolation. I have further cause for guilt when the first thing she does when we're in the store is tell me to go and choose something for myself as a treat. 'Anything you like. It's my gift to you for getting your promotion.'

'You don't have to, Mum. It's okay.'

'I insist, darling. Go and get yourself a nice dress or suit, or some jewellery—both if you like. Shoes too. Go the whole hog. I know you've bought some nice things already but nothing was from me, and I want to know my favourite daughter is beginning her new career with something from her mum.'

'Thanks Mum.' I give her a kiss on the cheek and feel a lump in my throat.

'I'll be in the food section. Oh wait, I'll come with you. I could do with some tops for work. We have a do coming up. Let's see if we can't find some bargains, eh?'

I laugh and nod in agreement, following her as she pushes the trolley eagerly into impulse-buying heaven.

# 7

IT'S NEARLY SEVEN—JUST MINUTES to go before Egremont's arrival. We're going to see *Tosca*, not *Turandot*. His brother got mixed up, although it's all the bloody same to me, of course. Ordinarily Mum wouldn't have been excited by the prospect of Egremont taking me out, but she's getting heady with all that's beginning to change in my life, so much so that now she's acting as if Egremont taking me out is something to celebrate. I'm not sure her buoyant mood will last when she sees him again (time having rose-tinted the memory and all that). She'll have no idea, of course, that she's looking at her future son-in-law.

That little gem can wait.

Right now Mum's readjusting my hair to her exacting specifications of a French roll. It's one thing—or *some*thing—she can do really well and the process is calming my nerves (or was). She dries my hair section by section and then rolls each division in giant rollers. She's now dried it again already taken the rollers out. She's just finished backcombing it all and I look like a demented cave woman. But now she's doing something miraculous and is turning straw into gold. Really, I'm not exaggerating—the finished effect is glorious. But Egremont—he'll be here in ten minutes! She needs to get a move on.

'If you stop fretting, I'll have it finished sooner. You're putting me off.' She yanks my head back as the comb gets stuck. I breathe deeply and force myself to be calm. At least I'm ready (make up and dress on).

Mum seems to have worked herself up into a maternal lather at the prospect of a man arriving in black tie and suit to escort her precious one (ha!) to the theatre. She's doing her best to convince herself that she's misjudged Egremont on those few occasions she met him before. 'Perhaps I underestimated Egremont,' she'd said vaguely as we pulled into our road.

'Okay, you're all done,' says Mum. The door!

Mum throws me into unknown emotional territory by running her hand along my face and saying, 'You look *stunning*'. I'm almost overcome with tears at the tenderness in her voice and the look of admiration in her eyes. Right now I dearly wish Egremont were somebody who would reward her motherly expectations. I have a surreal desire to leave the door unanswered. But go to the door I must.

I could burst with happiness when I open the it. Egstasy looks amazing—suave, sophisticated, even handsome in that rugged way some men have. He looks like a James Bond—well, an older version, with a twist. Oh that suit is *phwoah*.

'You look out of this world,' he whispers, stepping in. I pull at the hem of my black velvet dress. It's just above the knee and the sheer black tights make my legs look terrific, as do the chic suede ankle boots (this is the stuff I got today, thanks to Mum). My hands look cool too, peeping out of the long elegant sleeves, showing off to perfection my fake diamond jewellery, and what with the perfume—Egremont won't be able to resist me later. His immediate admiration of me, however, is soon eclipsed by his need to concentrate on negotiating the bags and boxes in the hallway, and because Mum's within earshot I'm unable to apologise for the obstacle course. He smiles in amazement at the hall-cum-grotto he's having to navigate. The contrast to his own hallway couldn't be starker—and that's probably exactly what he's thinking himself right now I shouldn't wonder.

When he steps into the sitting room and stands before the mother-in-law-to-be, Mum's mouth opens and closes several times like a feeding goldfish's and she's glued to the spot, unable to speak, just staring at Egremont. When she coughs and snaps out of her trance, I can't tell whether she's pleased, horrified, repulsed, astonished, mildly perplexed or has merely returned to her usual state of exasperated scorn. But it's clear that she's experiencing some kind of emotion. 'You remember Egremont?' I say as if I'm talking to a geriatric.

'Yes! Egremont.' She gawps at him. 'You're taking Evelyn to the opera. Very good. You look very nice. Would you like a sherry?'

She doesn't like him.

'No, thank you. We're running a little late, I'm afraid.' I daren't look at her again.

'Well well, off you both go then.' She nods her head and shoos us out with flapping hands (yes she's actually shooing us out of the room). Her behaviour is outrageous. I'm so embarrassed. I'm getting angry too that her new-found love and respect for me can be gone in a puff. Egremont steps on a bag as he turns to leave. He apologises.

'Just watch where you're stepping on the way out,' she says in high irritation.

I suddenly feel completely justified in my illicit clear-out of her stuff yesterday. Serves her damn right, cranky fickle cow.

When Egremont and I are seated in his car he looks at me meaningfully, his small mouth forming a hesitant smile. 'You look so lovely,' he says, blinking rapidly.

'Thanks, and so do you.'

'I scrub up well.' He laughs. 'I hope your mother didn't think I was clumsy.' Phew! But did he really miss my mother's signals of hostility?

'You could hardly avoid stepping on something.'

'Someone certainly likes *to shop*.' I want to apologise for Mum's rudeness in telling him off but he begins pulling on absurdly oversized tan-coloured gloves. The sight of them temporarily suspends my ability to think and before I know what I'm saying, the words, 'What do you wear *those* for?' escape.

He looks at his gloved hands, then at me. I can tell my outburst has stung him. I feel terrible. But the gloves—they are seriously ludicrous, and distracting.

'My brother—Robert—he bought them for me. They're driving gloves.' He looks wounded. What have I done?!

'Yes, sorry, so they are. They're very nice,' I lie stupidly. He attempts to smile but a frown prevents it from forming. He places his gloved hands on the steering wheel, then turns to me. His face is relaxed again. More than that—he's looking at me admiringly.

'You really do look lovely—beautiful.' Oh, the gentleness and awe in his voice—I could slide off the seat with the *arrrrrrrrrh* feeling it gives me.

\* \* \*

Walking into the theatre I feel good on Egremont's arm. Now those gloves of his are off, he looks impressive again.

'Here, let me put your coat in the cloakroom.' I hand it over, loving that he's taken the initiative.

'I'll get some drinks then. What will you have?'

'Just a mineral water please.'

'Right you are.' It's a poor complement to the large G&T I'm about to have!

Moving among the interesting-looking theatre-goers makes me positively beam with satisfaction. Everywhere I turn an eccentrically dressed person nods hello. I squeeze past a young gay-looking guy in a trilby to get to the bar. He's with his mother (has to be) who looks like a Russian tsarina in her array of furs. She's hysterically snooty and can hardly look her son in the eye her nose is stuck so far in the air. But I love it! There are all ages here, mixed together. And so many hats! Everyone is dressed up. It's fabulous. It was worth coming just to see this lot alone.

With a mineral water in one hand and a long gin in the

other, I look around for Egremont. He's nowhere to be seen. I go a little further into the throng. Still no sign—then I spy him. He's in conversation with—no, it can't be! I look again. It *is* them. He's talking to the ski-resort couple like they're old friends. I almost drop the drinks with shock. How the hell do they know each other? They've obviously told him I'm approaching because Egremont turns around. I plaster a smile on my face as I go towards them.

I hand Egremont his drink and take a glug of mine in between saying, 'Hi'. Tilly's partner has a very amused smile on his face, although hers isn't much different. God, to be the object of their amusement—*urrrrrgh*.

'Eve, this is Tilly—and her fiancé, Ben,' Egremont says, beaming with delight.

'*Eg-re-mont!*' says Tilly slowly, as if telling him off for something.

'Oh—sorry, I didn't think.' He looks panicked.

'It's fine,' says Ben. 'It's time we told the world we're engaged.'

I look on bemused.

'Their engagement is something of a secret,' says Egremont, quickly adding, 'Sorry, can I say that?'

Tilly laughs. 'Don't worry, Eggers.' She winks at him. Her warm smiles clearly show the gaff is forgiven. Ben, on the other hand, if I'm reading him right, is annoyed at this exchange.

'But tell me, Eggers, who is this again?' she says, looking at me.

'It's Eve—Evelyn, from work.'

'This is *Evelyn*?'

'Yes,' says Egremont looking a little lost.

'Hi Eve.' She puts out her hand for me to shake, but not before darting a look at Egremont that seems to say *you can't be for real*.

'Hi,' I reply taking her limp hand. I'm the only one who does the shaking. Ben's grip, by contrast, nearly crushes my knuckles.

'We know Evelyn—or we've seen her about. She's normally with a *friend* in Vern's,' says Tilly with a smile of innuendo. I don't like the tone of her 'normally' either.

'She means Adam,' I say to Egremont who nods eagerly. 'He's a good friend of mine from work.'

Tilly nods her head but her eyes seem to suggest that she believes Adam is something more than that to me. I'm grateful that Egremont is oblivious to such meanness.

'So you're engaged?' I say, desperate to change the subject.

'We haven't made it public yet,' says Tilly rather archly. She screws up her nose at Ben affectionately. He doesn't reciprocate and I see a troubled look, or a trace of one, on his face. Hmmmm, looks like there's a story there.

I notice with some irritation that Tilly's hair is also in a French roll, and exquisitely done. An abundance of hair allows for undulating curls to fall prettily around her chokered neck, which sets off her green medieval-style dress to tasteful effect. In contrast, I feel like Patsy from *Ab Fab* with my extreme bouffant. No wonder the eccentrics were drawn to me.

'How do you guys know each other?' I ask before Tilly has time to ask another question (she was getting ready to, I could tell).

'We met in Tuscany,' says Tilly smiling indulgently at Egremont.

'On the slopes,' adds Ben, now looking as dopily happy as Tilly.

'On the slopes *in Tuscany*?' I query, thinking they must have got something confused.

'Why is that strange?' asks Tilly, narrowing her eyes at me.

'You don't mean you ski in Tuscany?' As soon as the words are out I feel my face getting hot because I know I'm exposing my ignorance.

'You haven't heard of the Apennines then?' she asks. My face burns full read as I admit my mistake. Of course, I should have known there would be mountains there. Why did I have it in my fucking head it was hot all the year round in Tuscany? Tilly laughs at my expense. I curse myself for not having asked Egremont about the bloody alpine pictures.

'Passo delle Radici, Monte Amiata, Casone di Profecchia. They're all fabulous ski resorts,' says Tilly still laughing at me. She also winks at Egremont, which makes me boil.

'They're on the Tuscan–Emilian range to be precise,' adds Egremont, seemingly blind to my humiliation.

'We're all mad for skiing,' Ben chips in, though not in a way that suggests he's saving me from the social quicksand I'm sinking in.

'What do you both do here, in Liverpool?' I ask quickly.

But Tilly continues as though we're still in Tuscany. 'It was a happy coincidence when we found out we all hailed from Liverpool,' she says, flashing yet another indulgent smile at Egremont who's now twinkling his eyes at her as though she were me—*grrrrrrrrrrrr*. I have more gin.

'In answer to your question,' says Ben, finally looking at me, 'I work for Channel 9.'

'Doing what?' Now I have to add the green-eyed monster to the other horrors I'm suffering.

'I do research at the moment, but one day, soon, I hope to get in front of the camera reporting on the things that matter.'

Tilly doesn't offer any information about herself and I leave it. No doubt she's a lady of leisure and I really don't want my nose rubbed in that.

'Do you live near here?' I ask, eager to complete their profile. I just know they live in Sofia Mansions or somewhere equally as grand and expensive. That's the equivalent of London's Park Lane—well almost.

'We live in Sofia Mansions,' says Ben rather archly, like he's Richard E Grant, or that's the accent anyway. While I'm trying not to look sick with envy, I see Tilly looking at her handsome reporter-to-be as if she's unsure of something.

'It's very smart round there,' I say resigning myself to the fact that they're rich and I need to get over it. Also, I'm quickly getting bored with the pair of them. But I'm intrigued by Tilly's continuing puzzled stare. Is Ben lying?

'It is very smart,' Ben goes on. 'The high point is the terrace. I have an enviable view over the estuary.'

A smirk spreads across my face at his use of the word 'estuary'. He can't bring himself to say Mersey—it's just too common!

'I practically live outdoors in the summer,' he says, sniffing in as if smelling the sea air.

'It's true,' says Tilly with the trace of a lisp I didn't notice before. 'We have *th*uppers out there constantly in the *th*ummer.' She sounds rather silly now.

'It's an impressive view,' repeats Egremont, laughing. I feel like asking what he's laughing about.

'And you—you're in sales, we hear?' says Ben in what I can only describe as a mocking tone. I look at Egremont.

'I was telling Tilly and Ben, Eve, how you're a natural sales woman. I was saying how you can *show the boys* a thing or two.' At this Tilly opens her eyes wide in a vacant stare. I think she's trying to indicate this news is no news to her.

'Fascinating!' says Ben. 'Do tell us more, Eve.'

I bristle at how patronising he is and wonder that Egremont can't see it. Tilly smiles on vacantly and in so doing is being needlessly rude. Egremont is looking at me expectantly. I wish I hadn't come tonight.

'There's nothing to tell,' I say, looking around.

'I was wondering why Harrison's don't organise trips to the theatre,' says Tilly, suddenly looking at me with a more interested smile.

'If Dick Whittington were on they might,' says Egremont laughing and sipping on his water.

'*Right*,' says Tilly laughing.

Ben throws me a look that seems to say Egremont and Tilly are outrageous snobs. I sigh inwardly at this confusion of characters. We're saved from further conversation by a call to take our seats.

'Maybe we'll see you in the interval,' says Egremont as Ben and Tilly move off in the opposite direction.

'Enjoy the opera,' Ben replies, then he smiles and gives

me an intense stare putting his arm around Tilly and walking away, although his eyes linger on me as he walks off. I get the feeling he thinks I fancy him and he's trying to make me envious. I'm envious all right, but not because I want his arm around my waist.

* * *

Well, what can I say except that I'm no Julia Roberts gasping at the spectacle and mesmerised by the operatic warbling, and I'm pretty sure I won't be going home and giving anyone a blowjob either, but that's another story. Honestly though, this is rot: seeing handsome men swoon at that fat-bellied ten-ton Tessie is nowhere near as captivating as Dick silly-hatted Whittington's quest to find fame and fortune in old London town. Frankly, right now, I'd plump for the latter.

A number of aborted smiles tell me Egremont has noted my lack of enthusiasm for *Tosca*. He's now straining his neck to see if Tilly's liking it any better—they're sitting a few rows in front. And what do you think? Yep, she's positively orgasmic as she erupts into ecstatic applause.

'I think she likes it,' he says, looking back at me with an intense smile as the curtains close and the lights come on. I find myself completely unable to reply. I had hoped my flash of cleavage combined with the scent of Gucci Rush would have distracted him from everything else, but he doesn't seem to be getting hot under the collar about me at all.

I'm not beaten yet, though. Far from it.

'It was Rupert who introduced us—in Tuscany or did I already tell you that?'

'Sorry?' I stare at his smiling bashful face.

'We all met in Tuscany through Rupert—my stockbroker brother.'

'Oh, your brother. Your brother introduced you all. Is that right?'

'They—Tilly's family—have a place not far from ours. We might never have met had Rupert not been there, "on the slopes" as Ben put it. That was our first introduction, before we traversed the blue run.'

'Oh—nice.'

'Even though their place is near, it's easy to miss people. And without an introduction, you've no idea who anyone is.'

'Yeah, of course.' I wish he'd shut up about them.

'I'm afraid we're ski bores,' he laughs, looking over at Tilly again.

'And cheese lovers?' I'm unable to keep the sarcasm out of my voice.

'Fraid so.' He laughs. I shake my head in astonishment. 'Would you like an ice cream? We don't have to go downstairs for the interval if you'd rather stay here.'

'I'd like a drink.' I get to my feet and don't wait for a reply. I begin stepping over the knees of those who prefer Cornettos to cocktails, although they probably haven't been subjected to all I have in the last two hours. I hear his somewhat breathless voice behind me but don't look. He catches up with me as I'm heading purposefully downstairs. 'Sorry, I didn't mean to go on about Tilly.' He's looking alarmed as we descend the stairs.

'Don't worry about it.'

'Sorry,' he says again, struggling to keep up with me.

Honestly, I could keep walking right out of the theatre.

But when I see his apologetic expression once we're at the bar I instantly relax. Poor Egremont! So he likes Tilly and Tuscany and cheese—and skiing. And why shouldn't he? In any case, I'd better try and like them all too. Well, at least three of them. Then again, if she's living in Tuscany half the year, maybe I'll persuade him Andalucía is a better prospect! He smiles at me with relief as if he's reading my thoughts. Oh, I do like him.

'Here, it's my turn to buy the drinks.' He gets his wallet out.

'G&T thanks,' I say directly to the waitress. He asks for a port. My! Behind his back I indicate to the waitress that I want a large one. She winks at me in confirmation.

'So what did you think of *Tosca*?' he asks.

I want to say that it's difficult to believe men would be dying of love for a big fat old moo cow of a woman (seriously, this Tosca is a fright—I can't stress it enough. In her case big is not beautiful). As for the performance (both singing and acting), I've no idea if it was shit or brilliant. It was just an endurance test for me. 'Trying to follow the story isn't easy, even with the surtitles.' I hope he'll be satisfied with that (and yes, I've just learned what surtitles are).

'You'll get used to the surtitles and will soon be able to keep up with the drama,' he says picking up our drinks from the bar and handing me mine. 'I used to be an opera virgin but now I'm a seasoned goer.'

I smile at the 'hot lover' analogy, all the more so because I know he'd be mortified if he realised his double entendre. Nor would he appreciate the image I now have in my head of him as a 'seasoned goer' on top of me, although the picture fades somewhat when he yawns. As his face settles back he looks older. I look away. No doubt he's tired.

We don't have long to have our drinks before the buzzer reminds us that the second half of the performance is starting. Egremont yawns again.

'Do you want to go for dinner after this?' he asks. I'm just about to say yes when he adds, 'Or are you happy to go home?'

'Do you want to go home?' I ask, my heart sinking. However, I can see that he does indeed want an early night.

Which is how the evening pans out. It's an extra blow to see Tilly and Ben heading into town arm-in-arm and animated, clearly heading to the bars and clubs for a night of fun, foolery and excitement. I think I envy them even more now because I dislike them.

'Oh, I nearly forgot—did you pick up the car?' asks Egremont as we turn in to my road.

'It's right there,' I say as we pull up alongside it.

'So it is!' he laughs. 'Didn't see it before. How is it to drive?'

'Great. I love it.'

'Good.'

'Not sure I'm looking forward to working with Mitchell though. And he's threatened to stay with me for two weeks.'

'His bark's worse than his bite,' says Egremont pulling over in front of my new car.

'You really think that?'

'Yes, he's all right.'

'But the way he treats you.'

'It's all bluster.' He tilts his head toward me. 'I've dealt with worse cases,' he says with a fake macho-man swagger of the head. I laugh. What a cool answer.

'You have a way of looking at life differently, Egremont. I like that.' At this he seems to melt.

'And I like you,' he says seriously. I nod my head not daring to think whether a good night kiss is on the cards. 'But I don't think we'll risk telling Mitchell about us.'

'Why not?' I ask teasingly.

'I think you know why. He's rather more into people's business than he should be.'

'But why is Mitchell making it—us his business?'

'He's always been *a bit funny* about work relationships.'

'That's rich coming from someone who married the boss's daughter!'

'I suppose that's his prerogative, him being *the supreme leader*,' says Egremont seeming to find the idea amusing.

'Fine, we'll leave it at that.' I undo my seatbelt.

'Tilly thinks Mitchy's a sweetie. Oh, sorry, I didn't mean to go on again—'

'*Tilly*? How does she know Mitchell?'

'Her mother's organising the big do for the Harrison's dinner. It will be *a grand affair*. Tilly's helping. She hasn't actually met Mitchell in person but—'

'So that's what she does, help with Mummy's charity?' I puff jealously out of my nostrils. I see Tilly's life as an endless parade of flirtation, air-kisses, limp handshakes and party dresses where she receives generous cheques for her bright smiles and polite syrupy chit-chat (which she has wisely substituted for the usual bitchy banter she reserves for people who can't further her career). And no doubt it's all captured in glossy *Hello* magazine for her endless amusement.

Egremont laughs nervously then a look of apology clouds his face.

'Do you want to come in?' I say without encouragement. I don't want him to now.

'No, I'm tired tonight, but perhaps we could have lunch at Modigliani's tomorrow. You liked their tiramisu.'

'Yes, okay, let's do that.'

He leans over and … kisses me. It's real, very real. It's a little awkward but all the same, the sensation is incredible. Moments later, his eyes droopy, he says somewhat hoarsely, 'Good night.' I open the car door, stunned and he drives off without looking back. I put the key in the door still dazed by that flurry of manliness. Stepping in I'm smiling. It doesn't disappear either when Mum appears in the hallway looking disapproving. No Mum, not even your frostiness could cool the fire in my body right now.

# 8

It's with a light step and bright smile that I follow Egremont into his favourite restaurant—sorry, 'trattoria'— Modigliani's. I've left my car—how I love the sound of '*my* car'—at his place. The kiss from last night is still burning on my lips. It wiped away all the silliness of what he said about Mitchell and his dopiness around Tilly. So what if he thinks everyone's lovely? No doubt his attitude works in my favour too.

The waiters greet Egremont by name and do a little 'talking Italian' too, but thankfully, because of Egremont's reluctance to parley Italiano, they knock it off. Good boys.

The waiters look between me and Egremont with genuine smiles of *good for him*. Their excitement for him suggests the novelty of the situation. It gives me an even more satisfied feeling.

'Zis table iss-a good-a for you, Egeremonte?'

'Yes, yes, thank you, Luigi.'

'Might-a I say-a, zis lady iss-a very nice-a. Whassa her name-a?'

'Evelyn,' I say, beginning to smile at the ludicrous English-with-an-Italian-accent. He seems pleased with my reaction. He bows, placing his palm on his heart. Egremont laughs and shakes his head. I smile on.

'Might-a I recommende ze cozze ripiene? Iss-a manifico for ze starter,' he says pulling out my chair for me to sit down. I look at Egremont for a translation, but he is, flatteringly, engrossed in looking at me, and it takes him a few moments to collect himself before sitting down.

'What is cozze ripiene?' I ask when he's seated.

'Oh ... er ... it's stuffed mussels. They're ... er, really good. They make a kind of sardine paste, then mix it with the mussels. Then it's deep-fried in breadcrumbs. It's ... really good.'

Luigi produces large menu cards for us—far too large. To my surprise Egremont doesn't look at his. Instead he looks over it at me and says, 'For main course, if it's all right, I'll order. They have something you should try.'

'What is it?' I'm trying to decide if I like him ordering for me.

'It's venison. It's fan-*tastic*.'

'Good, I'll have that then.' Yes, I think I do like this decisive Egremont.

'Due filetto di capriolo, Luigi,' says Egremont with confidence.

'Zis man-a has-a greata taste-a. Ze capriolo is-a manifico.' Egremont shakes his head in self-deprecation. 'And you like-a to order ze drinks-a now-a?'

'A bottle of Chianti,' he says making me smile more. The evening is beginning to feel promising!

'Per*fecto*,' says Luigi.

When Luigi's out of ear shot Egremont leans over. 'His accent is a *bi-ta much-a*.'

'I *know*,' I say laughing. 'It has to be put it on. It's too ridiculous.'

'No, it's quite genuine.' Egremont says this like he's telling me off. In the same tone he continues: 'and I think it's impressive for them to speak English at all. They weren't born here. They come from Naples.'

'It was you who said it was a *bit-a much-a*,' I remind him, feeling a bit put out.

'Yes, it's just—' He doesn't finish. Amazingly, there is awkwardness now between us. I want to say don't you hate it when you run out of things to say? But at the same time I know it's not up to me to say anything. He caused this. What a puzzle of a man!

Mercifully, Luigi appears again. 'Would-a you like-a to try-a ze wine-a?' Egremont, heaven be praised, throws me an apologetic smile, and laughs when Luigi says to him, '*Zee lady* shall have ze privilege, no?'

'Yes, Evelyn should have the privilege,' Egremont says, smiling indulgently once again.

'Verry good-a. *Here*,' says Luigi putting a little wine in my glass. I pick it up and take a sip, conscious all the time of Egremont's gaze, and indeed the expectant Luigi's. But it could taste like turps and I wouldn't complain.

'Very nice, thanks.' I flash my eyes with appreciation (I don't know why I felt compelled to do that). Luigi nods and proceeds to fill Egremont's glass and to top mine up again. Then, with an air of gravity, he places the bottle on the table and leaves us. Another waiter appears with our starters and a bottle of water. This could be a quick dinner!

'I really enjoyed our evening at the opera,' says Egremont putting his nose into the bowl of mussels. After a long inhale of the aroma, he comes up, saying, 'Tilly said it was the best production of Tosca she's ever seen. But then she does know some of the cast so perhaps she's biased.' I look at him with disappointment.

'You spoke to her this morning?'

'I saw them all at church. We're *good Catholics*.'

'Them all? You mean her family?'

'Yes, all the family. Tilly just has the one sister, Lydia. They're very different, but she's very nice. A nice girl is Lydia.'

'Ben was with them too?'

'Ben wasn't there, no.'

'From what I could glean last night, Ben didn't look that pleased about having to keep their engagement a secret. Do her parents know that Ben's her fiancé?' I watch his reaction to my question.

'It's a bit awkward,' he says pulling a face, but looking as if the situation amuses him.

'Why awkward?' I fork an unwilling mussel out of its shell and hope he'll dish the gossip.

'Tilly's father wants to know a little more about Ben, that's all. They haven't met his family yet and until that happens he won't entertain the idea of an engagement. It's really nothing more than that.'

'Sounds reasonable,' I say hiding my disappointment at not hearing tales of bitter family feuding.

'Oh, I almost forgot.' Egremont bites his bottom lip and smiles excitedly.

'What is it?'

'I have some news for you.'

'You do?' A smile spreads across my face.

He nods with significance. 'You have an invitation to *the house*,' he announces as though he's dropped a bomb shell.

'The house?' I repeat completely clueless.

'Tilly's house. Well, her parent's house—in Heswall.'

'I have an invite to Tilly's house—with you?'

'No, I'm not invited.'

'Then why has she invited me?'

'Okay, I'll tell you. Her sister's having a make-up party. Tilly asked me to invite you and your colleagues.'

'It's a sales' party then?'

'Is that bad?' He looks panicked.

'Not necessarily. No! It's fine.'

'Sure?'

'A make-up party in a grand house sounds good.'

'It is very grand.' He picks up his water.

'You know a lot of people with grand houses. When is the party?' I was about to drink some of my wine but I follow his lead and take the water.

'She hasn't fixed on the date, but soon I think. And if you'll excuse me I just need to use the little boys' room.' He dabs his mouth with the starchy napkin and gets to his feet. When he's gone I sit back and stare at the space he's left.

In less than a week to have advanced so far in his life—the fact astonishes me. And now to be a guest at Tilly's, to actually know Tilly when a week ago she was an object of mysterious envy to me. Granted I'm not going as a friend of hers, and that's fine by me. In fact, it doesn't matter at all what relationship I have with her—it's getting deeper into his circle of friends that's the plus—that's got to be a plus, right?

When Egremont returns I ask him a bit more about Tilly's mother and her involvement with the Harrison's annual dinner cum charity fundraiser.

'Pru—Tilly's mother—knows absolutely everyone. Many Premier League players from all over will be there.' He pauses for me to smile at this. I don't. He carries on: 'Their shirts alone will raise thousands, tens of thousands—if not more.'

'Seriously?'

'Oh yes, and there'll be some signed balls too.'

I instantly crease with laughter at the idea of autographed scrotum. Egremont frowns at my toilet humour. 'Eve, *please*.' I'm relieved, however, that he at least got the joke.

'Sorry, that was childish of me.' I try to force back a fit of giggles—though it's not easy with my head full of images of tattooed tessies. But his look!—I have to stop laughing.

'I think Mitchell's getting nervous about how big the night's going to be. He's never had the TV cameras there before, nor that number of celebrities.'

'So the Annual Dinner really is a big deal?' Talk of TV cameras is enough to bring me back to serious mode.

'It is. Channel 9 are covering the whole night.'

'I probably won't be giving a speech then. Things must have changed since he asked me.'

'No—you *are* giving a speech. I've seen the itinerary for the night and you're pencilled in.'

I look at him with disbelief. 'When did Mitchell share this with you?'

'On Friday. We had a last-minute meeting. I had to go back to the office for it.'

'Mitchell seems to vacillate in his attitude toward you. He's so ambivalent you must get confused.'

'Someone's swallowed a dictionary,' he says laughing a little.

'What I mean is that Mitchell blows hot and cold with you and he treats you very badly—in public.' At this Egremont's smile disappears. He whispers something I can't quite hear. I shake my head to show I can't understand him.

'It's not that bad.' He's looking uncomfortable. Yet, he needs to hear this.

'What I'm getting at, Egremont is that Mitchell has no right to treat you the way he does just because you're an easy target. When you tipped coffee down his shirt—by accident—his reaction was grotesque. That outburst was psychotic but the next moment he's patting you on the back like you're his best pal, and you just accept it.'

'Come on, grotesque is a bit strong.' I'm amazed—he's now laughing it all off.

'Is it?'

'Someone in the office was distracting me. I should have been looking where I was going. It was my bad luck he wasn't drinking water for once.' I have to smile at this come back. I also marvel at his true unconcern. He really doesn't care about the verbal assaults. And here's me fretting over the slightest hint of hostility from anybody.

'Okay, you've convinced me, Egremont. And in which case, it's impressive how you handle him.'

'Years of practice.' He wobbles his head and yanks his mouth down like he's a macho man. I like the joke.

'I'm sure *I* need to learn the art of indifference.'

'What do you mean?'

'I let people—things—get to me.'

'Stick with me and I'll rub some of my coolness onto you.'

'It's a deal.' I'm laughing and smiling. I love him! A moment later, still high on how I'm loving this sassy Egremont, I say, 'So my speech is on? And I'll be on TV?'

'Yes, it's on—very much so. Mitchell likes the feature—that's what he called it. You're *the face of Harrison's*. Or one of them. He says he wants to "keep it real"' Egremont makes bunny ears with two fingers.

'I'd better be good then.' I feel buoyed by the idea of me in front of celebrities and cameras.

'I know you'll do us all proud.' He's looking at me with respect and affection. I beam a smile back at him

'How were your mussels?' he asks self-consciously breaking our moment of indulgent intimacy.

'Excellent, thanks. I really enjoyed them.'

'I think it's always good to try something different. You know, break out of the mould.'

'Right.' Is that a dig?

'I imagine you're quite a *creative person*,' he says with a wobble of his head. 'So tell me, what are your ambitions for the future?' I gawp at him, taken by surprise. What should I say? *You're my ambitions for the future*. Ha—imagine!

When he continues to look at me for an answer, I decide to reveal what I wanted to do before I settled on him.

'I've thought about trying to get into television actually—talking of television.' I laugh. He nods seriously and I carry on: 'Documentary journalism appeals to me.'

'So whatcha doing stuck in sales?' he says in a sing-songy way, breaking off some bread and dabbing it into his empty mussel bowl as unconcerned as if he'd asked me if I think it's going to rain.

My head jerks back involuntarily. Is he serious? He picks up his water glass and is clearly waiting for a reply. Doesn't he know that you don't graduate from Shitty Comp High as Artistic Director of the Royal fucking Opera House? Okay, wrong choice of career but you get my drift. Really, what am I meant to say? His continuing expectant look is irritating beyond anything. I gasp inwardly at so sudden a sea-change in the conversation and atmosphere between us. Where was our mutual love and understanding of moments ago?

'Forgive me, but aren't you *stuck in sales* too?' I reach for my wine.

'I'm an area manager but—sorry, my sense of humour. I wasn't criticising you. My mother's always telling me I'll cut myself with my sharp tongue one day.'

My eyes ping open and I fight the facial spasm that wants to crease up in a scowl of disbelief at Egremont thinking he has the rapier wit of Oscar Wilde.

'Oh, it doesn't matter.' I push away my bowl wondering at my fit of ill humour. I'm getting him wrong. I have to be. I'll ruin things if I carry on in this temper. Talk about mercurial! I'm worse than my mother.

'It's just that I've always imagined, from things you've said over the years that—I don't know, but you've always struck me as being artistic, or creative. You *speak your mind*,' he gushes in an apologetic tone.

OH, I LOVE HIM

'And you like women who speak their mind?' I'm teasing—and thankfully relaxing again.

'In moderation,' he laughs.

'What does that mean?'

'It means I like women with their *own mind*.' He wobbles his head again and laughs. 'Tilly's mother is a strong woman.' He has admiration in his voice.

'You obviously spend a lot of time with her?'

'Because of the charity work, yes. And then there's church. And they do like to invite me for dinner. And then there's Tuscany.'

'I get the idea.' I wonder if he's joking.

'We have lots in common, I'm afraid.' He looks around— I'm guessing for a waiter.

'Why afraid?' I'm afraid myself that he's on to me in my intuitive dislike of them all.

'Because you might get sick of hearing about Tuscany, cheese and skiing.'

I laugh at his insight, and protest that he couldn't be more wrong. He smiles too. How handsome it makes him look. He's James Bond renewed: suave and confident.

Luigi returns to the table and refills my glass. He goes to pour some for Egremont but sees he hasn't touched his. He places the bottle down and removes our plates. We both say how delightful the mussels were and he bows his head in appreciation.

Our main arrives almost without a break.

'This is clearly a fast-food restaurant,' I quip as the waiter puts a plate in front of me. Egremont doesn't seem to hear—he's too busy doing a nosedive into his dish.

'Ah, that is *handsomely fragrant,*' he says looking up at me, his head still bent.

I poke my nose down and inhale. 'Umm, it is nice.' I want to add that it would have been nice to have had a break from the starter but I leave it.

'Have you had venison before?'

'Yes,' I lie (don't know why—well, I do but let's not go there).

'My brother lived off it when he was up in Scotland.'

I'm about to ask if he's talking about Rupert but that would risk more talk of Tilly and her family in Tuscany *on the slopes*. No more!

'So what's going into your speech?' Egremont asks when he's finished chewing a mouthful of deer.

'I don't know yet.'

'No, sorry, of course. You'll be gathering material for it in the coming weeks.'

'Yes, I suppose I will.'

'I'm sure you can make it interesting. You're a strong, opinionated women.'

'Opinionated?' I gasp.

'Well, I mean you have strong opinions that are good.'

I laugh a little at his faith in me. I wonder what he would think if I voiced my real thoughts?

'You could say something about the charity night itself too. You know, talk about the footballers. Do you know anything about football?'

'I think they earn too much money and I don't like the culture generally.'

'Why, what's wrong with it?' He darts me a worried look.

'For one thing, tickets are so expensive that the core fans have to go to the pub to see the match. The Miller near where I live looks like Anfield on match day. They actually go in with their shirts and scarves on and leave when the match is over. It's a weird thing to see. It's sad.'

'Maybe they prefer to have a beer while they watch—and it's warmer indoors.'

'Somehow I don't think that's the case.'

'I'll let you into a secret.' He leans in. 'I'm not really much of a football fan myself either. I prefer cricket.'

I'm saved from replying by Luigi asking how our dinner is. I tell him it's lovely. When he's gone Egremont jokes that I should avoid football in my speech.

'Don't worry. I will.'

'You'll be wonderful,' he says softly. And the way he's looking at me now, it makes my stomach flip. There's something about Egremont—he can go from nerdy to utterly cool and sexy in a heartbeat. He reaches across the table and takes my hand, giving it a squeeze. It's as if he knows that I'm occasionally—well, disappointed in him. He's asking forgiveness for his awkwardness. I swear that is what he's doing. 'You look so lovely tonight. You're very beautiful. I'm a lucky chap—if I can say that. Can I say that?' I gasp. This I wasn't expecting.

'Yes, you can say that.' He smiles contentedly.

'Will you have some dessert?' he asks when we're finished.

'Not for me, thanks. I'm stuffed.'

'You'll have some coffee, though?' When I tell him I'd love some he begins looking around and shouts, 'Due espresso!' adding, 'Il conto per favore.'

We leave the restaurant with many entreaties from Luigi to return-a veeery soon-a. Just out of the door, Egremont holds my hand. I look down in surprise at our clasped hands. The coarse texture of his palm feels good again in mine as I explore it a little more.

I wonder what I should do when we get to his house. Will he invite me in? We drive home virtually in silence, save for a few pleasantries about the meal. But when we pull into his driveway, he says what I want to hear: 'Would you like to come in for coffee?'

'Yes, thanks, I would.' He doesn't look at me as I reply but smiles nervously.

As he puts the key into the lock of his front door, I can see that his hands are slightly trembling. Oh God, this is going to be our next kiss. He holds the door open and I step past him, my heart racing. Inside it's deathly silent. He closes the door. I turn to face him. He doesn't move. It's my cue to go to him.

'Evelyn.' He puts a hand on my shoulder.

'Yes?'

'*Evelyn* ...' He puts his other hand on me. I throw my

arms around his neck and we kiss. Oh how we kiss!

He breaks away and clutches me to him like a boxer trying to halt a fight. His chest heaves. It's frustrating and exhilarating. I have a vague feeling of having something from the past in my arms, something that no longer exists—a man with a sense of honour.

I, on the other hand, have no such scruple, and take him by the hand to the sitting room. I practically shove him on to the cottage suite. To my delight he pulls me on to him. Finally, *finally*, it's happening. I begin undoing the buttons on his shirt like a wild thing. I have to have him NOW—But what? What's this? He's stopping me! His hand is pushing me away. His kisses are getting lighter. I try to persist but little bird pecks are all I'm getting back. I open my eyes and look at him. The expression on his face—it's one of horror.

I push him away and get up.

'I'll put the coffee on now,' he says fastening his shirt.

'Not for me, Egremont. I'll go home.'

'I'll get the door,' he says, unable to look me in the eye. We go through the hallway awkwardly. He presses my arm gently causing me to turn. 'Sorry about that, Eve. I won't be so—*so silly* next time.'

I'm unable to say anything but I can't help holding his gaze. No, Egremont you won't be so silly next time I think with conviction.

# 9

THE PUNGENT SCENT OF STRAWBERRY jam is strong in my nostrils as I step out of Mitchell's straight-out-of-the-showroom, shinier than shiny yolk-yellow Porsche. I have to say, the smell of jam is a welcome change from the competing bouquets of Mitchell's Eau de Lacoste (he squirted in the car) and the brand new overly aromatic leather upholstery.

But on a more positive note, Mitchell did not attempt to perve me in the confined, intimate space of his car. Nor did he glance at my legs, or inappropriately brush against me or even attempt any kind of a lewd comment. He was not libidinous, lascivious, lecherous or lustful. That folks is a result.

I breathe in again as I look at the imposing art deco building I'm about to enter. Our—or rather *my*—first port of call is Jessop's, a biscuit factory in Wallasey.

'You ready?' asks Mitchell somewhat aggressively pressing the remote lock on his key ring, prompting his car to light up like a Christmas tree and emit a noise like a vuvuzela.

'Yes,' I say, reeling a little from the deafening sound of the car alarm.

'That'll keep the bastard scallies off it,' he says with a sniff as he comes toward me.

I clutch my stiff briefcase to my chest. I can't help wishing it was a little older and more worn in. I wish it wasn't pale brown too. I prefer black, but this was a present from Mum. Perhaps I'll get another one, or try and change it. Would she be offended? I NEED TO STOP THINKING ABOUT THE DAMN BRIEFCASE.

My palms are getting sweaty at the thought of shaking hands with the chief buyer. I look down at the handles of my briefcase and see there's a stain developing on the parched leather. 'I feel nervous now.' Mitchell rolls his eyes in irritation.

'What the fuck are you nervous for? I told you all you need to know. You haven't forgotten what you need to say already?'

My mouth parts slightly in disbelief at what I'm hearing. His ten-minute training session told me he knows nothing about selling, and I mean zilch. He started telling me about the difference between a 'selling point' and 'a feature' only to get them confused. Then he told me that I should go in asking the buyer, 'Would you like to see if Harrison's can beat your current supplier on price?' I pointed out that the person could just say 'No.' As diplomatically as I could I showed I'd be asking open questions like, 'For what reasons are you so sure you're getting the best deal from your current supplier?' And, 'Go on, impress me. How do you go about sussing the competition?' To this he shook his head slowly and said sneeringly, 'Keep it simple, stupid. It's not shitting Master Mind. Don't pester a customer with complex fucking questions.' Jesus.

'You remember their current supplier?' he asks, chewing gum aggressively.

'Oh ... er ... Jessop's is Lancton's, right?'

'Yes. Remind Lynn they're expensive. And don't forget the money-back guarantee we're now offering if we fail to deliver on time.'

'Are we really offering that?'

'For returning customers we are. And when you say it, sound like you mean it.'

'I will!'

'Now *go*,' he barks and walks off in the opposite direction. 'I'll meet you back here in half an hour. And don't forget to flag up the copying paper and next-day delivery times with orders before twelve! Oh—and the printing.'

'Gotcha!' I say to his retreating figure, although I have absolutely no faith in these promises we're making. It's been done before to absolutely no effect.

I step into Jessop's imposing foyer. 'Can I help you?' asks a suspicious voice from behind a vast counter.

'Is Lynn Shanks in?'

'Who should I say's calling?' asks the receptionist with more than a trace of annoyance in her voice as she picks up a phone.

'It's Eve Widdowson from Harrison's.'

'Are you a rep?' she asks with disgust in her voice.

'Yes,' I reply haughtily, standing as straight as I can. 'But we don't use you,' she says, hesitating with the phone receiver.

'I know, but if you could just tell Ms Shanks I'd like a word.' With a shake of exasperation the receptionist puts the receiver to her ear.

'Hiya, Lynn, there's a rep from Harrison's. I told her we don't use—oh. Oh, okay.' She puts down the phone. 'You can go in. It's the office there.' She nods her head to the right with a sniff.

'Thanks for seeing me, Lynn,' I say enthusiastically as I step into the office.

'Not at all. Do sit down, Eve,' she replies, smiling more than I'd expected. 'So how can I help you today?'

'When was the last time you looked at a Harrison's catalogue?'

'Not sure I can tell you. It was a while ago.'

'Then I'd like you to take a look at some pages I've highlighted.' I open my briefcase. 'I think you're going to be surprised. While Harrison's has been remodelling itself, other firms have been getting expensive. Lancton's is no exception.' She looks at me with a trace of a smile at the mention of their suppliers. 'Just look at our copying paper.' I hand her the catalogue. 'And while you're there, look at our prices for printing. I know Lancton's charge way more.'

'But they're reliable, Eve—and good.'

'We're just as reliable, especially now.'

She smiles again and I wonder if I've accidentally said something funny.

'Look, if we don't deliver on our agreed time, you'll get the order for free.'

'You're kidding?' She's now eyeing the catalogue with interest.

'Not at all.' I conceal a smile and think *now who's smug*? When I return to the car park, I'm swinging my briefcase as I approach Mitchell's Porsche. I'm carrying an order worth over four hundred pounds with a view to Lynn considering a permanent switch, which will mean hundreds more.

'Someone's pleased with themselves,' he says as I get in the car. I tell him the good news, 'And, yes, she is *very* interested in having us do her printing too. It was a breeze, Mitchell.'

'Good, you've got something between those ears after all.' He starts up the car. 'See if you can do as well at Karter & Co. It's just across the road but I'll drive you.'

'I'll try my best.' I laugh at him under my breath.

\* \* \*

The morning continues with success after success. Before I can say, 'So tell me how you go about sussing the competition,' I'm walking out with an order. I know I shouldn't say this, but I'm beginning to see why Mitchell needs me.

'There's a little caff round the corner. Does the best meat n' tater pies in the world,' Mitchell says, looking at me with—if I'm not mistaken—respect.

'Pies? Sounds all right,' I lie, trying to conceal my surprise at his choice. I had him down for nouvelle cuisine, or sushi—pasta at least.

'Don't fancy it then?'

'No! I'm sure they're great.' I need to be careful not to put him in a bad mood again.

'They do baked taters and sarnies too.'

'Great.' I'm loving his softened mood. What a difference my success has made. Perhaps he was scared this morning that he'd made a mistake in putting me up for promotion. And maybe, just maybe, Egremont is right in his more ... sympathetic judgement of him.

Twenty minutes later we're stepping into Get Stuffed. 'Sit there, Eve.' Mitchell points to a spare table that looks less greasy than the rest. 'I'll get the teas.' He stops and turns, 'Did you say steak and kidney pie?'

'Just steak, thanks.'

In between his 'power calls' in the car he had raved on about the pies so much I thought I'd better show willing. I couldn't quite believe my ears—Mitchell Harrison, never out of the gym, always drinking water is a closet pie-gobbler. He must train doubly hard to keep that washboard stomach and tight little bum.

A group of plaster-bespattered labourers eye me with varying degrees of sarcastic interest. They clocked us getting out of the Porsche and are now smiling lewdly to each other and at me. No doubt they're putting two and two together and getting five. I feel uncomfortable as my not-too-long skirt has become positively short now that I've sat down. Several of the workies subtly (some not so subtly) bend their heads for a better look up my skirt. Mercifully, they keep their comments low, but it's obvious what kind of scenarios they're putting together for me and Mitchell.

It's my turn to laugh when they recoil sheepishly as Mitchell walks past them, giving an aggressive stare (he jutted out his face right at them). They turn their attention back to their newspapers and I gather from their exchanges they're now going over footie scores. Interesting that Mitchell can have such an effect for not being such a big man. Mind you, he does look like a gangster. Perhaps it's the scar over his eye and his pockmarked complexion that adds the intimidating air of menace. But what's the betting he'd run a mile if one of them challenged him?

'There ya go,' says Mitchell, placing two mugs of tea on the table. 'Looks a bit rough this place, but wait till you've sampled the fare. Beats any posh nosh and they don't fleece you. And believe me, you'll need the carbs—you're going to be on your hooves all day.'

'I'm sure it's good.' I pick up my tea and try not to bristle at the casual insult.

'So, you must be pleased, Eve, with all that you've ... *achieved* this morning.' The word 'achieved' seems to come out of his mouth as if it's a difficult compliment to give.

'I am pleased—very pleased. Thanks for the opportunity again.'

'I can spot potential, Eve, and I knew that with just a little coaching in the art of persuasion, you'd be as good as the next guy.' He winks at me and squeezes my knee. His hand lingers there and he's now looking at me with suggestive eyes. I look away and snatch my knee from his grasp. So much for the new leaf. I refrain from saying, *Why, gee thanks* to his now empty praise.

'This afternoon we're going into Birkenhead because I

want you to concentrate on getting printing orders. These companies are in the dark ages and still do a lot of their correspondence by snail mail—and that means letterheads. You have the printing catalogue on you now?' he asks.

'No, it's in the car.'

'Can you go get it?' He's staring at me with wide eyes that scream *now!*

'Sure.' I get up and the labourers immediately elbow each other, alerting their mates to the fact that 'the bit of skirt' is on the move. They focus themselves in readiness for sport. I roll my eyes and show extreme fatigue as I walk past. I also say 'fucking grow up,' which gets a few laughs from some of them.

\* \* \*

It's almost five o'clock when I get back to the office. Walking into Harrison's as a rep (even with aching 'hooves'), I have to say, has made the place look more inviting somehow. Talk about beauty being in the eye of the beholder!

Around telesales phones are ding-a-linging off the hook and it's as noisy as hell as usual. 'Afternoon—Harrison's—Telesales—Tired and Emotional speaking—How may I help you?' is ringing out from all around their desks. How wonderful the solitary life on the road is in comparison—or it will be when the racket of Mitchell on his mobile ceases to be a constant in my ear.

I see Laetitia and Adam. Her outfit has shifted geographically. She's French today: blue and white striped shirt, necktie and black beret complete the picture. Neither of them see me, though they're not on the phone.

I go over to them.

'Hey kiddo,' Laetitia says looking up and smiling her toothy smile.' (And yep, her teeth are red with lipstick). 'How's life on the road?' she asks looking back at her screen and frantically keying in some figures.

'Life on the road is very good thanks, Laetitia. Got fifteen orders today.' One shouldn't brag, but *I can't help it*.

'Knew you'd be a star, kiddo.' She hits a key with finality before turning her full attention to me. She eyes me up and down. 'And don't you look luuurvly.'

'Thanks. I updated my wardrobe over the weekend.' I give her a little twirl and hope I don't look self-conscious. The truth is I feel totally transparent all of a sudden, as though my weekend with Egremont—my failed attempt at seduction, the kiss we finally had—can be seen in my face.

'You Business Barbie now?' says Adam dully, looking thoroughly fed up. 'All you need are the black-rimmed glasses to complete the picture.'

'Not having a good day, dear boy?' I won't tell him that secretly I'm liking his Business Barbie comment. Quite funny!

'Something like that.' He picks up his ringing phone.

'And what's Mitchell like to work with?' whispers Laetitia.

'He's been invaluable.' Adam gives this a dismissive *humph*. Laetitia and I look at him. She creases her nose indicating I should ignore him. I wouldn't have been quite so full of praise of Mitchell if a couple of reps hadn't sauntered past. 'Invaluable, eh?' She smiles suggestively. 'Wow, you really are in like a dirty shirt. So, come on, Kiddo, give us all the goss.' She leans over in readiness for my answer.

'Sorry Laetitia, I don't have time to talk. I've got to set up my new accounts and get these printing orders in.'

'You're taking printing orders *now*?' She looks startled.

'Yes,' I say hesitantly. 'Shouldn't I?'

'They haven't set up the press yet.'

'What press?' I'm wondering if we're talking about the same thing.

'The printing press.' She pulls in her chin as if I'm mad not to know.

'We're not using J. Renton anymore?' 'No honey, we're not.'

'I'll give Mitchell a ring,' I say more to myself than to anyone else.

'A ring about what?' asks Mitchell walking past. 'About the printing. I hear we're not—'

'My office now, Eve.' He clicks his fingers into a point toward his office. I follow. I see Adam shaking his head and eyeing me with—with what I'm not exactly sure.

'So what's your problem with the printing?' asks Mitchell sitting down and rocking back in his chair.

'I didn't realise we were printing in-house now, and I just heard that the printing press is not set up.'

'Printing *press*?' he scoffs. 'We've moved on a bit since Gutenberg, love. I've bought in state-of-the-art digital printing. We can have the customer's order—no matter how big—done the same day.'

'So I can go ahead and place my printing orders now?'

'Yessssss,' he hisses through closed teeth. God he's maddening.

His phone rings and he jerks his chin toward the door, dismissing me. As I step out I almost bump into Egremont.

'Egremont!'

'Eve.' He looks flustered and looks rapidly about. I inwardly roll my eyes at his gawkiness. It's going to be obvious to anyone with half a brain that we're involved, and—oh I don't know why—but right now I don't want anyone to know. Or do I? God I'm confused.

'How was your first day?' he asks gently pulling me to one side.

I take the opportunity of moving right away from Mitchell's office. I notice Adam staring at us, and now I'm a little flustered. 'I got over fifteen old customers back, or a mixture of old and new. I did all right. Mitchell's pleased.'

'He's pleased with you?'

'Well, he was.' I laugh weakly.

'That's terrific. Mitchell's like that—blows hot and cold. Listen'—he lowers his voice—'I was hoping that you'd have dinner with me tonight but I have to go to Scotland for a few days—maybe until the end of the week.'

'Oh—why?'

'It's part of our bid for world domination,' he says laughing. 'I'll tell you about it when I get back.'

'I'll look forward to that.' He smiles at me and I feel my awkwardness is melting clean away, and suddenly I don't care who sees us or suspects we're together. I glance over at Adam but he's busy with his calling-card box. If he had been looking I was going to give him something to chew over. Indeed, enough of this skulking around. Soon everyone will know that Egremont and Evelyn are a couple.

# 10

CLIMBING THE STAIRS TO THE OFFICE next morning, I'm amazed by how many reps can now see me! I've been said hello to more times in the last few minutes than the last two years.

Automatically I walk toward the telesales desks before remembering that I'm now in a different part of the office. 'Look at her swinging her flashy motor keys,' says Colin jokingly as I approach. I decide to go and have a chat.

'I wasn't swinging them,' I jest back looking around to see if Adam's in—his desk is vacant. Laetitia isn't at hers either, but her bag is there so she must be around.

'Bet you're glad to be out of telesales. Nothing doing here,' says Colin shaking his head. Poor Colin. Another fundamental he'll never grasp is that sales is more about the dark arts of the rep than the needs of the client.

'And doesn't she look the part. That a Chanel suit, girl?' says Adam behind me.

I turn to greet him. 'Hardly,' I say, surprised at the lack

of warmth and humour in his banter.

'Here's the star of the road,' says Laetitia. 'Ready to knock 'em dead again, kiddo?' She pulls out her chair. I stare open mouthed at her. She's dressed head to toe in khaki camouflage!

'What the fuck's with Desert Storm?' I'm immediately convulsed with laughter at Adam's quip.

'Can you share the joke?' asks Laetitia expectantly, looking frankly ridiculous.

'Think they're skitting your fashion sense,' says Colin— an evil smile playing about his small mean mouth. Adam and I look at him.

Laetitia shakes her head. 'Children,' she says dismissively. But I can see she's rattled and feel ashamed at our cruelty. I dart Colin an angry look who stares back in defiance. I mouth the word 'loser' at him. Now I hope he does get the sack. Little bitch.

'There's no need to have a go at him,' hisses Adam in my ear. 'What does she expect, coming in looking like fucking GI Jane with weight-gain.'

'You're a bitter little bunny this morning.' I'm puzzled by his acidity. And as for standing up for Colin. Huh!

'*Bitter little bunny*?' Adam repeats with contempt while sitting down like he's fed up.

'Hey you.' I push him gently, trying (and failing) to laugh it off.

'Think you'd better get to your work station. Herr Mitchell's on the prowl.'

I look round and see Mitchell coming out of his office. He catches my eye, holds his palms up at me and shrugs his shoulders, his way of asking what I'm doing around telesales. I take the hint and head in the direction of my desk.

When I get there, I feel the meanness of the situation more forcefully—the desk, I'm talking about. Why have I been shoved into the darkest recess of the office? With a little manoeuvring, room could have been made for me in a brighter area. But there's no point in stressing over this now. It's something I can look into in a few weeks. I don't want to rock the boat yet.

'So, who are you smitten with—Eggy-bread or sulky-knickers Adam?' asks Mitchell offloading what look like maps onto my desk. Without giving me time to answer (thank God), he carries on talking at me: 'That's what you'll need to help you around the Arlington estate today and Wallasey for the rest of this week.'

I stare at the bundle of maps he's referring to. 'I'm not going out with you today?' I pray I haven't missed something.

'I'll come to that in a minute. First you can answer my question: are you smitten with Eggy-bread or sulky-knickers?' He smiles at me.

'Is that a serious question?' I ask, picking up the maps.
'It is serious, yes. I need to know if you've got your head focused.'

'I'm not smitten with anyone.' This is not the time to 'come out'. I look through the maps and put them down again. I was expecting him to give me back the orders he took from me yesterday. I didn't get to file them in the end because he wanted to have a look through them first. I thought they might have been among the maps.

'Are you going out with either of them then?' I want to tell him to mind his own business but something tells me to hold off. 'Eggers is on important business up in Scotland. I need to know he's concentrating on *Aaarrison's* and not on you.'

'I'm not involved with anyone.'

'Good. That's good, Eve. I like that because'—he moves the maps aside and cocks one buttock on the desk—'you'll need all your energies for the coming months, certainly for the charity dinner. Your speech needs to get written ASAP. You'll talk about how I coached you and how you were rewarded with sealed deal after sealed deal.' He rubs the back of his neck with both hands, but it's as though he's displaying his chest at me. I notice he doesn't have any trace of sweat marks under his armpits. But then he wouldn't, he's so reptilian.

'Base it around our first day—well, yesterday, but talk generally in terms of time span because what I taught you yesterday was concentrated coaching. Those eight hours were worth two weeks, let me tell you.'

I nod in response, though I can't quite keep a frown completely from my forehead.

'You needn't mention the steak pie or Get Stuffed though.' He laughs and gets up again.

'No, I wouldn't have thought to mention that.'

'Talk about my mentoring to begin with. Really give a picture of how *Aaarrison's*—me—yeah?—how I'm like a guru, nursing new talent; work to a theme about nurture and talent and new shoots, and growth.'

I nod like I'm interested as he rattles on.

'Which reminds me,' he says, distractedly pulling out his phone. 'I need to call Chaz. I'll be back.'

He walks away a few paces, his phone clamped to his ear. After a moment he says, 'Chaz, call me. We'll do lunch at my hotel. I've made a decision about the art work—and it's looking good for you. Just need a few questions answered.' He comes back. 'Okay then, you're all set. You've got the Arlington estate today, and I've emailed you a breakdown of your week's targets. You've got the maps, and you've got GPS so you have everything you need.'

'You're not coming with me?'

'I've got too much on, what between printing and decorating this place I haven't got time to scratch my arse.' He looks around at the stripped walls. 'And you've proved you don't need me to hold your hand.'

'Have you given me any details about the clients I'm targeting today—who their current suppliers are, that kind of thing?'

'Ah—no. You're going in cold. I don't have time for that now. And keep pushing the printing orders. Think, *Aaarrison's* are stationery.'

'Okay, will do. Do you have the orders from the accounts I won yesterday?'

'I'll take care of them,' he says looking around like he's turned his mind to something else.

'Sorry, Mitchell, I don't follow you. Surely you don't have time to key in those orders. Is someone going to do it for me?'

'You concentrate on bringing in new business.'

'Am I not taking care of the accounts I won yesterday?'

'No,' he says sharply, darting me an impatient look.

'Then who will manage them?'

'I've got Colin to keep those customers supplied. We'll review the situation later.'

'Colin? *He'll* be handling my accounts?'

'You've set the ball rolling. He'll just be making sure they've got what they need. He's better at handling existing customers.'

'But he'll be getting a percentage of their orders—my orders.'

'We're more of a team here, Eve—a family. You'll get your percentage too, don't worry. It's all good. You've been singled out for better things. Now don't let me—the firm—down.'

'Fine—okay.' I can't disguise a sigh of frustration. 'Now go get us more business. You've got your area to cover and a car. What are you waiting for?'

'Nothing.' God, I'm confused.

But I'll try not to think about it. Perhaps allowing me to concentrate on drumming up new business isn't a bad idea. I can negotiate my pay and accounts when I've seen what my pay cheque looks like.

Adam and Laetitia are both on the phone when I pass by, but I hear Adam's voice a moment later: 'Take it easy out there, girl, and sorry if I was a bit off earlier.' I walk back to him. 'Juggling rehearsals and this shit is doing my head in, Eve.'

'I hope this is your break, Adam, and fingers crossed it launches you onto the big screen.'

'Some hope,' he says picking up his phone again, but then he takes my hand, squeezes it gently and mouths,

'Good luck out there.'

'Thank you.' I'm so happy he's back to his old friendliness. 'Now piss off,' he mouths again. I leave laughing, which is only broken momentarily by the dirty look I shoot Colin.

\* \* \*

The stately marble lobby looks the same as Jessop's (the biscuit factory I was at yesterday). This company makes jam. It might even supply Jessop's for all I know. I was hoping Mitchell would have given me this kind of information but I have absolutely nothing to go in with. I don't have a contact name either and I know nothing about their current suppliers—nada—zip. The only thing I know for sure is that we don't supply them. I guess if yesterday was cold-calling, this is frozen calling.

'Can I help you?'

'Yes—thanks.' I approach the reception desk. 'Can you please give me the name of your chief buyer—the person in charge of buying your stationery.'

'Are you a sales' rep?' She eyes me suspiciously.

'Yes, from Harrison's. We have a new catalogue out and I want to discuss it with your buyer.' I have a feeling the woman wants to tell me to go away but she's not rude enough.

'Just a minute.' She disappears into the back. A full five minutes later she comes back.

'Mr Dunn will see you. His office is on the first floor, to the right of the stairs. His name's on the door.'

'Thanks.' I make my way to the stairs, rehearsing my opening lines for Mr Dunn.

I enter with my brightest smile and I'm rewarded with someone showing a surprised smile back. 'Mr Dunn, thanks for seeing me.'

'How can I help you?' he says, sitting up a little, though not inviting me to take a seat.

'I'm Evelyn Widdowson, a rep for Harrison's. I know you don't use Harrison's for your office supplies *at the moment*'—he darts me a look which seems to say, don't jump the gun, love—'but I'd like you to take a look at some pages I've highlighted in our new catalogue and compare the prices with those of your current supplier.' I step closer to his desk.

He takes the catalogue. I don't say anything as he turns the pages thoughtfully. 'Yes, you've got some good deals on here, but the problem is'—he closes the catalogue—'deals are just that. They don't last.'

'They're not discounts I'm showing you but yearly low prices.'

'They look like loss-leaders to me, your paper anyhow. We're trying to go paperless here.'

Ignoring his inconveniently commendable green policy, I say, 'How long have you been with your current supplier?'

'Ten years.' He folds his arms challengingly.

'What would you change about them if you could?' He smiles at my pitch. He knows the game I'm playing.

'I would change many things. But I've no doubt whatsoever that if I switched to you, within a month I'd have a whole new set of problems, and many of the old ones too.

'Not at all. Harrison's is the largest supplier in the North West and we—'

'*One* of the largest suppliers,' he corrects me.

'Okay, one of the largest suppliers, but we're the best, and if you switch to us I can guarantee next day delivery on orders before twelve and much more besides.'

'For the orders my company places that would be impossible, and by the way, almost all companies offer next-day delivery to new clients. My present supplier, if I threatened to switch would also come down on price—*never knowingly undersold* and all that. Price matching is the new firewall. In fact, I'm grateful to you for showing me this catalogue'—he shakes it at me—'because the next order I put through will be making specific reference to your bargains.'

Damn, he's strides ahead of the game.

'Why don't you try us for one week and see if we can make a difference?'

'And upset my supplier for no good reason?'

'You won't go back.'

'Look, I wish I could help you.' He gets up. But there's not a chance of us changing unless my supplier really screws up or folds, which isn't likely to happen any time soon. I'll keep the catalogue though—just in case,' he says cheekily. I've been had!

'What about your printing? Can I ask who does your printing? Harrison's have gone into printing in-house and aim to be the best and the cheapest—also the quickest. We've got state-of-the-art technology. Here, have a look at this catalogue.' I search in my briefcase and pull out the catalogue. I hand it over with an encouraging smile.

'Actually, on the printing you could give me a quote. I was let down last time. Okay—sorry, I didn't get your name?'

'It's Evelyn. Eve Widdowson.'

'Okay, Eve, leave your card and I'll call you with an order for printing.'

'Great! I look forward to getting your call. You won't be disappointed.'

He leans over and shakes my hand.

Walking out I can't help but feel that I let him get away. I had his attention; he was looking at the catalogue. But all is not lost. I'll make a note of everything he said and call back after he's got his printing order. At least I can chase that up, well if Mitchell lets me.

I resolve to do better in the next place. I look at the map. Mitchell's highlighted a car showroom. Ah, there it is.

\* \* \*

It's now almost five o'clock. My feet are hurting so much I could cry and I've had virtually no success in drumming up new business, save for that promise of a printing order from Mr Dunn at the jam factory. I got orders for paper and other cheap stuff, but nothing significant—no major order or a promise to switch supplier. Printing seems to be the only thing anyone's interested in, which is making me nervous about the terms Mitchell's offering.

How could I be so monumentally inept today when yesterday I seemed to be able to sell a farmer his own gates? What powers of persuasion did I possess then other than those of being more knowledgably equipped? It was as if Mitchell had sprinkled fairy dust over me to make me a sales goddess but only made it last twenty-four hours.

Now it's worn off and I'm an average Joe who no one listens to.

It was uncomfortable too: as the day wore on people's smiles wore off. It felt as if I was bothering them—a nuisance. And this is what Mitchell wants me to do permanently? The other reps manage accounts. They go and have lunch—dinner even—with their clients and discuss kitting out entire offices, even in different parts of the country.

I take a deep breath. I'm just tired, cranky and frustrated. Mitchell said he'd review the situation later. I need to keep my head. It's only been one day. Tomorrow will be better.

When I get home there's a full scale row going on next door. The mother's screaming at both boys, while the dog barks and yaps. I hear Tommy's little voice protesting that he didn't take 'it'. His mother's yelling 'you're a lying little fucker,' over and over. I sigh when I hear his alarmed voice saying, 'Mummy, I didn't take it. Honest.' Poor kid.

I offload my briefcase and head upstairs. The argument next door carries on. The 'it' is something missing from the mother's room—oh wait—it's her iPad. I won't depress you with anymore of the details. Poor Tommy. I wish more than anything I could help him out. And I'll bet any money the big lug of a brother took the damn iPad.

The door shutting downstairs tells me Mum's home. 'I've just got to make some calls in my room, then I'll be down,' I call out over the landing railing.

'Okay,' she says distractedly (she'll be picking up her post). I close my door and then the curtains. I'm going to lie down for half an hour and shut out the world.

\* \* \*

I'm woken up by my phone ringing. Egremont!

'Egremont—hi.' I blink the sleep out of my eyes and try to sound awake.

'How are you? How was your day?'

'It was okay. Well, I didn't get to keep my accounts from yesterday. I'm not sure why. Bloody Colin's taking them over. And I was cold cold-calling all day, but it isn't forever—Mitchell says. I did get lots of printing orders. Sorry, I'm babbling on. I'll stop.'

'It's okay,' he says, laughing a little. 'You've obviously had a very busy day.'

'I have, but I'm sure you have too. What about your day. How was it?' I look at the clock and see it's only six. Good, I haven't slept too long.

'Oh, not bad. Business as usual, you know.'

I'd like to tell him that I don't know. 'When will you be back?' I ask instead.

'Not sure, probably Friday. Mitchell says he might join me but I think he won't. He's going to be busy overseeing the makeover of Harrison's.'

'I don't get why this means so much too him. What does it matter what the walls are covered in?'

'I think his hotel has given him a different perspective. He likes the idea of branding the inside as well as the outside. He wants more people to *come through the gates* as it were.' I imagine Egremont's head wobbling as he says this but I dismiss this thought as I pass my hand over the bed. I wish he was here. Well, not here exactly—just on the bed, on *a* bed, with me.

'Is your hotel room nice?'

'Er … yes, it's fine.'

'As nice as Mitchell's hotel?'

'No—nowhere near. Harrison's aren't generous with expenses I'm afraid, but that's all right. I'm happy with the bog-standard inn.'

My heart sinks a little. I want him to like a bit of luxury. 'The reason I was ringing—apart from to talk to you—is to tell you that Lydia's make-up party is on Friday.'

'Oh, Tilly's sister?'

'Yes.'

'Good. Great. I'll go. Do I need to take anything?'

'Just yourself. And maybe your purse.' He laughs.

'Of course. What time?'

'You're to be there for seven thirty. I'm sending you the details as we speak.' My phone vibrates.

'I think that's it coming through now.' I look at my phone and see the download waiting.

'Sorry, I have to go. Mitchell's calling.' He sounds panicky.

'Okay, no problem. We'll talk soon.'

'Bye.' The phone goes dead.

I lie back on the pillow. When he comes back from Scotland I'm going to have him—every inch of him. Just let him try and stop me.

'You coming down for your tea, Eve?' shouts Mum (she'll be at the foot of the stairs).

'Yep, won't be a minute.' I spring off the bed with vigour.

# 11

I'M ON MY WAY TO ADAM'S FLAT. I've never been before. 'I'm bad with the flu, babe,' he'd said. He was absent at work again and I phoned him thinking he was 'throwing a sickie'. But it turned out he is actually sick. I wanted to know how the play rehearsals were going but he could hardly speak he's so full of cold.

I've finally finished the Arlington estate. It's now Thursday and I fared a little better than Tuesday. I have to steel myself, though, before I go in to a new factory or whatever it is. I force myself to wear my best smile and I have to rally all my enthusiasm to get past some of the hostile receptionists and reluctant buyers, but I'm developing thicker skin—I think, I hope.

I'm going to Birkenhead today via Adam's place, which is in Anfield by Liverpool's ground. It's on my way, although I'd have gone in the opposite direction just to check on him if I had to (he sounds seriously sick). His ill humour the other day was probably him coming down with the flu.

He must have been feeling rotten then. I've got some Jewish penicillin for him out of the freezer. Mum cooks nourishing chicken broths and, like her shopping purchases, she hoards them for later use.

I wonder whether I should let him know I'm coming. But if I do he'll only put me off (he's done it before). Still, perhaps I should have given him warning. Perhaps he has an army of actresses mopping his fevered Scouse brow.

I park the car. God, it really is depressing—boarded-up pubs and houses, hard-looking scruffy women in pyjamas smoking in doorways, hoodies hanging around aimlessly, and all in the shadow of Anfield, the stadium of Liverpool Football Club. Heaven only knows what the foreigners think when they visit this, one of the richest clubs in the world and take in the devastation surrounding it. I would say I wonder what the posh ones make of the surroundings (let's face it, they're the only ones who can afford the tickets), but I know already: 'It's grim up North'.

What's that joke about the difference (for a Scouser) between a cow and a tragedy? Answer: Scousers know how to milk a tragedy. This is one tragedy they need to milk. Although, to be fair, this area is waiting for re-development and I gather some of the locals aren't playing ball by moving out. On the other side of the stadium there are really nice roads with delightful houses, far nicer than where I live. Still, they should get a move on and sort this out.

Jeeeeze, what's the noise?

Two fluorescent police cars, lit up like grottos, fly past.

I press the intercom at Adam's door and eventually his voice croaks 'hello'.

'Adam, it's Eve.'

'*Eve*! Nice one, girl. Come up.'

I smile with relief at his friendly manner. The door buzzes and I push my way into a dark, dank hall. I hear Adam's voice again and look up to see his head peering over the stairwell.

'Adam! Don't stand there, go inside.' I think he just told me to shut up.

When I reach his landing, I could cry. He's stooped all woebegone in a dressing gown and matching pensioners' slippers. And I mean I really could cry—my eyes are stinging. I have to bluster not to show him. The screech of cars and more sirens distract us.

'This place is overrun with police.' I pray my hoarse voice doesn't betray me. Don't know why I'm so emotional.

'Tell me about it. Like Miami fucking vice round 'ere with all the fucking bizzies.' He starts coughing and signals with his head for me to follow him.

Stepping through the door I'm impressed by his book collection. Place looks like a library. He has guitars too, electric and acoustic. 'Didn't know you played guitar.'

In answer he groans, but manages to say, 'I'll make some tea.'

'No, you won't! I'll do it. Get back on the couch.'

He nods obediently and returns to slump on to the makeshift bed, pulling a box of tissues from a table onto his lap. The pages of a script lie scattered on the table, *Jill's House* plainly marked on each page.

'I take it you've had to stop rehearsing for now.' I take out two mugs from a cupboard. I'm relieved and impressed by how clean his place is. He has choices of tea as well. Spearmint, no less. Ah, but that's maybe a feminine touch I think turning over the box. 'Wow, you have honey too,' I shout.

'Got everything you need in there, babe,' he wheezes.

On entering the sitting room with our tea, I repeat my question about his having to give up rehearsals.

'Yeah, they sent me home. I'm gutted. Just want this bastard virus out me system now. You shouldn't be here, you might catch it.'

'I'll keep my distance. I'll be fine. Had it not so long ago. So—how are you, apart from generally rotten?'

'Be alright if I could sleep.'

'I found that the easiest part. I guess you're stressing about the play. But it'll go. I brought you some home-made chicken soup. Can I put some on now?'

'Ah, hun, thanks. I'll have some in a bit. Let's just have this tea for now.'

As soon as Adam picks up his mug thumping music begins to vibrate through the walls. 'God, doesn't that get on your nerves? No wonder you can't sleep.'

'Yeah, but you forget about it. Well, no you don't. Fucking hell, the noise some people make round here, *period*, screaming their fuckin business all hours of the day—they sicken me, girl, they really do. I won't be happy till the whole shower o' shite is corralled into walled estates with frigging watch towers, where the unroooly denizens will be shot in the buttocks for as little as dropping litter.'

He puts his tea down and makes the action of aiming a rifle. 'Yeah, keep them all in one big fuckin ghetto till they can learn to behave themselves, that's what I say. Think I'll get a petition going.'

'Ah, you're funny.' His fascist rants (fake) are one of his specialities. He smiles at me before letting his head fall back again.

'You wanted to do something about it once.'

I stare at him.

'Well you did. You had dreams of becoming a—a what was it? A ground-breaking journalist championing the underdog?'

'Championing the underdog? I *am* the underdog.'

Adam looks over at me and shakes his head. 'Far happier touting paperclips, eh?'

'Ouch.'

I hear a faint, 'sorry, girl.'

'I'm just a spectator now. I drove past some kids the other day. I don't know, it was the redundancy of them all. My car excited their attention and they all started whooping and grinning with that hideous cheeky delight, looking like escaped lunatics.'

'Arrrrh, I hate when they do that.' Adam makes a strangling gesture round his neck which turns into a coughing fit, but he signals for me to go on.

'They're not that bad really, I'm sure. I'll revise my opinion, of course, if they scratch the car.'

'Mitchell would take it out of your pay.'

'I don't think so.'

'Oh yeah?' He looks at me quizzically. 'And talking of sadists, how's the bastard treating you?'

'He's his usual pig self. One thing that surprised me though—he took me to lunch in a greasy spoon caff called, would you believe, Get Stuffed.'

'Humph, that's not like the gastro freak we know and love.'

'Exactly. He's mad for the pies there.'

'He's mad full stop, babe.'

I laugh weakly at this observation. 'Get Stuffed is the name of the caff?' asks Adam looking at me like he's trying to think of something, or remember.

'Yep.'

'That rings a bell, but I can't think why. Where is it?'

'In Wallasey, near the tunnel.'

'Nah, don't know it,' he wheezes breathing out heavily and letting his head fall back. Poor thing, he's exhausted.

'Can I get you anything?'

'Just talk to me, babe. Pour some of those mellifluous vowels over my sorry soul.' He lifts his head of the pillow and gives me a cheeky smile.

'Shall I read some of your lines to you?' I pick up a sheet of the script.

'No, I can't deal with that now.' I put it down again. 'You were talking of the redundancy of those lads in your road. I had posh friends once, and I'll never forget their sports bags.' He opens his eyes and sits up a little.

'Oh?' I wonder whether to tell him to lie back and rest but by the looks of his sudden animation it would be pointless.

'They were the size of fuckin caravans—their sports bags. I couldn't believe my eyes. They were bursting full of tennis rackets and cricket whites with bats and batting pads like wardrobe fuckin doors. Trainers, footie boots, school blazer and tie thrown in for the after-tea party.

Different fuckin' world, girl. There was no such thing as redundancy in their lives.'

'How did you know them?'

'One of my foster carers—they were minted—lived over on the Wirral.'

'Foster carers?'

'I was taken into care on and off for a few years. This family were a cut above. They had two sons.'

'Do you still keep in touch with any of them?'

'Naaaaaaaa, wasn't with them that long in the end, but it doesn't matter.'

'You know, I don't think I've ever seen Tommy with a sports bag.' (I won't press him for details on his foster-care stint right now, but wow, poor guy).

'Probably his school doesn't have a playing field anymore,' says Adam reaching for the tissues again. He gives a glance at the script and looks like he's reading some of the lines.

'They must be missing you at rehearsals?'

'Ah, this is doing my head in, girl. Me first break and this happens.'

'Sorry, I shouldn't have brought it up. Have you been to the doctors?'

'Naaa, no point. Got the flu, and that's it. You look nice, by the way.'

'Thanks. I like dressing up for work.'

'Always had you down as a closet Barbie.'

'Did you now?'

He nods his head solemnly. I ask how many visitors he's had.

'One or two.'

'You cut a sorry sight, my friend in your hospital attire.'

'Don't know when I've ever felt so shit, hun. My head's got fuckin Big Ben in it.'

'I'll go and heat up some of that soup.' I get to my feet. He gives me a weak thumbs up. Bless bless BLESS. He then drains his tea and falls back onto his pillow looking totally exhausted. It's all I can do not to kiss his clammy forehead as I pass him on my way to the kitchen.

'You're a good friend, Evie.' He sounds like he's drifting off. He's never called me Evie before. It's what my dad used to call me.

Leaving the soup to warm gently, I step back into the sitting room. He's asleep. I take a seat opposite him. I should really be getting to work, but well, another half hour won't make much difference. Mitchell went up to Scotland for the day (or down to London—he had to decide which). He's not around anyway, thank God. And maybe today will see better results—for me—in terms of sales. If I'm super positive surely it'll make the difference that's needed.

'Sorry, babe, was I out for long?'

'No!'—I turn to Adam with a jolt—'You only just nodded off. Your soup should be just ready to eat. I'll get it.'

'Shouldn't you be back at work?' he says yawning. 'After I've got your soup, I'll go.'

'Thanks, girl. You're good.'

'You'll never guess who I was introduced to at the weekend,' I shout from the kitchen.

'Who?' He coughs.

'The ski-resort couple from Vern's. You think they're students.' I put my head around the door to see how he takes the news.

He sits up a little and frowns at me. 'How come?' he asks blowing his nose.

'They were at the opera and we were introduced. He works for Channel 9. He's training to be a reporter.'

'I hate him even more now,' says Adam, letting his head fall back on the pillow.

'She works in charity with her mother,' I shout pouring the hot soup into a bowl. 'He's called Ben and she's Tilly.' I carry the soup into the room.

'The names fit,' he says with an undercurrent of disgust as he sits up to eat. 'And who were you with?' He eyes me suspiciously. Shall I confess?

'I was with Egremont,' I say casually, giving him the spoon and putting the bowl on the coffee table.

'*Egg-Salted*? What—just you and him?'

'Yep.' I wish now I hadn't opened my mouth.

'That's a bit risky, isn't it? You know, the way he fancies you. How come you came to be going to the opera together?'

'He asked me and I said yes. I also went to dinner with him on Sunday. Well lunch—a late lunch.'

'*Evelyn*,' he almost growls as he takes a mouthful of soup.

'I'm seeing him.'

He nearly chokes on his soup. And now he's laughing and coughing so violently I think he might burst an artery. His invalidity fooled me into thinking that he'd be more compassionate.

'*Adam*,' I plead, feeling my cheeks burn with annoyance or embarrassment.

'No, sorry girl, but you've got to be kidding.' This he just manages to get out before collapsing into another bout of coughing and laughter. He eventually comes right, but keeps convulsing with laughter, clutching all the while at his chest, obviously in great pain.

'Look, I've got to be going. I hope you feel better soon.' I make for the door. He tries to stop me, but hysteria gets the better of him. I let myself out and can still hear his muffled croaky laughter as I go down the stairs.

# 12

I'M ON MY WAY TO TILLY'S for the Venus make-up party. It's miraculous that I'm going at all, after the day I've had. Sapped of energy and wondering if I've caught Adam's cold, I decided, after walking through just three doors (super-sorry sales performances by me), that there was nothing for it but to head home at lunchtime. I almost fell asleep in the car park of the industrial estate.

I know I should have tried a few more cold calls but I was craving my bed and Horlicks like I've never known before. But I didn't want to miss a chance to see Tilly's house so I've dosed myself up. I feel fine—really. I feel a little *too* fine, but the medicine didn't say anything about not handling heavy machinery.

Oh, a text message. It's from Adam:

TA VERY MUCH FOR SOUP, GIRL. EXCELLENT IT WAS. AM SORRY ABOUT EGG-SALTED. YOU RAN AWAY BEFORE I COULD EXPLAIN THOUGH YOU CAN'T BE SERIOUS. PLEASE SAY I'M FORGIVEN

I chuck my phone on the car seat. I'm too fatigued to beat myself up anymore. It's the sort of reaction I'm going to have to get used to. There's no point fighting it or apologising for it or defending it. Eventually they'll accept it.

Egremont's on his way back from Scotland today and I'm having dinner with him tomorrow at his house. He's going to cook Italian, of course, but 'something simple'. I don't care what it is as long as dessert is him!

Despite the way I'm feeling, I'm very much looking forward to our girls' night out—or in—tonight. I shall probably be clubbed round the head by the envy stick when I get to her house on the Dee side of the Wirral peninsula. I have no intention of buying any of the over-perfumed tat for myself—I have sensitive skin, thank you very much. I'll have to pretend to fill in a form at the end so no one will be any the wiser (I think I know how these things go), and when she finds that there's no order from me, I'll just tell her not to worry about it.

It's pitch black along these country lanes. I'm beginning to think I'll never get there. Oh, wait a second, the satnav has just piped up again and told me I've arrived at my destination though I can't see anything. No wait. Something's lit up in the near distance.

I stare in awe. A multitude of latticed windows, ablaze with orange light are just discernible through a long line of fir trees as I pull off the road. The house looks like a Tudor mansion. Something nasty whispers, 'this is what you want from Egremont'. I turn the car into the open gates.

Stepping out onto the gravel drive I hear a familiar voice calling my name. Ben's posh vowels. But what the— Something's on me. God, I'm being mauled by a fucking dog. Huge paws are scratching at my neck. Urrrrgh, it's on my shoulders. A great wet nose or tongue slides across my face and it's all hairy and oh—disgusting. I scream in frustration and try to push the thing off.

'Down! DOWN!' yells a commanding voice. I open my eyes and see Egremont, his face contorted with anger yanking the dog off me by its collar. 'Bad dog,' he scolds holding the dog down but keeping his grip on its collar.

'Egremont! Thank you.' I try to catch my breath and look down to see what damage has been done to my coat, although it's too dark to see clearly.

'Oh, don't mind Bananas. He's just a big softy,' says Ben laughing and taking the panting Alsatian from Egremont. Egremont lets go, giving Ben a look of strong disapproval. It's a look I've seen before—a diluted version of it—that Egremont has shot Mitchell after mein Fuhrer has had a go at me. Thankfully Mitchell has never noticed it, but the fact that Egremont takes such risks on my behalf is a massive turn-on.

'You should have shut him in, Ben. He nearly knocked her over,' shouts a voice from the door.

We all turn to see who it is.

'Sorry, Mrs Dev,' says Ben dragging the drooling two-ton mutt away by the collar.

'Very gallant of you Egremont for coming to the lady's rescue—though of course Bananas was only being playful. Again, send our best to Rupert,' says Mrs Dev from the door.

'You're leaving?' I ask him as he turns to me shyly.

'Yes, I came to see Pru'—he indicates the woman at the door—'We had the Harrison's annual dinner to discuss. Mitchell wanted me to see her ASAP. Looks like our dinner is going to be quite *the charity event*.' He's wobbling his head, clearly growing more relaxed again. I feel a pang of annoyance at myself for finding the head wobble silly. In every other respect he is manly.

'Thanks again—for getting the dog off me.' I give him my warmest smile.

'Oh it was nothing.' He drops his head modestly.

'I'll see you tomorrow?'

'For dinner? Yes! Can you come for seven thirty?

'I can.'

'Great. I'll see you then.' He nods but seems reluctant to leave.

'Are you coming in dear?' asks Mrs Dev from the doorway.

'You'd better go in,' he says in a whisper, lifting his brow a little and twinkling his eyes at me.

'Bye,' I say equally quietly. It's the kind of goodbye we often say at work when we don't want anyone to hear. It's incredibly intimate. At those moments his eyes seem to bore into my soul. Ever cautious Egremont—just in case there's a Harrison's rep spying us from a window right here and now.

'Not everyone is used to dogs,' says Mrs Dev as I approach the front door. She's Tilly's mother all right. It's Tilly in thirty years' time. She must be fifty but looks in great shape in her country casuals. 'Of course animals are sensitive to that. They're remarkably intuitive—dogs—

although Bananas was probably being mischievous. I do wonder at his being out though. That was rather remiss of Ben. Are you quite recovered?' She closes the door as I step into a spacious hall, which looks like it belongs in a cathedral.

I marvel at the high ceiling and a sweeping staircase in the centre. The place smells of polished wood and good carpeting (although the floor I'm standing on is stone). A large grandfather clock chimes in the corner. I'm about to tell her I'm fine when she asks my name.

'Eve,' I tell her running a hand through my ruffled hair. Thankfully my coat isn't stained, not that I can see anyway. I begin to take it off.

'*You're* Eve?' she says quizzically, taking my coat from me and putting it in a room nearby. When she comes out again, she says, 'Are you the Eve who is stepping out with Egremont?'

'Yes.' I suddenly feel awkward. I can tell by her expression that she's surprised by my appearance. Whether good or bad I can't tell. 'But please don't mention that in front of—'

'Oh, I know it's quite the secret. I shan't breathe a word in there.' She nods to one of the doors leading off the hallway. I hear some laughing coming from behind it. 'Ahhh, that's why you were "saved" from the savage beast. Egremont was trying to impress you.' She laughs at the thought of this.

I smile but it's constrained. I'm standing next to her and she's not showing any sign of moving on to the party room. 'So, what sort of a day have you had, dear?' she asks, eyeing me up and down with undisguised interest. Before I can answer, she carries on. 'You must be exhausted after all that canvassing. I don't know how Egremont does it and still has time to help with our charities. And he's on so many of the boards now. Occasionally his brother Rupert helps out. Have you met Rupert, the stockbroker?'

'No.' I'm about to add that I'm looking forward to that, but she continues eagerly.

'Don't remember at which event he demonstrated his skills in the charity department—perhaps the Merryweathers.' She pauses and screws her eyes as if trying to picture it. She shakes her head. 'Mmmm, anyway—we've been firm friends ever since. He's an absolute *angel* when it comes to getting money for worthy causes. At the Parker ball last year we raised almost a million for the orphaned children of Africa. Or was it Romania, that one? Anyway, he's a *rock*. I mean *a million*. But do tell me something about you, Eve.'

'There's not much to tell, I'm afraid.'

'Oh, I'm sure that's not true. Do you ski?'

'No. I've always—'

'Do you ride?'

'No.'

'Is there an instrument that you play then? Perhaps you're an indoors girl?' She looks at me with one eyebrow lifted and an expectant smile as if she must have finally hit upon the one thing I do.

'No, I'm not musical.'

'Well, I bet you speak another language—several perhaps? You look like a linguist.' Her smile begins to disappear as she's guessing my answer will be in the negative again.

'None,' I say through closed teeth.

'What, no languages *at all*?'

'No.' I wonder whether she's being deliberately offensive or if she's just rude out of stupidity. Or that classic combination of both?

'You and Egremont must talk a lot of shop then.'

'I should be getting to the party.'

'Oh yes! I quite forgot. Lydia will be *dying* to get started. Lydia is my youngest daughter. She's like me, entrepreneurial. Tilly is creative like her father. They are quite chalk and cheese my two, although they're peas-in-a-pod alike in their ambitions. One way or another my girls will do the Devanthy name proud.'

I nod feigning interest.

'They're both very accomplished too. They speak Italian *and* French fluently, and although Lydia can't draw—well her silhouettes aren't bad—she can bring tears to the driest eyes with her violin recitals.' After the last sentence, she rolls her lips together and opens her eyes wide as if she's made a gaff at my expense.

'Let's go through then,' I say, helping her out. Jesus.

'Yes, lets,' she says with staged enthusiasm. 'Gosh, I don't think I have ever had so many Liverpudlians in my home at one time.' I wonder whether to say she ought to lock away the silver. I follow her in the direction of noisy chatter saying nothing. Moments later, she opens up a double door and we enter a room stuffed with Harrison reps. How they all smile at me! I see Laetitia. She's dressed in a purple ball-gown with a massive red feather boa around her neck. And—this is something new—she's wearing a large brown wig!

Interesting. She looks like a tranny. She's got super-glossed purple lips to match the dress. I'm wondering how her teeth look.

I can't see any other telesales. Tilly must have considered them too poor to buy anything. Not worth their weight in nibbles it would seem.

'What would you like to drink?' asks Mrs Dev.

'White wine, thanks.' I hope she's got some good stuff.

'Excellent.' She looks at me intensely as if trying to get all the details of my face so that she can recall them at a later time. Seriously, I've never been so scrutinised. When she's done, she smiles again and leaves, saying, 'White wine for Eve.'

I see Tilly. She's coming to greet me, I think. '*Tilly*, hi,' I gush. Don't know why.

'Thank you for coming.' She gives me an air-kiss near my cheek.

'Thanks for asking me. Your house is beautiful.' I'm struggling to keep the awe out of my voice. Seriously, you could open this place up to the paying public. It has floor-to-ceiling latticed widows on three sides. There's a roaring fire in an inglenook fireplace big enough to camp in. The birds-of-paradise patterned sofas are sumptuous and gigantic, like something you see when the royal family are relaxing 'at home'. There are ornate tables here and there with beautiful fat vases of flowers on them.

'Property is awfully cheap here compared to Surrey.' She laughs at this and adds, 'It's a wonder everyone doesn't live like this up north.'

'Ummmm,' is all I manage to respond with.

She turns her gaze to pictures on the wall that show her and her family in numerous stages of expensive play and posing. I spot one taken with the Liverpool team at a black-tie event. Tilly's in the middle of the line-up looking stunning in a silver dress. Several of the players are looking at her adoringly.

She smiles at me with her eyes when we look away from the pictures but she says nothing. I guess she knows the pictures say it all.

'There you go, Eve,' says Mrs Dev, holding out a glass for me. As I'm taking it, Tilly asks me to come and meet her sister.

'Lydia, this is Eve, another rep from Harrison's.'

'Pleased to meet you,' says her very plain and chubby sister who's dressed in clashing floral patterns and a vile blouse with too many frills. When I thank her for inviting me she snorts with piggy laughter as if I've said something hilarious. I involuntarily look at Tilly. She bristles with annoyance at my obvious surprise that this goofy girl is her sister. I can't help but smile. Too good!

'Well, let's get started,' says Tilly with undisguised irritation (perhaps her sister has had too much wine already and is sillier than normal—she's still giggling).

'Oh yes, let's get started,' says Lydia squeezing her fists together and putting them in front of her mouth. She shuts her eyes at the same time as if she'll burst with excitement. I laugh—I think it's a release of tension, but I pretend to be laughing with her sister.

Everyone, I now see, is sitting expectantly, catalogues open on laps. A woman with a glow-in-the-dark false tan coughs to get everyone's attention. She's behind a table filled with make-up products.

Many of the reps wave at me again and say hi as I sit down next to Laetitia who has just patted the seat next to her. The warmth from the reps toward me is amazing—how they smile now, and with no hint of apology at having ignored me for so many years. I smile back at them all. Their altered attitude doesn't allow me the satisfaction of calling them hypocrites because each and every one of them would readily admit that, formerly, I was simply beneath their notice. You can accuse Liverpool women of many things, but dishonesty or self-deception is generally not one of them. No. Be they vulgar ('God, I'm fucking crude'), bitchy ('I've got more faces than the town-hall clock'), loud ('I know, I've got a mouth like the Mersey Tunnel') or stupid ('Thick as shit, me'), they'll happily announce that they are so to the world in the manner I've just indicated, and I *sincerely* mean no offence by such comments. I love them for it, and hope it's rubbed off on me.

'Okay, ladies, before we get to sample the delights of all these beautiful guilt-free pleasures you see around you'—our host sweeps her arm over the products on the table—'I would first like you to give yourselves a nickname that best sums up your personality. And it must be *alliterative*. I hope I said that right.' She lifts her shoulders nervously.

Lydia bursts into snorts of piggy laughter again. Everyone looks in her direction and I can see most of the reps have raised their eyebrows in astonishment at Lydia's nice-but-dim laugh. Mrs Dev must have done some persuading to get Tilly to organise this—she's in agonies of embarrassment at her sister. Mrs Dev, however, is oblivious to her elder daughter's distress and is laughing too, as if the glow-tan hostess has said something incredibly funny. 'What do we have to do again?' asks one of the reps (I forget her name). We can just about hear her above the sound of Lydia's snorting—yep, she's still going.

'I'll give you an example,' says the hostess. 'I'm Cutie Claire.' She points to a badge on her jacket that says just that. This makes a few eyebrows raise even higher. I'm afraid she's not very cute at all, though her face is very shiny like a newly-minted copper coin. 'Using all these beautiful guilt-free products has certainly made me feel cute. Once you start using guilt-free luxury products like Sheer Indulgence you'll all be cute too.' Cutie Claire laughs. 'Okay, who'll go next? Tilly?' She nods encouragingly at Tilly.

'Erm, right, okay. Let me think. I could be Talkative Tilly?' I frown inside. She hardly opens her mouth. I could suggest Tiresome. Ha!

'Okay, Talkative Tilly it is,' says Cutie Claire writing Tilly's name-tag out. 'If you could just pop that on.' She gives the sticker to Tilly.

'And Lydia. What about you?' she asks. All eyes turn to Lydia.

'Mucky Lydia,' she says before bursting into snorts. 'Very nice, but it has to be alliterative,' says the hostess trying to maintain her smile.

'Happy Lydia,' says Lydia through laughing grunts.

'Lovely Lydia. Write down Lovely Lydia,' says Mrs Dev, smiling and shaking her head indulgently at her daughter's continuing silliness.

'Okay, Lovely Lydia it is,' says Cutie and hands the badge to Lydia who immediately stops laughing to put it on. Amazing how she can switch it off like that! 'And next?' asks the hostess looking around the room.

'Delectable Debbie,' says a rep.

'Oooooooooh get you,' says Claire, hurriedly writing out the badge name.

'Seductive Suzy,' says another.

I'm beginning to panic about my turn. I can't think of anything fitting to go with E. Enigmatic? No way, not in front of this lot. You have to be careful when using big words in Liverpool—some Scousers violently object to them. I was once in Sainsbury's looking for some bottles of Orvieto Classico. Sorry, but I was, although, if you know anything about wine you're probably laughing at me. So Sainsbury's. There I was, standing in front of the wine aisle. The wine bottles had just been newly stocked. I removed the two I wanted, which left this gaping hole in the shelf-stacker's arrangement, so I brought some bottles forward in order to re-establish the shelf's neatness. The shelf-stacker was watching me, and seemed to want an explanation for what I was doing. So I said to her, 'I was just restoring your symmetry.' She screwed up her face and said, 'Ya wha'?' in a menacing voice. Needless to say, I beat a hasty retreat.

Oh, it's my turn. Cutie Claire is looking at me expectantly. 'Errr, Edible Eve?' I suggest vaguely. Edible Eve—

I ask you!

'I like it,' says Claire, writing feverishly. Laetitia is up next.

Removing her boa, and with a naughty smile (yes her teeth are stained purple) Laetitia, running the boa seductively under her chin, says, 'Oh, I'm definitely *lovable lusty lickable Letty.*'

This makes a couple of the reps shriek with laughter but interestingly doesn't produce so much as a giggle from Lydia, who seems aghast at what she's heard.

'I can see I'm going to have to keep my eye on you,' says Claire looking like she's a little fearful of our *Letty* (I've never heard Laetitia use that version of her name before). 'I've gone with Lovable Letty, if you don't mind.' She sticks the badge on Laetitia's chest.

'Spoil sport,' says Laetitia with a pout.

'Now *before* I show yourselves the whole range of these amazing guilt-free and marvellously indulgent Venus products, I would like to tell you that I *used* to spend in excess of sixty pounds on my essential daily face creams—you know, having to buy separate cleansers, toners, moisturizes. Different ones with different serums. But *now* thanks to this Venus *all-you-need-in-one* cream, which you can see is in glamorous high-end packaging, I now only spend *twenty-five pounds* on one bottle. My skin never looked better or felt smoother. Really, people have commented on it and I'm not just saying that. And I've saved all that money. This is where the *guilt-free* bit comes in. We all have financial commitments and whatever they are it's easy to feel guilty about spending so much on yourself, but I know that like most smart working women, you just won't compromise.'

There are murmurs of agreement. To my amazement her pitch is working.

'What's it tested on? You don't, like, torture animals or nothing?' asks a rep.

'Oh, great question! I was just coming to that. Another reason why it's a *guilt-free* pleasure is because it's *not* tested on animals. There is *no* suffering involved.'

The rep seems satisfied, but most look indifferent to this added bonus.

'But please, today, you aren't obliged to buy—'

What? Did I hear correctly? Oh, bad sales technique, Cutie Claire. Never, but *never* give people an excuse to keep their purses closed. Venus Cosmetics, whoever the hell they are—no doubt some little cupboard on a Widnes trading estate (not tested on animals, not tested on *anything*)— would not be pleased.

'Right, now I'd like a volunteer please. I have this *Hayekian* facial glow for yourselves to try today at no expense to yourselves. We all have those days when we're not as radiant as we'd like to be—say, after a night out.' There are a few ripples of laughter at this insight. 'Well, this product, when applied as I will show you in a moment, when—'

'I'll have a go,' says Laetitia, getting to her feet. She tosses the boa on my lap.

'Sure, Lovable Letty,' says Claire, looking a little deflated.

'Yeah, let's see what you can do for lusty, lickable Laetitia.'

I take a sip of wine, which tastes like vinegar. As Laetitia is getting seated someone sits next to me. I've never seen her before.

'I'm Eve,' I say as she plonks herself down, almost causing me to spill my drink.

'I'm pissed.' She laughs through a closed mouth. There's a passing resemblance to the family in looks and accent so I'm gathering she might be an aunt. I put my drink down.

I need the loo so I excuse myself.

Crossing the hall I see Ben in an adjoining room. He's holding a snooker cue. He's clearly in the games' room.

'Hey!' he shouts. 'You recovered from the Banana attack?'

'Yes.' I'm praying the bathroom will soon present itself. I'm not in the mood to talk to him.

'How's the party going?' he asks coming to the doorway.

'It's going well. My boss is getting a makeover.'

'The drag queen?'

'No comment,' I reply looking for a door that fits the description Mrs Dev just gave me.

'She's quite a character,' he says chalking his cue.

'She's that all right, but a great boss.'

'Sorry about the dog, but then your geek in shining suit rescued you.'

I'm about to reply when a commotion across the hall interrupts me.

'Mr Dev!' says Ben suddenly looking much less cocky.

'You still here?' says none other than long-tall-Chaz. That guy is Tilly's dad! He gives Ben the briefest of glances that borders on contemptuous. Now that he's not wearing a suit I notice his legs are long and muscular and my eyes are drawn to his strong buttocks straining the pockets of his country cords. Looks like he was bred for riding polo horses.

'Where's Tilly?' he barks looking around. 'Tilly!' he shouts and repeats her name several times as he steps in and out of rooms.

I move into the recess of two corner doors. He doesn't appear to see me.

'Pa! You're home,' says Tilly coming out of the party

room and rushing forward to greet him. I notice that her run is skippy and babyfied. The spot I'm in allows me to see them but they clearly can't see me. Ben's disappeared too.

'You got it darling,' he says planting a kiss on her forehead and taking her in his arms.

'Oh Daddy, I didn't?'

'You did, darling, as I knew you would. You're to do the whole building. It's a massive commission. It seems we didn't need to put on this bloody farce after all,' he says indicating the make-up party room.

'Really? Oh well, Lydia's enjoying herself. It shouldn't be more than another hour.'

'Good. They're all in there, are they?'

'Yes. Lydia is very pleased about it.'

Her father grunts dismissively.

'When will I meet Mr Harrison to show him my work?' She's asking in an absurd baby voice. But wait— Mr Harrison?

'You're to meet the Mitchell character next week—I can't remember the details. It's in my notebook.'

*She* is the artist? Simpering Tilly is selected to transform Harrison's? No, I've got this wrong. They must be talking about some other deal. She's involved with the charity night. Must be.

'He's going with the branch theme. He loved your portfolio.'

'Really? Oh, I'm so happy. Thank you Daddy,' Tilly squeals and claps her hands excitedly.

She didn't do her own pitch? Nothing? And she got that job? Really—she is the Picasso?

'He balked a bit when he knew you were a girly and my

daughter but some promo shots with the Chelsea strikers holding your artwork soon brought him round.'

I lean on the wall for support.

'Oh Daddy, come and tell me more about it. I want to know everything.'

'We'll go over it all tomorrow evening. Now, I have to run.'

'You're going out again?' Her voice is sulkily pathetic. 'But we haven't seen you all week.'

'Don't whine, darling. It doesn't suit you. I could ask where you've been half the week—gallivanting with whatshisname no doubt.'

I look to see if Ben is around again but he's still gone, though a giveaway shadow tells me he's listening too.

'But yes, in answer to your question,' continues her father, 'I'm out tonight. I have to go to the club.'

'Won't you look in on the party?' lisps Tilly.

'Haven't got time. I'm still looking for my overnight bag. I asked Sal to put it in the boot room, but I'll be damned if it's there.' He looks around frantically. I brace myself for him seeing me and realising I've been earwigging, but he crosses the hall without noticing.

'She's usually very efficient, so if she said she'd put it the boot room, it'll be in there,' says Tilly walking across the hallway. She disappears into a room next to the front door, the one where Mrs Dev put my coat—of course, the boot room.

Tilly emerges moments later with a smallish leather holdall.

'You. Are. A. Doll, Tilly-mint,' says her father taking the bag. He kisses her forehead again and whispers something in her ear. She nods her head sulkily but seems to like what he's just said to her, judging from the smile on her face.

'Shall I tell Ma you're home?' asks Tilly in the same simpering baby voice while watching her father run up the stairs three steps at a time.

'No need. I'm running late. I'll see you all tomorrow at supper. Let her host and keep an eye on the silver.' My jaw drops slightly at the timely cliché.

To my astonishment Tilly goes back to the party without having acknowledged me, though she did look my way. Talk about being invisible. I stand in the empty hallway feeling frustrated—feeling a number of things actually for I still don't know where the loo is and I'm getting desperate. But now I have Tilly's conquest to think of. That lisping brat has been selected to *launch Aaarrison's into the twenty-first century* with her branch sculptures.

A more disturbing thought enters my head—she'll be good.

'It's right in front of you,' says Ben coming out of the games room. 'Can't you see Manneken Pis?'

'Eh?'

'The pissing cherub there.' He nods at the wall. I see a brass cherub right in front of me.

'Oh. Thanks.' I have seen the image before. I guess it is famous. The cherub is somewhat camouflaged because it blends in with the wall panelling but a handle beneath reveals it is in fact stuck on a door. I look down at my brown woollen dress. Perhaps that's why they didn't see me either. 'Why didn't you come out sooner?' I ask him before going in.

'Sooner?' He's feigning ignorance.

'Never mind.' I try the handle. But before I can enter I have to steady myself a little. I pinch my nose in an attempt to offset a sudden pain in my head and a feeling of dizziness.

'You okay?'

'I dosed myself up with medicine before I came out. Got a bit of a cold or something. I think it hasn't agreed with the wine. I'll be alright. I'll have something to eat shortly.

'You're a delicate little thing and should take care what you imbibe.'

'Right,' I say dismissively and go into a bathroom, which is bedecked with more pictures of the Devanthys at play. They're mostly skiing pictures. I'm too desperate to pee to inspect them.

So she's Tilly Devanthy then. It sounds absurd, like a caricature. Certainly doesn't have the same cool catchy, easy ring as Tracey Emin. And Tilly's 'Unmade Bed' (if she herself ever had to make one) wouldn't be covered in unsightly stains, used condoms and empty wine bottles, or whatever the hell Tracey had lying around on that genius piece of homespun hoodwinkery. I laugh flatly at the thought of Tilly's slightly ruffled Egyptian cotton Queen-size on display at Tate Britain. People would think they were looking at a Harrods' window display.

When I'm done in the loo, I have a closer look at the family pictures cluttering the walls. I can't see Ben in any of them. I notice that Lydia is invariably obscured by either the father or the sister. Not nice. I have a squirt of one of the many perfumes on the windowsill.

When I re-emerge Ben is still outside, and he's blocking my exit.

'Again, I'm sorry about Bananas. Look, there's a bit of a scratch on your face.' He touches my cheek.

'It's nothing.' I move my face out of his reach and wonder at his behaviour. I can't quite put my finger on it but he seems like he's trying to be intimidating. No, that's the wrong word. But he's imposing somehow. 'Can't believe he went for you like that—though he was only being playful. That was lucky for you. It could have got nasty. If I'd have signalled a threat—mistaken you for a burglar, say—then Bananas would have gone truly bananas.'

'But that wasn't likely to happen, was it, there being a party here tonight?'

'No, not likely to happen at all. Anyway'—he moves aside so I can pass—'Glad you're unhurt. I'm just playing snooker—by myself. Mr Dev, as you saw, doesn't care for it, not tonight at least. He has better things to do—*the club*.' He flares his eyes at me. I don't react to the suggestion that there's something amiss with Mr Dev's visit to 'the club'. No doubt Ben is sore that 'Mr Dev' doesn't care for his company or can't even remember his name. Interesting that he's now admitting he was listening and deliberately didn't come out, though perhaps he knows I saw him hiding.

'So, I'm playing on my lonesome.' 'Enjoy,' I say heading back to the party.

'What do you think of Lydia?' he asks when I reach the door.

I turn to face him. 'She's not much like her sister.' 'No,' he laughs. 'That she isn't.'

With a hmmmm buzzing about my lips I go back into the party.

'I think you'll agree, she looks *luuurvly*,' says Cutie Claire as I enter the room. I laugh when I see Laetitia's face—it's copper-coloured and shiny as a new coin like Claire's. She looks positively clammy.

'It feels amazing,' Laetitia says, running a hand over her face. 'Where's a mirror?' She flaps her hand impatiently.

'Here,' says Claire, handing her an oversized hand-mirror. 'There you are.'

Laetitia has a good look and frowns. 'Doesn't it look like I'm a bit sweaty? And surely that shade is too dark for me?'

I'm amazed. Laetitia can see it!

'That's the richness of the oil base from the bee serum. It'll settle in and any excess moisture will penetrate the skin, turning back the clock and giving you that enviable softness and glow just like honey …' Claire continues valiantly. Laetitia begins to relax and buy into it.

'She looks like a melted Malteser,' says Ms Pissed next to me.

'Right, ladies, what I propose to do now is let you all sample the different guilt-free pleasures on offer today. So I'll circulate them and also give each of yourselves a Venus cosmetics order form. Again, I want to stress that no one is under *any* obligation to buy.'

Ms Pissed attempts to refill my glass with an empty bottle. A moment later, she nods at me and winks as if she did actually succeed in her mission. I put down the vinegar wine. No more! I grab a sandwich from a near table (I'll get the hell out of here soon).

# 13

I'M JUST BACK FROM DROPPING MUM in town. I could tell by the spring in her step that it's going to be a happy day for the tills around Liverpool ONE. Thankfully she's meeting some work friends for lunch so I was spared having to traipse around with her.

'That yours?' asks Tommy as I get out of the car. He resumes kicking a ball against the wall (he'd stopped to let me park).

'It's my work car,' I say shutting the door.

'It's dead nice.'

His brother comes out of the house. After he's closed the door he leans on it and puffs out his cheeks like he's bored. I look at the car. It's splattered with mud thanks to that country drive to Tilly's. I have an idea.

'Do either of you, or both of you, want to wash my car? I'll give you a tenner each?'

'Yeah, I will,' says Tommy excitedly and picks up his ball.

'Okay,' says his brother pushing himself off the wall

in surprise.

'I'll get you some buckets and sponges,' I say with enthusiasm.

When I come back out with two buckets half filled with soapy water both of them are standing by the car in readiness. I hand Tommy's brother a bucket first.

'Thanks,' he says gruffly. I can see he's a little embarrassed and maybe shy.

'And that's yours, Tommy. But do you need to change out of your football kit first? It looks new.'

'My dad got it for me, for me birthday. He's coming over later for me party.' At that moment Tommy's mother stands in the bay window of her house and sticks up a large red sash reading HAPPY BIRTHDAY SON. She looks at us all and frowns. Getting on her tiptoes on the window sill she opens the top window and attempts to stick her head out.

'What are yous two doing?' she asks, her face screwed up looking at the boys as if they're about to break into my car instead of wash it.

'We're washing her car,' says Tommy holding up the sponge.

'Not in your new kit you're not. That cost a fortune. You'll have it filthy. I told you it was for your party. Now get in here and change it.' Tommy immediately puts down the sponge and runs to the door, although he doesn't seem in the least bit fazed.

As his mother's letting him in she hisses in his ear. 'You never listen to me, you little fucker.'

I look at the birthday banner again. They must have run out of the ones with 'Happy Birthday *Little Fucker*' on them.

'And you watch your gear too, Reese,' says the mother coming out with arms folded. 'Hey, I hope you're paying them well,' she says and bursts into a cackle. 'I'm only messing, love. That's it, you put the little sods to work.'

Some of the neighbours across the road come out for their afternoon sit on the wall. She immediately forgets about me and goes over to see them.

'I'll get the hose set up, Reese.' I'm so happy to be reminded of his name. Already up to his elbows in suds, he nods from across the bonnet.

As I attach the nozzle to the tap, I'm grateful Mum got a good hose. I know the boys will have fun with the jet-spray trigger. I carefully unravel it as I go through the house. When I get it outside Tommy's there again and soaping the wheels (doubtless Reese gave him that job). Reese immediately takes charge of the hose. He pulls on the trigger and he's taken aback by the force of the water that comes out.

'This is boss, this,' he says blasting one of the lathered fenders.

Tommy protests as he gets caught by the spray, but when he sees the shiny wheel he says, 'Ah, giz a go.'

'Later. It's not a toy,' says Reese, aiming it at a passing cat, which meow-squawks and leaps away. Tommy mutters something and ducks back down to carry on cleaning. Their mother, obviously having seen them, does another cackle and yells, 'You're a shit shot. Should have drowned the bastard.' She's joined by her friends on the wall in hoots of forced laughter. Reese shakes his head at them.

'I'll leave you to it,' I say and go back inside.

To my amazement, they haven't finished after one hour. I bring them tea (three sugars each) and biscuits too, which they appreciate. I put out some polishing cloths after they asked for them. Watching them busily and happily buffing up the paintwork it's clear they love having something to do, something that gets results. It probably doesn't occur to them that they're working.

A huge sigh fills me. Why is it that they never have anything to do? At the weekends they hang around in gangs or twos, play fighting, spitting, kicking stones aimlessly. Tommy's football kit is just fashion. I've never seen him in football boots. He can't play for any team. I sigh again. I'll get them some lemonade and crisps.

\* \* \*

I'm driving to Egremont's and trying to dismiss the thoughts that his not telling me about Tilly being potential artist-in-residence at Harrison's is unforgivable, worrying, a betrayal—all of the above. Yet I can't get certain questions out of my head, like why didn't he want to tell me? and after I had specifically asked him what was going on that day in the office with 'Chaz'. He didn't think to tell me the guy was Tilly's father either?

I know I mustn't get carried away with bad feelings towards him about this. It could ruin everything—well, our evening at least. Is it just jealously? I pull up in front of his house and breathe deeply to calm myself. But with a head still full of resentment over his silence about Tilly, I say to my reflection, 'I will get over this; it's not that big a deal'. When he opens the door, Egremont juts his chin at me and peers closely at my face. I frown. He moves his head from side to side as if contemplating something. 'Egremont? What are you doing?'

'I'm checking to see if your newly acquired Venus make-up serums have turned back the clock yet.' He smiles and then moves aside for me to go in.

'Ah, the make-up party.' I frown on the inside.

'I hear it was a roaring success.' He's clearly in a buoyant mood.

'It was a night full of surprises,' I say to his back as he closes the door.

'Oh?' His eyes are encouraging me to expand.

'Tilly is the fated artist who's got the Harrison commission. I had no idea she was even an artist or that Chaz or Charles was her father. I'm surprised you never mentioned anything about it.'

'No, I ... er ... I was a bit sworn to secrecy. She's very private about that side of her life. Sorry I didn't say anything, and I didn't click on you didn't know her father. I thought that had come out at the opera. But, please, go through to the kitchen.'

'I was a little hurt that you needed to keep Tilly's secret from me.'

'Oh, maybe I shouldn't have. Sorry, they all told me not to mention it and I didn't think about it again. I mean, I made a note to keep the secret, and, well, it sort of kept itself.'

His explanation satisfies me. I laugh and say, 'Your way of thinking is incredible. I wish I could be that straightforward—and I'm hopeless at keeping secrets.'

'Remind me never to tell you one then.' He looks at me with a concerned expression.

'Oh, I can keep serious secrets. I was only talking about things that—' I'm struggling to find the right words.

'Things that you consider important?' he suggests, and I don't care for his tone. It's a tad critical.

'I don't think I'm a bad judge.'

'No, I'm sure you're not,' he says quietly. He smiles again.

'So what are you preparing for us tonight? Something smells good.' I try to peer into the pan on the stove.

'It's a modest bolognese with tagliatelle. I decided to forgo the starters and just have a simple supper.'

'Great!' I suddenly realise I've left the wine in the car. 'I bought some wine. It's in the car. I'll just get it.'

On my way out I wonder that his reaction wasn't to say I shouldn't bother because he's got plenty of wine. But should I be having such thoughts? Not that I want to get away with not bringing wine, but it's just that his instinct wasn't to—I need to switch this off. Returning to the kitchen I hand over the Rioja.

'You didn't have to bring anything.' He turns it around in his hands nodding appreciatively.

'Please, feel free to open it. Rioja goes well with bolognese I believe.'

'It does indeed.'

'I got it from Waitrose. It was on their Customers' Choice of the Month, or something like that.'

'It's a good quaffing wine,' he says, unscrewing the top. 'I'll just let it breathe for a while.' He puts it on the counter top. 'So what was the make-up party like? Did you buy much?'

'I got a few things, yes,' I lie.

'If you ever want repeat orders, I can give them to Lydia for you. I have one of her catalogues here I think.' He opens a drawer and searches through it.

'Thanks. Hey, the party was very good. Lydia and Tilly were great hosts. And the house is amazing, like you said.'

'Isn't it? And you've recovered from the shock of having Bananas maul you?' 'Yes! Thanks to you.'

'I'm glad I was there to minimise the damage.'

As he says these words I have a desire to be close to him, to put my arms around his neck and kiss him—and to be kissed, properly. It would make up for all the conversational awkwardness between us. Who knows, once he's made me squeal he might even be willing to make me privy to a few of his deeply guarded secrets.

'I think it's safe to try the wine now.' He takes two glasses from a cupboard.

'Goody,' pops out of my mouth. I hope that didn't make me sound like an alcoholic child.

'I wanted to ask about your job,' he says and hands me a glass. 'Are you enjoying your new position?'

'Very much. I love the challenges it presents.' My heart sinks at the sound of my own lies. I want to tell the truth, or voice my doubts, but I know it would disappoint him. It's early days yet. We'll get to that place later—I don't need to worry about the white lies yet awhile.

When we're seated in his little dining room looking at each other over plates of bolognese I venture another conversation about Tilly.

'Do you know when she'll start work at Harrison's?'

'Next week some time I think. I don't know for sure.'
'Has she already made most of the sculptures or pictures?'
'I think so, but again, I don't know for sure.'

I'm guessing he's holding back. I get the feeling I'm trespassing on this area of his life—his secret life with Tilly. How long before he lets me in?

'You haven't told me anything about Scotland,' I say swirling the fork around my plate. 'Did you achieve much?'

'I'm not sure.' He pulls a thoughtful-looking face. After a long pause, he adds, 'What we were doing was more of a *testing-the-water*, *sussing-out-the-competition* kind of thing.' He includes two full head wobbles, pulling his mouth down at one side. It is not a flattering look and I dearly wish he'd knock it off.

Half an hour later we're in the sitting room, back on his cottage suite with a book between us. It's yet another book on Tuscany. This time it's one about mountains. I try to look like I'm genuinely interested as he points out where his brother likes to ski off piste.

'And what about you, Egremont? Where do you like to ski off piste?'

'I'm afraid I'm not good enough for that. I can manage a blue run on a good day, but the ski school needs to watch out. I've been known to scatter a few children who cross my path,' he says laughing. I laugh too, though I don't find it funny.

When he gets up to fetch the coffee, I look at the snowy scenes. What would it be like to go skiing with him—and Rupert and Tilly et al? Will I one day be smiling in a colourful photograph holding skis and flanked by the whole lot of them?

'There we go,' says Egremont setting down two small coffee cups. 'There's a few biscuits there as well.' He fusses over the tray. His mobile rings. He takes it off the table and mouths 'Mitchell.' I nod and pick up my coffee.

'Did he? ... Really? ... No, I'm sorry, I didn't.'

I look at Egremont and see he's getting panicked. He puts the phone down after apologising several times.

'Trouble?'

'I'm afraid I've got a bit of work to do—sorry.' He looks dejected.

'What—*now*? Do you need me to go?'

'It might be best.' He seems overcome with thoughts connected to the phone call. I down my coffee and get to my feet.

'We'll do this again—soon,' he says with a sigh.

'Hope you don't work too late.' I head out of the room. He catches up with me by the front door. 'I really enjoyed tonight. Thank you.' He stands awkwardly in front of me.

'Me too. I can't wait to come again.' He breathes with relief and nods his head in agreement. I tiptoe up and kiss him. He responds warmly and we have a long kiss.

'Come back soon,' he says hoarsely as I leave the house.

# 14

I GAVE MITCHELL THE FIRST DRAFT of my speech today. He looked it over, sniffed and told me to bathe him in more glory—his actual words—so I'm going to go over the top now. I'll tip over into total mockery and bet you any money the dickhead won't catch on.

I'm not in the best mood to tell you the truth. Egremont didn't call yesterday. I was expecting an invite to Sunday lunch and for him to tell me all about the urgent work that Mitchell forced on him. All I got was a text saying, 'Hope all is well – still busy my end x'. Somehow I've got to get some fire in that man's belly with regard to me. Or rather, I've got to ignite it!

I pull the car up alongside the railing wall of the industrial estate I have to do today, but I'm overwhelmed with feelings of reluctance to begin. The thought of walking into those offices and trying to persuade busy or bored people that they need Harrison's in their lives seems like more effort than I can muster.

That first day with Mitchell, walking into established firms armed with information, it offered some excitement. I don't know, I embraced … welcomed … was galvanised by the challenge. But now I'm just cold-calling on row upon row of shabby little businesses. Mitchell and Colin are still 'taking care' of those big accounts I won back and showing no signs of giving them back to me.

I pick up my samples case from the passenger seat and take a deep breath. I open the door and get out. Glancing around it's hard to know what half these small-traders are actually selling or offering. Not that it matters. They all have an office.

I push open a mud-smeared glass door and a bell pings. I hear a choked voice saying, 'Be right with you.' A minute later a guy holding a steaming pasty walks into the reception area. He sits down behind a battered desk. 'What can I do you for?' he asks, eyeing me up and down and wiping the grease from the pasty on the lapel of his tatty suit.

'I'm from Harrison's Office Supplies. I wanted to let you know about our new catalogue and fill you in on the competitive rates and the all-improved customised stationery service we offer.'

'Don't tell me,' he says in a voice loaded with sarcasm, 'you've come to deliver us the best deal on clip boards, arch files and copier paper. And you've got the cheapest buff flaps in town. I'm talking foolscap wallets of course—nothing seedy.' He grins broadly and takes a bite of his pasty. A blob of pale shiny cheese oozes out and drops on his shirt. I avert my eyes only for them to encounter a naked calendar woman straddling a motorbike. He follows my gaze and grins.

I leave.

I walk into another ten offices and get to leave our catalogue in a few. I have some orders for the loss-leader copy paper. After coffee from a burger van, I do the rest of the estate and fare much the same. By late afternoon, I haven't much to show for six hours' work, though in truth it wasn't six hours I'd put in. I spent at least two sitting in the car watching traffic go by then I decided to knock off for the day.

I'm sprawled on the sofa at home now. Oh, that's my phone. Could it be Egremont? It's Mitchell. 'Are you busy right now?' he asks aggressively.

'Just finished the Lindin Industrial Estate. I'm about to head home.' I'm praying I sound convincing.

'Good, you're still in Birkenhead. Listen, the vans are all out so I need you to go to the depot and collect some orders, then drop them off at Jessop's.'

I curse myself for the needless fabrication. Now I've no choice but to go back. I tell Mitchell I'm on it and leave the house again.

Great. Just great. I'm snarled up in rush-hour traffic on the wrong side of the tunnel. If this carries on I won't make it to the warehouse by six. I could tell Mitchell there's been a serious crash and I'm stuck because of that. Too risky—any one of the reps could be at the warehouse and he'd check his super satnav for those ultra-quick traffic updates. 'AND SEE THAT I'M LYING MY FUCKING ASS OFF' I shout at the dashboard. I notice a guy in the next lane staring at me. Yes, sir, yet another loser in meltdown. I look away, a little red in the face.

'Come on, come on,' I beg through gritted teeth as I edge towards the roundabout that leads to the tunnel entrance. There's a deafening honking of horns when I cut up three cars as I jump out into the wrong lane. I blithely ignore the yells and wild gesticulating as I race toward the tunnel. Now I know why reps deserve their poor reputation for driving. My phone keeps ringing too but it's in my bag on the back seat.

When I get to the depot, there's a pissed-off store guy standing outside next to a stack of boxes. He's on his phone. When I approach he hands me his mobile. I know its Mitchell on the other end.

'I've been calling you. Why didn't you pick up your phone?' he says angrily. 'You've been nearly a fucking hour.'

'Sorry, I didn't have the hands-free set up. My phone was in my bag. And then I got a bit lost. These roads—'

'Just get your arse over to Jessop's and apologise to Lynn whose waiting round like a spare part for you. Remember, you were the one who promised her the next-day delivery, so let her know it was your fault, not Harrison's, that she's been kept past six.'

'Okay,' I say to a dead phone. I give it back to the guy, who now looks sorry for me. 'Sorry about this.' I take some packages from the stack.

'Open up your boot,' he says kindly, picking up one of the larger boxes.

When I get to Jessop's, Lynn is far from being the welcoming, charming lady I encountered a few weeks ago (which seems like months ago now). Silently she watches me struggle with the boxes.

'Just put them by the door,' she says curtly.

'I'm really sorry about this Lynn. It's totally my fault, and—'

She nods dismissively and walks away to take a call. When I'm done, she's still talking on her phone. 'All finished here. Sorry about that,' I say to her back. When she doesn't reply or even acknowledge my apology, I get the message and leave. As I get into the car, I can't help thinking that if Mitchell had let me handle the Jessop's account myself this wouldn't have happened. I'd have made damn sure they had their order in time. My phone rings. It's Egremont.

'What are you doing this evening? I was wondering if you wanted to come over to my house for coffee. We could have a game of Scrabble or something.'

'Erm, we could do that.' I can't help but smile. Scrabble or something? He has to be talking about something else entirely, right? He finally has to be talking about sex.

'You could come over about eight?' he suggests. 'I'll do some supper. Nothing fancy—just a little pasta.'

'Sure, would love to.'

At eight on the dot I'm knocking on Egremont's door. In the car is my overnight bag because the next time I hope to leave this house is seven in the morning. When he opens the door, I see an old woman cross the hallway behind him.

'I've got some company,' he says smiling and holding the door open wide for me to come in.

When I go in, to my dismay I discover a huddle of pensioners in the sitting room holding cups of tea.

'They're from my church. You don't mind company tonight do you?'

'No, no,' I lie, wondering how long I have to stay before I make my excuses.

Two hours later I'm back in the car going home. It's only a hiccup though. We'll get there. One way or another I'll overcome his shyness, the pensioners, his workload. Whatever it takes, as God is my witness, I will get that man into the sack, 'After all, tomorrow is another day.' Ha!

\* \* \*

I open my eyes and stare into the darkness. A smile crosses my face. I've just had the most pleasing dream about Egremont.

We were being playful, like lovers, with no embarrassment whatsoever, like two people who had—you know. He was pretending to fend me off, catching at my hands as I attempted to pull his shirt. He kept kissing my neck all through our play fight and making little jokes. His laughter was wonderful. I was enjoying myself so much—enjoying him. He was telling me about his new house:

'I've moved house,' he said, looking at me with a seriousness I'd never seen before.

'Really, moved? Where?' I asked.

'I've bought an old rectory,' he said, smiling like he knew how much I'd like the news. 'It's quite remote and is a little too big for one person.'

I stared at him wondering if he was going to pop the question.

'Can you guess what I'm going to ask you?' he said taking my hand and putting it to his lips.

'I—'

'Do you love me, Evelyn?'

'I do.'

'Then come back with me to the house. We'll marry from there. Come back to my home—*our* home.' He pulled me to him and kissed me passionately. When he broke away, he said, 'Yes, come with me now and prepare to be my wife. Let's be happy together.'

The dream is a sign. I am Egremont's saviour as he is mine.

# 15

As I walk into the office with Egremont—just a coincidence that we came in at the same time—Adam's eyes are on us immediately (and no Eggers and I haven't seen each other all week – Mitchell's had him running all over the country). Adam looks away without reaction—no 'hi', no scoffing, no nothing. When I say hello, it's only Laetitia who responds. Egremont overtakes me to go to his office, whispering, 'Have a great day.'

'Okay, talk later.' I smile after him as he goes. 'You're all better now, Adam?' I ask his back.

'Yes, thanks, completely recovered.' He picks up his phone and begins making a call. He hasn't looked at me. Laetitia darts a puzzled look between us.

'You're looking luuuuurvly, Eve. I'm liking you in baby blue,' she says, eyeing me up and down over thick-rimmed glasses (Adam reckons they're fake—they only come out when she's wearing secretarial-type clothes).

'Thanks. You look good too,' I say truthfully. She's in

plain black with white blouse and it suits her.

'But, kiddo—' She's dropped her voice to a whisper. 'I think you're late for the Friday meeting.' She inclines her head toward the conference room, as Mitchell's taken to calling it.

'Shit!' I quickly take off my coat and hear Mitchell calling me.

'Hey, get your arse in here, Widdowson.' I look over at him and he points aggressively at the meeting room. He promptly disappears back into it. 'Don't worry, kiddo, he's all bark.'

Adam blows through his mouth contemptuously but finally gives me a friendly look. I smile at him warmly.

'Thanks again for the soup,' he says gently. 'It was amazing.'

'Glad it helped. Are you back at rehearsals?'

'Yes.'

'Eve, are you deaf? Get over here now,' shouts Mitchell having popped his head out again. Adam calls him a fucking wanker as I'm leaving. I truly hope Mitchell didn't hear that.

'You got that purchase order for me?' asks Mitchell as I step into the packed conference room. I look at him blankly. 'The purchase order from Jessop's—Lynn's order from Monday. You did deliver it?'

'Jessop's order! Mitchell, I'm sorry. I forgot about the delivery receipt.'

'You didn't get Lynn to sign the purchase order?'

I shake my head and brace myself for the onslaught. 'THEN WHERE IS IT?' he screams.

'It's er—'

'She's claiming half the stuff's missing, but I can't do much about it if I don't have the fucking receipt. You didn't check the stuff in?'

'It was late. She was in a hurry to go home.' As the words come out I feel utterly stupid.

I look around and see smirks on the faces of the other reps. 'I'll call the warehouse now and find it.' I'm staggered at my incompetence.

'You'll do better than that. You'll go over to Jessop's now and find out what was delivered and what still needs delivering.' He looks as if he wants to punch something. I catch Egremont's eye. He's looking like he wants to cry on my behalf. I leave the room, grateful to escape from everyone's delighted looks. I'm also glad that Egremont saw that. Soon he'll understand that he's the only one who can save me from all this.

As I pass Adam's desk he grabs me by the hand. I look at his hand in mine, then at him. He stares at me without saying anything.

'What is it?'

'It's my last day,' he says flatly.

'Really?' I sit down in my old chair (my desk is still vacant). 'Does Laetitia know? Does anyone know?'

'Yeah, I told her. I basically quit today. I've got work as an extra. There's tons of acting work going begging at the moment.'

'I wish I could act,' comes out of my mouth, surprising me.

'You still here, Eve?' shouts Mitchell. Adam grimaces and mutters something with lots of F-words.

'I best go.' I get up and take my hand out of his. 'Look, if I don't see you before you go I'll see you at the opening night of your play.'

'You're deffo coming to that, aren't you?'

'Of course I am. I wouldn't miss it for anything.'

'Sound,' he says, smiling at me as I walk away.

'Actually, Eve, get your slack arse back in here,' shouts Mitchell. 'You can sort your mess out after the meeting.' I turn on my heel and head back towards the conference room. Adam shakes his head in sympathetic disgust.

'Okay, back to business,' says Mitchell as I re-enter the room. 'The first thing I want to say is that you can all get off my back about the printing orders. There is a backlog but it will be cleared. There's a revolution happening behind the scenes and that's all you need to know. So far no deadlines have been missed and none will be. Next week the all-new *Aaarrison's* printing orders will begin rolling of the presses. You should deliver the first batches yourselves so you can go over the quality—which will be first-class—with your clients. That clear enough?' He looks around the room with a sharp eye and is met with murmurs of unconvincing approval.

'Good. And now to the other business—our annual charity dinner,' he says more confidently. 'Despite Eve here acting like a real dippy drawers, she's still delivering a speech.' All eyes are on me again, but this time I'm guessing they're not so mocking. 'And I want to see a new draft of it by the end of the week, Eve. You got that?' He snaps his fingers at me. 'Don't want you letting the side down that night.'

'Yes, I'll have it for you.' I can barely disguise my annoyance. I feel like telling him to shove his speech.

'Good, we want to hear the voice of the successful newbie talking about how we promote and foster talent.' He flashes a less than sincere smile at me. 'And the rest of you need to prepare too. We've only got a few weeks before the event, which is, as you know, at my hotel, The *Aaarrison* Plaza. It's gonna be big. We've got some serious celebs coming so there'll be security up the kazoo. You need to make sure you're on time and that you've got your ticket. You've got to be in there before seven or you won't be allowed in. The hotel will basically go on lock-down after seven. And look smart—black-tie smart for you guys; and girls, I want ball gowns—spend your bonus on something designer for the cameras. Make *Aaarrison's* look like the class operation it is.'

There are squeals of delight from the female reps and excited laughter from the rest. Egremont raises his shoulders at me and pulls his face into an expression that shows nervous anticipation. I'm prevented from feeling anything about the event by the arrival of Tilly outside the meeting room. She's carrying a large flat black leather folder, one of those artist's portfolios. It's a wonder I've never seen her with one before. Oh, but why would I? Her father's the one who totes it around for inspection.

She looks cool as hell in her leggy 'skinny' jeans and little white T-shirt. She wiggles her fingers at me. I wave back in an effort to be friendly. God only knows what I actually look like (sick as a dog, probably). Mitchell's face visibly brightens on seeing her.

'Meeting over,' he says getting up and heading out of the room. With a hand on Tilly's shoulder he walks her to his office.

Meanwhile I get ready to sort out the delivery that should never have been my responsibility in the first place.

I whisper 'good luck' in Adam's ear before heading out. He's on the phone, but he gives my hand a squeeze whilst it's on his shoulder.

As I let it go and walk on I feel miserable. Adam's last day and we're not going to mark the occasion. I also have a sinking feeling that I won't be seeing much of him again after today.

\* \* \*

It's almost the end of another unproductive day. I got the Jessop's order sorted out and that's about it. Now I have the prospect of an uneventful weekend ahead with no invitation from Egremont to spend it with him. I did ask what his plans were. He was vague, saying something about dull church work 'and a few dinners that will be a yawn.' He said something too about needing to tie up loose ends in Scotland before he went away. I didn't get chance to ask him where and when he was going away (think it's Tuscany). He's going to call me. Of course, things could all change.

I have, at any rate, written my new speech. I'm looking over it now (I just printed off a copy). It's a dangerous parody but some devil goaded me to carry on in high-blown exaggeration. If I do go with this, it's possible I won't be able to read it and keep a straight face.

'That your speech?' asks Mitchell, approaching me while looking distractedly at his phone.

'Yes, but it's not finished.' I try and cover it with some papers.

'Looks long enough.' He swipes it off the desk.

I prepare myself mentally in case I need to give an offended reaction for when—if—he susses it's a piss-take.

I watch his head bob up and down with what I assume to be approval, although for all I know he might be brewing with indignation and only making it look like he digs it until he explodes with outrage and fires me.

He begins reading out loud: 'There is no superlative too full of praise or one that could over express my gratitude to Mitchell and Harrison's for the opportunity, nay opportunities they have given me. But it is to Mitchell in particular that I owe direct thanks. I wish there were a trophy or special accolade I could bestow upon this selfless good man who has the patience of Gabriel. He's a mentor, a guru, the best boss and a killer salesman who can spin straw into gold when he puts his brilliant mind to it. That's what he did with me.' He stops reading and looks at me.

'This is all right, Eve. This is not bad at all.' He reads on and I begin to shake a little with laughter. I cough to stop myself and feign seriousness. 'Can I keep this?' he says when he's finished.

'Sure.'

'I might need to tweak a few things, but good job well done, Eve.'

'Thanks.' I watch him leave. 'Dip-shit' I add under my breath.

# 16

Is that Adam? It is! What's he doing out this way? I pull down the window and yell out his name (I think a weekend of doing nothing but reading a novel and lazing around has made me desperate to talk to someone). He turns and sees me after a few moments. He waves back. He shouts something I can't quite hear. On impulse I turn into a slip road. He comes bounding up to greet me.

'Hey Mzzz Snazzy pants, what choo up to?' he asks, smiling broadly and putting his hands on the open window.

'Snazzy pants?' I repeat, grimacing. He laughs. 'What are you doing over here?'

'Was just visitin Anna.'

'*Anna?*' I question, forcing a smile.

'She's the leading lady—Jill.'

'Ah, Jill's House—she plays your wife. So it's you and Anna, eh?'

'Nah, it's not like that. We were just rehearsing.'

'Oh, sure you were.' Before I can say anymore my phone

vibrates. I see Egremont's number flashing. I hit the off button before Adam sees it.

'Who was that?' he asks, straining to look at the phone.
'Just Mitchell. He'll want to know if I dropped an order off. Don't feel like speaking to him.'

'Hounds the life out of you, does he?'

I puff with contempt and Adam laughs. 'Do you fancy a walk around the park?' he asks encouragingly. I look over at the entrance to it.

'Sure, why not? I'll just park up.'

When I'm done he opens the car door for me. I grab my coat and get out.

When we're just about at the entrance, I notice a group of scallies approaching, a dangerous dog straining at the leash. Thankfully they pass 'without incident'. Adam doesn't even give them a second glance.

'How are rehearsals going?
'Good, very good, thanks.'

I wonder whether to press the point about how well things seem to be going with Anna, but as he clearly doesn't wish to be drawn on the subject I leave it. But it's interesting that they're putting in extra time together—very interesting.

'Do you fancy sitting down for a bit?' he asks, suddenly stopping in front of a bench.

'Yes, why not?'

'Bet you've been on your feet all day, have you?' he asks, looking sympathetic as he sits down.

'It's not too bad. These shoes are more comfortable than they look.' I refrain from telling him I do more sitting in the car than traipsing around industrial estates. I scan the bench and see that it looks clean enough not to stain my coat.

The lake is dotted with people fishing. 'Can there be any fish left in that lake?' I ask.

'God knows.' He thrusts his hands in his pockets. 'Funny hobby, fishing,' I reflect, looking around.

'Can't say I get it.'

'Glad the park's busy, though.'

'There used to be boating on it.'

'Really, on that lake?'

'Yeah. Not in our time but yonks ago. I seen pictures of it somewhere.'

'But now they've gone.'

'What's up?' he asks, scanning my face.

'Nothing. Just tired—end of the day. And I wish it was the end of the week instead of the beginning, that's all. Hey'—I badly want to change the subject—'did you notice the Victorian lamps at the entrance as we walked in?'

'I did,' he says, frowning a little.

'Did you notice they weren't vandalised?'

'I didn't think about it.' He pulls his head back in surprise.

'Well, all three lamps on both posts are intact, and have been for as long as I can remember. But the yellow bus shelters and the ugly silver phone boxes are bashed in with wilful regularity. What does that tell you?'

'Think I see what you're getting at. There's an aesthetic appeal in the old lamps that makes the bastards stay their destructive hands?'

'Exactly so, dear Watson.'

Adam laughs.

'Those bus shelters and phone boxes are so ugly they make me want to turn into Wreck-it Ralph myself.'

'Steady on, girl.' He raises his eyebrows at me.

'Seriously, to look at them injects me with a kind of depression. You ever get that?' I look at him.

'It can happen, sure. I get that feeling when I'm eagerly awaiting emails, or messages, or responses from people I don't even like.'

'Jane Austen wrote something to the effect that *the anticipation of happiness is happiness itself*. For me I think it sometimes works the other way round.' As I'm saying this, Adam is looking at me as if he doesn't quite believe I'm serious.

'Okay, that's going too far. But ... I mean ... well, as I said, it's like being injected with depression.' I mime a needle going into his arm. He looks at it as I'm doing so. I carry on. 'You're going about your day happily enough, and it can happen at any time. You see a scruffy kid looking neglected and sad, or it's a beggar shuffling about in the cold.'

He takes over: 'Or you walk into McDonalds to satiate a hunger you know not whence it came.' A smile begins to play about his mouth.

'Monosodium glutamate?' I suggest. He nods, agreeing.

'Of course,' he goes on, 'it was your feet that carried you in there, for your heart and mind said *absolutely do not try this insidious fare*. But you give your order all the same—to some acned youth who you try not to pity, hoping all the time that it's not him pitying your sorry ass.'

It's my turn to nod, although I'm smiling, enjoying our impromptu *Whose Line Is It Anyway?*

He continues: 'And in minutes—for 'tis fast food—you take your tray and sit down, dispirited as any prisoner. Naturally, you've tried not to look at the clientele, but inevitably you do. What a woebegone looking bunch. Nothing like the bright young things in the Ad—'

'No, they're not.' I force my smile to fade. 'Then there's the gaggle of legging-clad single mums with their grey-faced, ignored offspring—'

'—who also come at the weekend when having "access" with their father.'

I nod in agreement again and then I continue: 'You divert your intrusive gaze before you get a mouthful of indignant rebuke, although the wha-the-fucka-you-luckun-a? would be entirely deserved.'

'Oi! You sounded like me then,' he says with fake offence at my Scouse accent.

'Sorry.'

'You really depressed?' he asks, taking his hands out of his pockets.

'No.' I laugh but it's unnatural. He looks at me with scrunched forehead.

'What about Egg-sal—Egremont? Are things not going well there?'

'He's so busy lately. He's great friends with the ski-resort couple and her family—her very rich family. That okay-ya tall guy, Chaz who was sizing up the office for artwork, that's Tilly's father.'

'He's spending more time with them than you?'

'I'm not sure.' I look at Adam and smile in thanks for this outburst of sensitivity around Egg-salted and me.

'Is he—Egremont what you really want?'

'I need him.' Adam's head drops and he shakes it ever so slightly. He's probably battling with not showing his despair at my pathetic state.

'I am getting cold.' I stand up. 'Shall we walk back to the car?' Then I have an idea. 'We could go to the pub for a drink—if you like, warm up a bit.'

'I can't, girl. Got rehearsals in a few hours.'

'Can I drop you at the Everyman then?'

He hesitates. 'Nah, you're okay, I'll get the bus. It'll be quicker, and it drops me outside.'

Not relishing the idea of rush hour traffic back into the city, I don't force the offer.

'We'd better head back then,' I say with a weak smile. We walk back in silence. When we pass the Victorian lamps I have a last look at their preserved elegance and beauty.

'I hate to break it to you, girl, but the lights on the other side of the park are all smashed in. There are no light bulbs nor nothing—haven't been for years.'

'No way!' I stop dead in my tracks.

'Afraid so,' he sighs, zipping his jacket up to the top. 'I'm not sure it entirely explodes my theory but we'll leave it there.' To this his nods with a sigh.

He sees me into the car and walks away, looking back only once. I wonder if he was glad to get away. He'd greeted me with a beaming smile and full of beans. He'd left with a sad look and a heavy step. What I do to men! I take out my phone and see there's a message from Egremont.

The message reads:

*Would you like to meet up before I go to Tuscany?*

I type back that I've got a cold coming on (don't know where that came from but I'm sick of being too keen only to be let down). To my surprise a message comes back before I've started the car. It says:

*Best leave it then. Don't want to be sniffling on the slopes.*

I stare at the message and picture his head wobbling as he says *sniffing on the slopes*. I feel incredibly cheated.

# 17

It's Adam's opening night and I'm outside the Drogar Theatre waiting for Laetitia to show. It's been a spectacularly uneventful few weeks. I've spent more time in the car listening to Radio 4 than I have 'door knocking'. Egremont has hardly been in touch, apart from a few dull messages telling me about the quality of snow and what food he's had, although he did suggest I'd like the place. But will I ever get there? Will he ever get down on one knee and let me start my life as Mrs Egremont, lady of leisure, the lady who does the ignoring instead of being ignored? And is it really what I want?

So, like I say I'm outside the unknown Drogar Theatre, because it isn't the Everyman staging *Jill's House* after all but this obscure little venue, although I'm sure it's hip and happening. There's certainly a buzz about the place (interesting that Adam couldn't bring himself to tell me until the very last minute).

And here she comes—in a very big overcoat. Naturally,

I'm wondering what's underneath, although judging by the beret, it will probably be her Parisian number again.

'Hey, kiddo, I'm not late am I?' She beams a broad smile (yes, lipstick-stained).

'No,' I reply, grateful she didn't plant a red kiss on my cheek. 'Drink?'

'Oooh yeah, I'm parched, kid. I'll have a Malibu and coke, and make it a large one.' We head in to the upstairs bar. When she takes off her coat, I'm struck by her outfit. She's a kind of rotund Marcel Marceau in white salopettes and short top with two prominent Mickey Mouse buttons. Her face is a mask of powdery white foundation, which makes her teeth look very yellow. My mother would have said something like 'Who got her ready?' or 'What's she come as?'

The first bell goes as the barman puts down our drinks. 'Damn, they're early.' I look round for a clock.

'No, it's 7:45, kiddo.' She winks and downs her drink in one. I shrug and try to do the same.

'Where we sitting, hun?'

'Lower centre circle—should have a good view.'

\* \* \*

Oh dear. Oh dearie, dearie dear. Adam's play is one of *those* plays. I should have guessed from the program that this was low-budget and obscure. Not one actor has been in *Casualty* for a start. The dialogue: 'Mam, will ya tell 'im t' shut it; ees doin' me 'ed in.' Making it worse is the fact that such lines, every last stupid one, is being met with uproarious mirth— all forced out, of course; nothing but Pavlovian responses.

This is also a gritty play, and Adam has said the line, 'Is it so wrong t' wanna make somethin' o' meself?'

Jill's reply: 'No, an I wanna come flyin' with ya.'

The play is staged around a small dining table in a cheap kitchen where various members of friends and family come in to have 'a cuppa' and dish out their own gutsy urban philosophy, as if such noble sentiments have never been expressed before by humble folk.

Adam (aka Jack) is coming back on stage. I'll let you listen to a bit:

> Jack: *A just wanna life, if that's not too much to ask.*
> Jill: *An' I just wanna new washin' machine.*
> Jack: *I wish I could just disappear over thee far off oceans un never 'ave te worry over nothin' again.*
> Jill: *An' I wish I could spin dry.*

I all but shouted out, 'Do me a fucking favour.'

Adam hasn't been honest with me. This is some sort of indiscriminately subsidised student effort, perhaps a lazy workshop collaboration. It's unlike Adam to have kept me in the dark, just like it took him till last night to tell me the venue was actually at this little theatre. Is he in denial?

Jill, his onstage wife (Anna), is very cute though. I'm sure he's loving that, if not the dopey things she's being forced to utter.

We're to say hello to him after the play (he insisted).

So I have to like at least some part of *Jill's House*. Despite the dialogue, Adam's acting is amazing. He definitely has presence. There! I have my praise. Alleluia!

Laetitia shifts in her seat—OH, I DON'T BELIEVE IT, but look who's here. It's only Tilly-mint and Ben. Shit, he's just seen me. He waves. Tilly's now looking over. She jerks a smile and looks back to the stage. I smile and look away, but it isn't long before I furtively look back. Ben is looking self-consciously handsome and debonair. Actually they both are. Bloody hell. He slips his hand into Tilly's and looks fondly at her as she continues to laugh like a drain at the nonsense. He smiles as he stares at her face. He seems to be gaining more enjoyment from observing her reactions than from the play.

'Adam's great, kiddo,' says Laetitia from the side of her mouth. I nod, unable to avert my gaze from Ben and Tilly. Why can't I have a relationship like that?

To my delight and relief the lights suddenly go out on stage. The first part is over. I clap along with everyone else.

'Let's get a drink,' says Laetitia, getting to her feet.

'I think I need one,' I reply, following her out, though not before having stepped on several feet, bags and brollies in the struggle to escape the inch-width aisle.

'Well, what do you think of it?' I ask Laetitia as we queue impatiently for drinks.

'It's quite funny, but I didn't see you laughing much, kiddo. Not your bag?'

'Doesn't seem to be, no.'

'Adam is terrif though.' She cleans her teeth with her tongue.

'He is,' I say firmly. I can't be bothered to slag the play off. In any case, it just might prove impolitic.

'Large G&T for you, kiddo?'

'Oh yes please.' I sneakily rubberneck for Ben and Tilly as Laetitia is shouting our order.

'I was speaking to Mitchell today,' Laetitia says, looking at me with narrowed eyes and a serious expression—one, frankly, I'm not used to from her.

'Oh?'

'It was more Mitchell speaking to me—about Egremont—and you.' She nods significantly, again looking—well, worried.

'Me and Egremont? What about us?'

'Mitchell's acting weird about you two. *I* know you're going out together—don't worry, I haven't said a word—I know because I've seen the way you are around the office, but is it serious? I promise I won't let on. None of his damn business anyway, controlling freak.'

'Well, Egremont's in Tuscany so it doesn't matter, and the truth is, Laetitia, I'm not sure if we are actually going out together. We haven't—' I stop myself. Why they hell am I blurting all this out to her?

'I'd fuck him,' she says with a sniff as the barman puts down our drinks.

'Good luck with that.' I snatch my G&T from the bar annoyed. What's wrong with me? It's like I can't keep any thoughts to myself.

'Ah, like that was it?' she says knowingly, a broad smile crossing her face (and GOD! the lipstick on her teeth).

'I tried my best and failed, several times.' What the hell—I need to get this off my chest.

'Big hands and big nose—got to be something worth having in those pants. But he's not putting out. Don't you just hate those religious types?'

'You think old-fashioned prudery is what's stopping him?'

'He may be a virgin.' I almost spit out my drink at the thought.

'Surely to God he couldn't be?' But as soon as I've voiced the words I see the bigger picture. That's why he's avoiding me now and has aborted every attempt of mine to have him. He's terrified of 'doing it'!

'Arrrh I've hit a nerve.' She pulls a face, which looks comical given her make-up. She leans in. 'I bet right now he's peering at the night sky above Tuscany and beating his meat to thoughts of you naked.'

'Laetitia!'

'My play on his name is Egg-beater because I know he's got to be a practised hand. He flogs more than stationary let me tell you. Yeah, it won't take him long to knock the top off.'

'Will you stop!'

'Sorry, kiddo, I'm crude. What can I do? Just remember to keep things discreet in the office when things crank up a notch. Mitchell's a loose cannon and would probably fire both of you.'

'Mitchell's got a fucking cheek. What's it to him anyway?'

'I think he fancies you himself.'

'I don't know what he fancies. He's odd, but God, he's a married man.'

'You know he has the penthouse suite at the Plaza?' she says with eyebrows raised.

'Yeah, I know.' This is no news whatsoever.

'And do you know that his wife *never* goes there—to the hotel?'

'How can you possibly know that?' She laughs. 'I'm all-knowing, kiddo.' 'And how so in this particular case?'

'Told ya, kiddo, I got *connections*.' She taps her glistening nose. 'Channel 9 is right next door to the Plaza.'

'Do you know Ben'—I thrash around for his surname—'Simmons?'

'Can't say I do.'

No, I think to myself, you don't know him or anyone else at Channel 9. 'His wife lets him get on with it,' Laetitia goes on. 'Mind you, she's probably relieved she doesn't have to put up with him.'

'Then why did she marry him?' I ask, suddenly dying to know the answer.

'Becky Harrison'—she leans in again and whispers—'Let's just say, she's visually challenged, and that's not the worst of it.'

I stare at Laetitia's whitened face and my eyes dart down to the sausage chubbage now peeping over her too-tight salopettes. The words 'people in glass houses' burn my brain. I bring myself back to our conversation. 'But what about her being a hot-shot business woman? I thought that was the reason for her absence—she's too busy crushing the Asian workforce to bother with us.'

'Convenient myth.' Laetitia sniffs to add emphasis. 'You said that's not the worst of it. What else is wrong with Becky Harrison?'

'She's got a drink problem,' she says, emptying her glass down her throat.

'Poor woman,' I say, downing mine too.

Laetitia jerks her head for us to leave.

Back in the auditorium, I see Ben and Tilly having ice cream—it looks like they didn't move. I'm about to point out Ben but leave it. I can do that later in the bar if they stick around.

\* \* \*

At last the curtain comes down on *Jill's House*. Now we just have to wait for the cast to trot out.

And here they come, one by one to rapturous applause. I whoop loudly when Adam steps forward. He looks in my direction and I clap even more furiously. He beams a lovely smile at me. Joy! Now we have to wait for them to come together in a daisy chain—which they're beginning to do— all bowing their heads in faux humble thanks once again. Adam is continuing to look very pleased with himself, but why shouldn't he? It might be a subsidised drama written by some over-ambitious artistically challenged ... (don't drag the word out of me) but he's up before an appreciative crowd and clearly the star of the show. And speak of the devil, the writer is now being presented and the audience is going wild. He looks about twelve. He blows us many kisses using both hands, then starts bowing left, right and centre, and finally trips off waving (again with both hands) as if it's been a royal gala performance at the London Palladium.

When the clapping is over, Laetitia turns to me. 'Listen, kiddo, I'm not stopping for another drink. Can you give Adam my best and tell him he was fab?'

'What? Surely you can have *one*?'

'No can do. Meeting some media people.'

'Right then.'

How will I meet Adam now? Will I wait in the bar alone or just go home? Maybe Adam won't come out for a drink after all. He may be exhausted. I watch Laetitia leave. Was she really meeting people or just escaping me? And if she *is* meeting media types why didn't she invite me?

Naaaah—she was going home to her cats.

I think I'll try and get back stage—see what Adam's doing. There'll be no bodyguards that's for sure.

I make my way to the rear of the auditorium and duck behind the curtain. After a few wrong turns, I find Adam in laughing conversation with his co-thesps. I'm a little nervous as I approach and hang back slightly. However, he notices me and breaks away from the group.

He gives me a big silent hug.

'You were marvellous,' I say into his chest.

'I was,' he replies with theatrical emphasis, making me laugh. I pull away wanting to ask if we're having a drink at the bar—but I'll be muscling in, surely. Would I?

'I just wanted to say in person that you were fabulous. Oh—Laetitia says exactly the same—that you were fabulous. Her exact words.'

'Are you two having a drink here?'

'No, she's apparently off to meet some *media* people.'

'Like fuck she is. But she's left you on ya Jack Jones. You should have—' He stops himself. He was going to say I should have come with other friends until he remembered I don't have any. By the way, I did have once (female friends) but they emigrated—say nothing!

'Look, give me ten minutes and I'll meet you in the bar.'
'No! it's fine. I was leaving.'
'Like fuck you are.' He puts an arm around my shoulder.
'What would you like to drink then?' I ask, disguising a smile.
'A beer to start, thanks. Got a shockin' thirst on me.'

I let him go. He walks into the arms of co-star Jill (Anna). She jumps up and down like she's sharing some exciting news with him. I pull myself away from the scene and head back to the bar.

When Adam joins me he's alone. Yesssss! I do a mental punch in the air. I'm sitting with a pint, some nibbles and a bottle of Chardonnay with two glasses.

'Nice one, girl,' he says as he sits down. He scoops up his glass and drinks almost half of the contents in one.

'You obviously needed that.'

'Too right, babe.' He lowers his glass to his lap and runs a hand through his hair. 'So, ya like the play, eh?'

I nod eagerly.

'Really?' He looks at me searchingly.

'Really.' I try to sound convincing.

'*Adam*,' squeals a guy who's approaching. 'You. Were. Fabulous.' He comedy minces in a camper-than-camp voice. Adam gets up and extends his hand whereupon the guy pulls him into an embrace, uttering praise after praise about the play and Adam's performance in it. Behind him the cast of *Jill's House* are filing past to the bar. Some sit at our table, many of them coming in for equally hysterical eulogies from this fan (who's out-acting them all).

Soon we're surrounded by many more people and indeed bottles.

Ten minutes later, I'm sitting quite alone, socially speaking. Everyone around me is engaged in lively conversation; Adam's completely swamped. I slip unnoticed to the bar for another drink, my bottle of wine having been 'shared'. The bar is packed out and it's bloody noisy too. As I'm carried forward in the surge, I delve into my bag to have the money ready. When I look up I'm face to face with Ben.

'Emily!' he says, smiling broadly.

'It's Evelyn,' I reply, dazzled momentarily by his broad fine-looking face.

'*Evelyn*, sorry.' He shakes his head and makes an I'm-a-total-klutz face. 'Let me buy you a drink.'

'No, it's okay—thanks.'

'You'd be doing me a great favour. Tilly's bolted and I'm left in the lurch.'

'Bolted?'

'She's off to Florence tonight—skiing. Her folks just picked her up on their way to the airport.' A barman impatiently motions for Ben to give him his order.

'Skiing? I thought she was getting paintings ready for our offices.'

'She needed a break from the pressure. She's only going for a few days. She'll be back to finish her work. Your boss gave her an extension. She finds skiing rejuvenating.'

'I'll have a large Chardonnay,' I say with irritation.

'Right, yes.' He's acting like he's suddenly recalled why we're here. He orders a bottle and two glasses.

'Egremont will be pleased to see her,' I say through gritted teeth, exposing my annoyance.

'Oh, he's on his way back. She made sure of—'

'Made sure he wasn't there? Is that what you were going to say?' So Egremont's a nuisance? Was he due back today? I thought he'd said 'sometime next week.' I wonder if he's left a message on my phone (it's at home).

'I was teasing. I meant nothing of the kind. Who could possibly want to avoid Egremont?'

'Right.' I suddenly feel hot with indignation. Does Egremont pester Tilly because he fancies her? The thought is abhorrent.

'So what did you think of the play? Ben asks, biting on his bottom lip and raising his eyebrows.

'I thought it was total dross. It's my guess the writer's inspiration for *Jill's House* was from watching back episodes of *Brookside*, *Bread* and *The Liver Birds*. He managed to out-cliché Carla Lane.'

'Thanks for the feedback,' says a caustic voice in my ear. I turn to see the playwright himself. Ben pulls a face that says 'awk-ward'. Before I have a chance to apologise he's moved on and is heading for the actors' table. He sits down where I was sitting. And now what's the betting he shares what I've just said with Adam?

'We'd better find you another seat,' Ben says and takes the wine and glasses from the bar.

We sit a few tables away and I look on with trepidation as Adam puts his ear to the author's mouth to catch what he's saying.

'Shame Shakespeare happened to hear you, but you were spot on in your analysis—a cringing yawn from start to finish.' Ben pours our wine. 'Tilly loved it though,' he adds, looking bewildered.

When he finishes pouring the wine, he flashes his large pearly whites at me as if he's pleased with himself and all the world. Over his shoulder I see Adam staring at me. He mouths '*Che-Gue-fuckin-vara?*' I heave a sigh of relief—he's frowning jokingly.

I laugh and shake my head then indicate that there wasn't a seat for me on his table. The playwright also looks over. Shit—he recognises me and now looks at Adam and is saying something. I know it's about what I've just said.

Oh no: Adam is looking disgusted with me. That bloody rat has told him. Adam turns away. It gives me the oddest sensation.

'Drink up,' says Ben, pushing my glass of wine nearer to me.

\* \* \*

Half an hour later I'm leaving the bar alone. Ben got into a conversation with someone else and that gave me the opportunity to slip away. I didn't dare attempt a good-bye to Adam.

Outside the theatre throngs of people are heading in different directions. I head off for Hardman Street where there's a taxi rank. A sharp whistle behind me makes me turn. It's Ben.

'Where you off to in such a hurry?'

'Going home.' I'm wondering why he's pursued me.

Oh—he's just having a ciggie.

'Want to come to El Bar with me?' he says walking alongside me, smoking.

'I don't know. Do I want to go to El Bar with you?'

'Yes, you most certainly do. What else is there?'

'Sleep?'

'Per chance to dream?' He smiles and makes me smile.

'All right then, I'll risk it if you will. You can tell me all about how Egremont is making a fool of himself with Tilly as we walk.'

'Ah ha, so that's your motivation is accepting my offer.'

'It is and I hope to be rewarded.'

'We shall see see,' he says laughing.

When we get to the club, El Bar (and he's revealed nothing), I'm disappointed to see there's a queue snaking around the building. 'It'll take us ages to get in there,' I say about to suggest another place.

'It won't,' says Ben who, with impressive assuredness, walks to the head of the line. He goes straight up to the bouncers and says something quite casually. Yes! Hey presto, he's signalling for me to follow him inside.

There are a few disgruntled huffs and puffs as I walk straight past people hopping from one leg to another to keep warm—queue-jumping never felt so good.

'What were the magic words you used to get us in here?' I ask him over the thumping music inside.

'Channel 9. I can drop names that would get me into the Bank of England. Here, give me your coat.' I notice a little window where someone is taking coats.

'Shall I get a drink while you're doing that?' I look to see where the bar is.

'Sure. I'll have a Red Stripe.' I watch him walk away. What I'm doing with him is probably trouble one way or another. Egremont wouldn't like that I'm out clubbing with Ben. Tilly wouldn't like it either. But what of Egremont—is he in love with Tilly? I need to know.

With two bottles of Red Stripe in hand I look for Ben. I see him talking to some people. I hang back. He sees me. It looks like he's saying 'see you later' to them. He is. He's coming over. He takes his drink and downs half the bottle. He puts it on a shelf and leans in my ear. 'Come on, let's dance.'

Before I have chance to decline, he's gone. What choice? I follow him onto the dance floor. We move further and further into the crowd, syncing more and more in tune with the music. He's a jerky mover but nothing laughable. He comes closer and we begin to dance more together. He's a bit clumsy with his feet so I'm having to watch my step. Our bodies begin to touch and his hands start to wander.

I dance away to wrestle free of his hold. He accidentally kicks my foot again, which puts me off my rhythm.

The pumping music transforms into screechy discordant banging. I stop dancing immediately and shake my head to show I don't like it.

'Come on, we'll go for a fag,' he says taking me by the arm. We pick up our beers on the way.

'So what's your boss like?' he asks when outside.

'Mitchell?'

'Yes, Mitchell. Tilly thinks he's cool but I can see he's a wanker. He flirts with her ma because she laps it up, but it's a front.' He pauses to light his cigarette, then takes a long draw before offering me one. I take it. 'He's just keeping her sweet so she busts her balls getting him what he wants, which is Chelsea strikers mostly.'

'For the Harrison's charity night?'

He nods and laughs with scorn as he lights my cigarette for me.

'You're not a Chelsea fan?' I ask, taking a drag on the Marlboro full strength—I instantly cough.

'Man U,' he says drawing heavily on his ciggie. 'No comment.' He laughs at my reply.

'You'd better watch out at that dinner event. You've been singled out. He'll try to get you up into his penthouse later.' Ben flashes me a suggestive smile. I smile to myself at the thought that I get talked about in Tilly's house.

'I doubt it, because—what's that song? "She Fucking Hates Me." Change "She" to "He" and that pretty much sums up my relationship with Mitchell.'

'Then why has he asked you alone to give a speech?'

'Because it's all about praising him to the skies in front of an audience. He likes the idea of himself as Daddy Warbucks—you know, giving the poor unfortunates a helping hand—me being the only poor unfortunate who he's actually helped. Not that he has helped me—' I stop myself. What the fuck am I doing? He'll blab it all to Tilly and I'm dead in the water.

'Chill sweetie, I'm not going to repeat what you say—to *anyone*.' He lifts his eyebrows up and down comically. It relaxes me instantly.

'And for the record he doesn't hate you. Far from it. Remember, I have insider information.'

'The artist-in-residence?'

'Precisely!' He gives me a cheeky grin. My mouth twitches with irritation at the thought of Tilly. That bitchy pea brain and her life of privileged nothingness—grrrrrrrrr. As for Mitchell fancying me, Ben's probably telling me this for his personal amusement. Tilly doubtless regales him with tales of my daily humiliations.

Ben throws his cigarette on the floor. 'He's a better catch than Egremont. I mean Eggers! You and Eggers. How's that working out?' He laughs like the idea is hysterical.

'Am I making a fool of myself; is that what's so funny? Tell me. I want to hear about his running after Tilly.'

His laugh subsides and he looks at me seriously. 'He probably fancies Tilly the way every guy with blood running through his veins fancies Tilly. Actually, I think he's in love with the whole family, so there's nothing for you to worry about. And I know he really digs you. But what is it you see in him exactly—if you don't mind me asking?'

'His maturity.' I pretend to shiver so I have an excuse to go back inside. He takes the hint and puts down his bottle. At the door we have to halt to let other people out. Two of them are Adam and the playwright. To my astonishment Adam blanks me.

'Adam!' I say half laughing. He turns and looks me full in the face, then says something that sounds like 'hi' under his breath but it's dismissive and he carries on walking. Next to pass me is Anna ('Jill'). She throws me a weak smile and bounces up to Adam who puts his arm around her.

God, what must Adam think of me? To his eyes I'm clubbing with Tilly's fiancé behind Egremont's back, and with someone I'm not even supposed to like. 'I'm going to head home,' I tell Ben.

'You could come back to my place if you like?' he

suggests staring at me with what I can only interpret as a seductive look.

'No thanks.'

'Well, if you're sure.' He searches my face as if he's trying to read me but isn't making progress.

'I'll need my cloakroom ticket,' I say impatiently. He shoves a hand into his jean pocket. He gives me the ticket and looks around, presumably for other people to talk to. And so I'm summarily dismissed.

'Thanks.'

He nods and walks off into the crowd.

Seeing an excited group coming into the dark club to the buzz of the music I feel depressed that I have to leave. The dance floor is heaving with people enjoying the music with abandon. There's now an intermittent strobe light sweeping over the floor, illuminating their hot exultant faces.

'EVIE!'

I turn to see who's calling my name. My face bursts into a relieved smile when I see Adam coming toward me.

'Sorry about that before, girl.'

'No, I'm sorry, Adam. I didn't mean to be rude about your play.'

'Oh shut up about that.' He's trying to laugh casually but he's looking unusually awkward. 'Where's Noddy by the way?' He looks over my shoulder.

'Noddy?'

'Che Guevara. Soft lad—*Ben*.'

'Oh—he's staying. I'd had enough, so I'm leaving.'

'But it's early.'

'I know.'

'Come and join us,' he says with flattering eagerness.

'No, it's okay, honestly.'

'Dance with me then. Just one and I'll let you go home—if you still want to.'

'Go on then,' I say, smiling.

To my amazement, Adam and I dance in almost perfect sync and his closeness feels wonderful. There's no stepping on my feet or clashing of legs as with Ben. The track changes and everyone squeals with delight—Adam too—and I follow him in jumping up and down with my hands in the air.

The music cranks up a pace and we get pushed together by a swell of dancers. Adam doesn't miss a beat and we continue moving in time to the thrilling pump-pump-pump. The strobe changes to flashes of grey-white light. When it hits us, I see Adam has beads of sweat all over his face and his black hair is getting curly. The shadowing effect of the strobe highlights his cheek bones. He looks like a male-model!

We dance more and more, and we're both sweating. I feel trickles running down my neck. Adam smiles at me then carries on jerking his head in time with the beat. I notice he has muscles everywhere—his arms, his chest, his shoulders. When did he get those? I marvel at my blindness.

How could I not have noticed what an amazing physique he's got? He lifts his chin in the air and my eyes are drawn to his fine neck glistening with sweat. I want to scream at him that he's too fucking cool, but I just laugh and keep moving, raising my arms again, not caring that my pits are like a lake.

When the music changes again, it's something we both instantly scowl at.

'Come on, babe, let's get a drink,' he says into my ear. I turn to say okay and for a second we touch lips. He pulls away looking shocked. I laugh it off and he relaxes, nodding his head toward the bar.

As Adam's getting served at the bar I see Ben heading out of the club. I smile with satisfaction at the sight.

'Fag?' says Adam handing me a beer.

'Sure.' I lead the way out. We pass by Anna who's sitting with 'the bard' and several of the other actors. She winks and blows Adam a kiss saying 'later baby'. The sight zaps me like a taser gun. I lost myself back there. I'm not sure what in, but it was some confused sense that Adam and I had connected on a new level, but ... I get it. He's with her and they're one of those hip Notting Hill type couples who don't suffer from jealously and encourage each other's Platonic friendships. He just came to my temporary rescue and she probably thinks I'm a worthy charity case.

When I turn to Adam it's like our closeness of moments ago has evaporated. We're galaxies apart again. In fact I feel like a trespasser in his life right now, and what am I doing here but neglecting my own life. I need to get home to see if Egremont has called me or left a message. Good, Tilly and her family think he's a joke. Perhaps he has just learnt a valuable lesson out there in Tuscany, like I have here. Damn, I need to get home. I need to tell Egremont that we're okay—that we have each other, that it's me he needs.

'What are you thinking, Eve, so seriously?'

'I'm thinking that I'm going to marry Egremont,' I say in the calmest tone I can muster.

'You what?' He pauses with the lighter. 'I'm going to marry him.'

'But why?' Before I can answer this, he says,

'No, you're joking. Ha!' He lights his cigarette.

'I've never been more serious.'

'*Marry* Egg-salted? No—you have to be joking.'

I shake my head slowly showing him that I'm serious. Then I ask, 'Why is it that you always prefer that particular nickname?'

'You're deluding yourself if you *are* serious.' He chews on his lip and scrutinises my face then shakes his head. 'Would you really go through with it? Really marry *him*?'

'Don't forget I know him, and there's a lot more to Egremont than you saw at Harrison's. He's sexy too.' I avoid his gaze.

'Oh God, *please*.'

'Well he is—to me. You know the fairy tale Beauty and the Beast?'

'Yes—your point?'

'I've always been drawn to the Beast. When he changes back into a young prince, all his charm wears off for me.'

'So you like a bit of rough with a sensitive side. I can go with that. But honestly, I think you're confusing Egremont for something he's not.'

'How can you know what I'm doing?'

He tuts and puffs out a stream of smoke. 'Marry Eggers—do me a fuckin favour. Seriously, Eve, you can't marry that Victorian throwback.'

'Oh, but I can and I will. Really, don't worry about me. I'm much happier and more sure of myself than you think.'

Adam opens his mouth but shuts it again without speaking.

'Okay then.' I put down the bottle. 'Thanks for the drink but I should be going. I'll let you get back to your friends.'

'Let's sit down. Come on. There's a table there, in the corner.'

'I need to go, Adam.'

'No, you don't. Come on.' He goes to the table, sits down and pats the vacant seat. With a sigh I join him.

'Okay, before I say anything more, I want to ask you again—just to be sure—are you seriously going to marry Egremont?'

'That's correct.' I take a sip of my beer. I won't put him straight about the fact that Egremont is completely in the dark about our upcoming nuptials, but that's mere formality.

'Can I ask why?'

I think about telling him to mind his own business but his frank, concerned expression won't let me. 'I can't be a saleswoman all my life. I'm failing out there, but I don't see what else I can do. My dreams of being something more are just that—dreams.' I look directly at Adam. 'I can't cope with my life the way it is. Egremont offers a way out—a good way out. We'll be good for each other—help each other out. So it's not an entirely selfish mission I'm on.'

'But if the main reason you're marrying him is so that you can be free or because you don't like the work you do, freedom may not necessarily follow—'

I get to my feet.

'Please, Eve, can you sit down?' 'Adam, it's—'

'Please sit.'

I sit down.

'Thank you.' He looks at me like I've wounded him or something. 'Just hear me out on this. Egg-Sal ... *Egremont* and his world could be detrimental to you. He's not modern, don't forget, which I'm aware is in his favour where you're concerned, but that's a romantic notion you have, and the relationship you've had so far will most certainly not continue as it has done once you're ...' He looks away from me.

'Adam, it's okay, you don't—'

'Look,' he says turning back, 'he may court you now and simper when you tell him off but that's because you're not *his* and he still has to woo you.'

I go to speak but Adam holds up his hand. 'All that would change once you got married. What a man likes in a mistress he will not suffer in a wife. And don't forget that your lord and master, as he would be if you marry under such subjugated terms, may not like what he sees.'

'Are you being sarcastic with this speech?'

'No!'

'Then get to the point please.'

'What I'm trying to say is that Egremont will probably play the tyrant once you're his and trapped in his house.'

'You don't know him.'

'I know he's not man enough to stand up for himself. That kind of person finds their manhood in other ways.' Adam stops and takes a drink again. He peers at me over the top of it. I smile. I see what he's doing with the theatrical language—trying to inject some humour into his lecture. 'I don't say he'll be bad all at once,' he goes on. 'He may even mean to be a good and doting husband, but you'll force his patriarchal hand. You'll spend too much time in your thoughts. He won't care for the way you laugh at his insipid friends or get bored in his company or look longingly out of the window lost in thought for the sort of life and freedom that through your own paralysis has eluded you.' He pauses. I don't respond.

'Okay, then,' he says with renewed vigour, 'Let's say that Eggers is a paragon of husbandly affection, so much so that no ill temper or demand for solitude on your part can diminish his ardour.'

'The thespian language is getting tiresome. Anymore of it and I'll be ill.'

'Be quiet,' he snaps. My eyes widen in surprise. 'Sorry. That is, *please* allow me this indulgence; it feels appropriate.'—I make fists to steel myself—'Anyhow, how long will it be before his puppy caresses and foolish adulation take their toll on your nervous system? He'll begin to wobble his head more and more, and then he'll maintain a strange sort of silence because he doesn't know what else to do, and you'll want to slap his silly face for it.'

'Have you finished?' 'Yeah, I think so.'

'So you think it's a bad idea then?'

'Yes, I think it's a *very* bad idea and now you do too.' 'I don't. I just let you go on.'

'Do you want to know what you are, Eve?' He's looking at me like he's in despair.

'What I do know is you want to tell me and I have no objection to hearing it.'

'That's nice. I like that.' He lightens up. '*Pride and Prejudice*,' I admit.

'You and Jane Austen.' He shakes his head. 'But to get back to my point.' He coughs and looks serious again.

'Yes?'

'*Yes*,' he begins, but hesitates. I raise my eyebrows and nod, urging him to hurry up. 'You're an odd woman,' he says finally.

'An odd woman!' I repeat, my face reddening. 'Is this the reason you and your leading lady pity me and treat me like a basket case?'

'Pity you? *No*. I don't know what you mean.'

'You've just said I was odd. What do you mean by that, exactly?'

'It was only a reference to a book. The odd women are women who can't find husbands—there being a dearth of men back in the late eighteen hundreds because of wars and God knows what else. The upshot is, almost half the population of women can't be paired with a mate—husband—so they're odd. I called you "odd" because you're like one of the heroines in the book who marries a man old enough to be her father just to remove herself from the burden of having to earn her own crust. Naturally, it's a disaster.'

'So that's what makes you so expert on my imagined future with Egremont.'

His face becomes a picture of disgust. 'Future—*you*—with Egremont. Do me a favour.'

'This is getting us nowhere.' I get up. 'But since it's a night for honesty, I'll tell you what you are: you're a good actor in a shit play and you know it.'

As I'm walking away I hear him say, 'I know it's shit,

and I'll write a better one someday.'

When I've got my coat I look to see if he's followed me. He hasn't. Within minutes I'm hailing a taxi. Once I've told the driver where to go, I sit back and wipe the tears of frustration out of my eyes.

## 18

It's Thursday—almost the end of a nightmare week. I'm in the office, wading through multiple complaints about messed up printing orders. I wish I had some good news to share about Egremont and me, like how he came straight to my house from the airport, took me in his arms and carried me out of my house like that scene from *An Officer and a Gentleman*, except he didn't get back from Tuscany until last night. When he found out Tilly and her mother were on their way out to Florence, he decided to stay on a little longer. So yes, he prefers their company to mine. Deluded loser.

I stare at the screen and can see plainly enough that the printing was correctly ordered. I look again at my purchasing orders and see what's actually been delivered. If it's not the wrong paper, it's the wrong colour. If it's the right colour, it's the wrong size. If they wanted embossed they've got smooth. If they wanted leather-effect they've got denim. If the quantity isn't lower than what was originally ordered, it's over by triple the amount AND ALL BECAUSE OF MITCHELL.

The boot of my car is full of expensive but completely redundant paper and envelopes. I blushed with shame when Mr Dunn (remember, from the jam factory?) came out of his office carrying a box containing an assortment of five thousand wrongly printed items (A4 letterheads, envelopes, compliment slips—the lot). They were not only the wrong colour, but the email address was all wrong.

Oh! You'll laugh when you know which customer placed an order for around the same amount as Mr Dunn and got an equally fucked up result. Remember Shazza, the receptionist for Barry, Semple & Moore who complained about receiving five boxes of Tipp-Ex when she only wanted five bottles? Well, Mr Barry left and those solicitors became Semple & Moore. She needed to replace all of their stationery. The new stationery read, 'Simple & Moore'. *Un-be-leeeve-able.* When I collected the stuff from Shazza, her sarcastic disgust made me want to shrivel up and die. I'm on my way to the print room now. I've been told Mitchell's there.

I stare at the chaos as I enter. You should see it! It looks like the set of a Laurel & Hardy farce. People are walking around bumping into each other and actually scratching their heads wondering what's going on. There are wobbly towers of paper waiting to fall over—some already have. I just need to hear 'That's another fine mess you've gotten me into' to make the farce complete. I can't see Mitchell. As I step back out of the room, I almost pump into Tilly. She tuts and pulls the sculpture that's in her hands out of harm's way (me being the harm). I stare at what it is. It looks like a pair of bleached deer's antlers sticking out of a sea of pink. Is this the famous 'branch' motif we've been holding our breath for? Ignoring me, she barks a command at one of her entourage, an army of antler carriers. They're all holding the precious cargo above their heads, presumably so as not to snap off those things that are sticking out so precariously.

I'm unable to refrain from shaking my head at the scene. So that's it, some papier mâché bullshit? It's like something we did at nursery school. And no doubt that nonsense is part of the reason Mitchell's neglecting the printing.

'Great! Today's the day,' says Mitchell coming down the office. On his tippy-toes he inspects one of the paintings. 'I love it,' he says to anyone who's listening. Tilly's father emerges from a room carrying a tape measure. 'You think you can get this finished today?' asks Mitchell when he approaches.

'Absolutely,' he replies grinning with satisfaction.

'Then we'll have our opening night of the new *Aaarrison's* tomorrow,' says Mitchell clapping his hands and nodding his head like he's pleased.

I stare at him in astonishment. Is he for fucking real?

'Opening night?' queries Tilly.

'Just a few drinks, love,' says Mitchell leaning out of the way of her antlers. 'It'll be mainly the office mob, reps and managers. A little toast to welcome my new look for *Aaarrison's*.'

Some of the telesales, hanging round the print room (Colin among them), look at each other with raised eyebrows and shrug, obviously wondering if they'll be invited.

'Yeah, you can come too,' says Mitchell. Colin pulls in his fist and says, '*Yes.*'

'Mitchell, I need to talk to you about my printing orders. They're nearly all messed up. I've got a car full of returns.' Others begin to add their grievances to my complaints.

'All of you, just take any duds to the print room and have them re-done. Easy.'

I stare at him. I want to ask 'Is that it?', but it's futile. In any case he's walked on. 'Fine, I'll go and get the boxes,' I say to his back. No one else speaks.

# 19

WELL, HERE I AM. IT'S FRIDAY afternoon and instead of sorting out my printing orders I'm in the office holding a glass of Champagne and raising a toast to silly Tilly's 'transformation of *Aaarrison's*'. The place is packed out with God knows who (Mitchell seems to have invited everyone who's ever bought anything from us). I'm at the back of the crowd, practically at my desk where one of Tilly's bloody antlers now sits winking at me. Everywhere has been painted off-white and this, together with the bleached antlers, gives the office a sterile, creepy look, as if we're sitting in the remains of a deer park after a nuclear attack.

'Here's where you've been hiding.'

'Egremont,' I say without enthusiasm. His smile wanes at my coldness. He's been texting and calling but I haven't felt like speaking to him. I can't forgive him for Tuscany, Tilly and all the rest of it. In fact, his presence sickens me.

'What do you think of the *new look*,' he asks wobbling his head on the last words.

'Not much.'

'Sorry, I forgot you're *not arty*.' He does another head wobble. I look at him and can't think of a reply 'She's worked very hard to meet the deadline.'

'The only deadline I'm interested in are the ones for printing and none of them are being met. I don't know what's got into everyone. The place looks like some big naff art installation instead of an office.'

Egremont gulps uncomfortably.

'The stupid things would be put to better use as coat pegs.' I put down my glass—I'll be damned if I'm going to drink to this. I pick up my jacket and throw it over a 'branch'. 'Look, works perfectly!'

Egremont looks on in shock as the antler snaps under the weight of my jacket, which is now dangling there stupidly. I pull it off and the antler comes off with it.

Colin, who's obviously seen the whole thing, puts a hand to his mouth as I struggle to free my jacket from the antler thing. When it's free I don't wait for the fallout—I leave. Mitchell's too busy smooching with Tilly and her cohorts to know what's happened. I'll let Colin fill him in.

No doubt that was not the wisest thing I've ever done. I'll probably get fired for it and now I won't be giving a speech or even going to the big charity night, but do I care? No.

\* \* \*

I've come to Crosby Marina. I'm going to take a stroll along the promenade and look at the Gormley statues planted in the sea. Gormley (he's the Angel of the North guy) calls it Another Place. Tilly's 'art', it would seem, has its uses—it inspired me to come and see the real thing. It's amazing how the sight of the bronze men stranded in the sea can transport you.

I nod hello to people walking their dogs. I envy them their free time. I wish I had a dog to take for a walk. God, what a pathetic ambition. But is it so wrong to crave a quiet civilised life? God, that sounds like something out of the script of *Jill's House*.

I've reached the sea but the tide's in so I can't walk on the beach. I can only see the heads of the statues. It's eerie because it looks like they're drowning without protest. Perhaps it's a metaphor for my life.

I take a seat on a bench and stare at the submerged figures. Beyond them, out at sea, are large wind turbines; to the side are the working cranes of Cammell Laird shipyard. Funny that there should be camel in the name. The sand dunes round about look like camel humps. And now I'm remembering a joke my dad used to tell. It went something like, 'How do you tell if he's a Cammell Laird docker?' Answer: 'He's the one wearing the camel-haired coat.'

My dad. We came for a day-out around here one summer. I must have been about eight. He grew up nearby and lived not far from the captain of the Titanic's house, Edward Smith, (and Ismay's too for that matter). Dad said the captain wasn't at fault at all and that he was a brave and honourable man to stay put. Could so many men these days be so self-sacrificing? I'm thinking of that snivelling Italian captain who jumped off the Costa Concordia after he'd capsized it. You have to love his excuse: 'I fell into a life boat.' Priceless! Dad would have had plenty to say about that guy.

I miss Dad. I think I can safely say that my life became emptier when he died. I wish Mum would talk about him more, but she seems to have forgotten his existence. I suppose it couldn't have been a happy marriage and yet I seem to remember they laughed a lot, unless my memory is playing tricks on me.

A seagull squawks in my face and startles me. A couple of passers-by laugh kindly at my fright. I hear my phone go. 'This is it,' I say when I see it's a text from Mitchell: 'Don't worry about the broken picture. Eggers explained it was an accident. See you at the Annual Dinner. Good luck with your speech.'

I read the message again. He decides to get human now? Well, it's too late. I'll never take another order for printing and I'll never walk into an office trying to sell copy paper or any other office shit ever again. I breathe in the sea air and get a taste of freedom. It's an illusion to be sure but it's a good one all the same.

What will I do? I don't know. It's funny to think of my plan to marry Eggers. What a notion. What a bonkers, idiotic, gutless ambition. Why did I tell Adam? He must have lost so much respect for me. Adam—I miss him too. I see his smile now and his handsome face lit up by the strobe light. He has to have the sexiest smile of any man I've ever seen, and those intelligent playful eyes. What thoughts they reveal *and hide*. Now they're all for Anna. Lucky Anna. In five years they'll be the hottest couple in Hollywood.

Where will I be watching them from, I wonder, as they pose on the red carpet: in my mother's sitting room with the sounds of yelling coming from next door? No, that can't be. I'll have to have moved on. I'll go to the agencies on Monday.

I get up and have a last look at the statues. Whatever I do I mustn't end up like them, isolated, lifeless, drowning. No, I mustn't end up like my father. I begin walking back to the car. I'll go to the dinner tomorrow. After all, I have the dress, and who wouldn't want to meet real-live millionaire footballers, rarely seen in public unless you're paying extortionate gate prices? It will make for an eventful farewell.

# 20

WHEN I ENTER THE PALATIAL FOYER of the Harrison Plaza I'm met with frenzied activity. The place is awash with scurrying bouncers, caterers, camera crews and flapping hotel staff. Among them are the excited and let-me-tell-you overdressed reps of Harrison's (including myself). We're so glammed up you'd think it was the BAFTAs. I'm glad I decided to come. This is the perfect end to an imperfect career, if you could call it that.

Trying to look casual in my long black imitation Valentino, I look around to see who I can speak to, which will doubtless be Egremont. I'm going tell him we're over and tell him in a way that will show I mean it. Not immediately but soon. This is a night for farewells.

Mitchell was right when he said this year's dinner would be WAY, WAY, WAY more prestigious than any of the previous ones, no doubt because Mitchell's at the helm and wants to show the world—since he married the boss's daughter—that he's got the biggest ship on the office-supplies seas. Such a display disguises spectacularly well the piss poor company that's footing the bill.

I seek out the dining room. Wow! It looks like a royal wedding: white-clad tables decked out with armies of shining glasses, glinting cutlery and oversized flowery centrepieces, all lit up beautifully by giant sparkling chandeliers. I move aside for caterers to pass. Some of them look familiar.

I have my speech and I'm going to repeat all the emetic clichés, like 'never ceasing to relish the challenge', and 'always striving to deliver excellence', and 'remembering that one doesn't *represent* Harrison's one *is* Harrison's'—oh, and all the bullshit about Mitchell. But at the end I'll wink and they'll all know it's a joke. I picture myself goofily stirred by my own eloquence, on the verge of tears as I recall my valiant daily efforts to flog their ropey stationery and then I'll expose the fraud and tell them what it's really been like for me.

'Evelyn!'

'Mitchell!'

'You gonna make a speech, or what?'

'Yes, I'm all ready to go.'

'You can give it after the charity auction.'

'After?'

'Yes, *after*. Why, is that a problem?' he says aggressively then looks around impatiently. His agitation amuses me, and such is the state he's wound himself up into, there are beads of sweat on his usually arid brow. The reptile is coming undone!

'I was hoping to get it out of the way, that's all. The auction could go on for hours, couldn't it?'

'I'll let you into a little secret'—he leans in—'the Premier League footballers—yeah, that's Premier League—have a window and we ain't scheduling shit till they're done. There's going to be a lot of money raised here tonight, and there's no way I'm interrupting that for your little five minutes of fame.' He stands up straight and says in a louder voice, 'That okay with you, Miss, or should I get on to FIFA and have them wait till you're done?'

'Of course that's okay.' I smile at his offensively sarcastic tone as if he's said something nice. He stares at me, no doubt wondering why I'm smiling. He pinches the top of his nose.

'Sorry, Eve, there was no need to speak to you like that. There's a bit of pressure on me tonight.'

I look at him with slightly narrowed eyes. He's afraid I'm not going to praise him in the speech now?

'Here.' He hands me an envelope from the inside of his jacket.

'What's this?' I ask, taking it.

'It's for the beauty salon there.' He points to a brightly lit room. 'You can have your hair and nails done and do justice to that dress.'

'Thanks!' Things *are* looking up!

'Now go tell Chantel I said to fit you in. Then I want you in there'—he jabs a finger at the dining hall—'no later than eight.'

'You got it,' I say, heading for the salon.

\* \* \*

Well, here goes nothing. Into the hall I go, walking as elegantly as I can on my diamanté-encrusted Manolo Blahniks (got them by exchanging the too-small-slingbacks Mum had bought herself but forgotten to take back). The sparkles on the straps match those on the straps of my dress.

Wowza, this place is 'buzzun' as Adam would say, although I can't see any of the footballers yet. A number of roped-off vacant tables, even more elaborately decorated, show where they'll be sitting (i.e. away from the riffraff).

Weaving around the tables I'm getting a lot of appreciative looks. I'm hoping it's not for the wrong reasons. Chantel has painted what are known as Scouse brows above my eyes. Thunderbirds came to mind when I saw the finished effect—and we're talking Parker, not Lady Penelope.

And that's exactly what Mitchell's doing now as I approach the table—staring at my face.

'Jesus, is that you, Eve?' he says, getting to his feet, to my astonishment. He sits back down when I do (I'm between him and Egremont). Was that an unconscious gentlemanly gesture he just made? Even if it was it won't save him (talk about *too little too late*).

Sitting opposite are Ben, Tilly and her mother, Pru. Tilly smiles broadly at me; it might even be construed as laughing at me. The bloody Scouse brows. Well, laugh all you like—it's the last time I'll ever have to be in your company.

I catch Egremont's eye. He's looking at me with a pained expression. There's no telling if it's because of my coolness or the brows.

'Sorry, Pru. What was that?' Mitchell says as a waiter gives me a glass of champagne.

'The footballers are almost ready. You'll have to excuse me guys—I need to do some last minute checks,' she says getting up and leaving us to look at each other.

We're saved from further awkwardness by a microphone announcement. I survey the table nearest to us. It's full of Harrison reps. I notice none of the females have had the Chantel treatment. Was I the only one Mitchell offered this to? It's the speech perhaps, 'got to look the part', although it's more the part of Groucho Marx!

Saying a general 'hi' to them all, I get a few raised glasses and lots of 'Good luck with your speech.' Oh how little they know. There's no one from telesales, not even Laetitia.

'Good evening, ladies and gentlemen,' booms an American with a full-on Texas drawl. I turn my chair to see the speaker. Woah! The guy must be over six foot five and is built like barn door! 'And how are we today?' he asks, looking around with a beaming smile.

He gets a lame 'good thanks' from a few people. Mitchell shuffles in his chair with irritation at the lukewarm response. 'Let me tell you good folks that my name's Herbert Bloomingdale, and I'm here today to talk not only about how to be successful, but how to build on that success ...'

A white-jacketed waiter tilts a bottle of white wine at me. I nod for him to fill the glass. Wine with dinner, why not? It's one of the caterers that passed me in the foyer before. He looks at me a little longer than necessary. Christ, is he scrutinising my eyebrows too? Then I remember. He's one of the waiters from Modigliani's. He smiles when he sees I recognise him.

He pats Egremont's shoulder a moment later and whispers something in his ear. They both look at me and as I look away, I immediately see Luigi directing operations in the background. Modigliani's are obviously the caterers then. I turn my attention back to Herbert Bloomingdale: 'What marks out someone who excels in life?' he asks.

Hands go up. He points in our direction.

A voice behind me says, 'Someone who never quits.' It's one of the reps whose names I don't remember.

'Someone who never quits,' repeats Herbert, nodding weightily at its profundity. I can almost hear an 'Amen' from him. 'What else?' he shouts, no doubt waking up a few people.

'Someone with a flash car,' comes from somewhere else in the audience, which gets a few laughs.

'Well, that's true, my friend. The successful man's best friend is not four-legged but four wheeled!' Laughter again (the wine is obviously kicking in). 'What else?' he asks, looking pleased with how his speech is going.

'Someone who's always positive,' says another of the reps. Herbert nods vigorously at this.

I ponder the question myself. Hmmmm, just what *does* mark out someone who excels in life? I feel like putting my hand up and suggesting 'public school' or 'rich parents'. If Adam were here he'd probably plump for 'a person with a brown nose.'

'Ladies and gentlemen, what we all need if we're to excel in this good life are rules, goals and guidelines.' He punches the air after each word. 'Constant vigilance against apathy, lethargy and darn right *negativity* must be maintained at all times.' More air punching.

I finish my champagne.

'Self-management is key. You godda laugh at defeat, pick yourself up, bounce back, because everyone who's excelling *now* ain't always been so—no sir-ree.'

There are a few raised eyebrows around the room at this over-enthusiasm. I'd raise mine too but fear the effects. Mitchell's surveying the room, I'm guessing to register who's paying attention and who's not. I pick up my wine (why wait for dinner?). Mr Bloomingdale is continuing with vigour:

'But when you're not pulling in the big orders, it's your ability to recognise that this ain't how it should be— that this ain't how it's gonna be. Coz this *ain't* you. YOU WIN. It's the golden rule you can never let out of your sight. Whether you're from Santa Fe, New Mexico, Atlanta, Georgia, Birming-*ham*, England or Birming-*ham*, Alabama, the same rules apply …'

He carries on in full *Wolf of Wall Street* mode. I look across at Ben and Tilly. Tilly's playing with her napkin and looking bored. Ben does a mock yawn and thumbs in the direction of Herbert B. I smile and look back at Bloomingdale. I decide I'll use his enthusiasm as a model for my own.

'And by hell,' he yells, 'you are privileged, *privileged* to be selling Harrison commodities.' I laugh when he announces that he merely sells printing cartridges—with all that dynamism thought it had to be entire office suites at least. Oh, he's bringing his speech to its grand conclusion: 'Which just leaves me to say that Harrison's is the quality outfit in this town. Really, let me tell you good folks.' He picks up his glass and raises a toast to Harrison's.

Mitchell stands up and takes a bow then announces orders will be taken for dinner, which will be served promptly. The audience begin to applaud. I do likewise, although mine is closer to being a slow clap.

Despite dinner having just been announced, almost everyone at our table starts leaving. They are answering a call from a shrill Pru who's calling them from across the room. Mitchell hears her and tells Egremont and Tilly he'll go with them. Egremont asks me to excuse him.

'Of course. See you later,' I say cheerfully, happy to have him leave.

'Might-a I-ya getta your starter?' I smile when I see Luigi standing next to me. 'I can-a recommend-a the minestrone. Made-a by my own fair hand.'

I'm tempted to correct him and say—'hand-*a*'—but settle for, 'Thanks, I'd appreciate that.' He bows and signals for my glass to be refilled before leaving.

'And-a for the main?'

'Sorry, I haven't read the menu. What can you recommend?'

'The pheasant,' he says looking comically serious and thoughtful.

'Sounds good.' He bows and leaves me.

'You inspired to go an' conquer the world yet?' says Ben sitting beside me. I shrug. 'As you saw, Tilly's gone to help the mater and no doubt she wants to see if she can muscle in with the WAGs. What does that stand for again?'

'Wives and girlfriends.' But I'm sure he knows exactly what it stands for.

'That's it! I think she's secretly impressed with all their *OK!*-magazine glamour. Who knows, I might lose her to one of the strikers if I'm not careful.'

'Well, you'd better be careful then.' I smile and sigh as he pulls his chair closer to mine.

'You don't mind if we have a little chat?' he asks.

'Chat—about what?' I have more wine; it's going down like water, but I'm actually beginning to feel nervous now. The bustle and excitement of the place, and how nice everyone is being is getting to me, to say nothing of anticipating the imminent invasion of super-famous footballers. And there's a huge video camera being set up on a tripod beside our table. I don't know what it is but I'm not sure I'll have the guts to do my send-up speech. Damn me for the spineless coward I am.

'I wanted to chat about you and Egremont, and to ask if you're done with him now?'

'That's my business.'

'Is tonight the night you're going to dump him? Shall I put some extra tissues on the table?' I shake my head but find myself smiling. He's quite intuitive. Still, there's something about him I don't trust. Herbert B passes our table.

'You got to love that Yank,' Ben says watching him. 'He really believes that shit.' He downs his glass of champagne and swipes Egremont's full wine glass.

'Yank, you call him—he's from Texas.' 'Yeah, whatever—they're all Yanks to me.'

'You're not part of the Channel 9 team covering the event tonight?' I nod at the camera guy setting up.

'I do the serious stuff. This is not my kind of gig. Neat eyebrows by the way.'

'Mitchell insisted I have a makeover.'

'They're not you,' he says in a low voice. Yep, no mistaking—he's flirting with me.

'I need the lav,' I say and get up.

'It's your nerves—that speech you've got to make to a room full of celebs, oh and four million viewers. It's enough to rattle the most seasoned of speakers, but you'll be fine.' I leave without answering him—sarcastic shit that he is.

Out in the foyer, there's what Bloomingdale might call a hullabaloo. Swathes of people are moving through the lobby like shoal fish. I stand aside for footballers, WAGs and paparazzi to pass. A bald-headed bouncer nearly knocks me over. He doesn't attempt an apology. But then how could he—he didn't even see me.

I recognise a few of the footballers (and I swear some of those men are wearing more make-up than the women). I notice too I'm no longer alone in the Scouse-brow department. Pru's trying to co-ordinate them all. Ha—she's got a walkie-talkie! But then she needs it. It's chaos. Mitchell is hugging all and sundry. My stomach flips. Oh God. I'm going to be too intimidated to speak. They're all so imposing. And those menacing bouncers. No! I need to remember, they're only here to flog over-priced polyester.

When I'm in the bathroom, I get a shock when I look in the mirror. The eyebrows are ridiculous, worse than on the WAGs. It's certainly not the look I wanted for my farewell speech. I won't be taken seriously. But then did I really expect I might be?

Returning to the table, I see Egremont is back. Ben is sitting next to Tilly once again. He raises his eyebrows at me and nods his head toward Egremont. I turn away.

'You look lovely,' whispers Egremont. 'Not sure if those eyebrows are you, though.'

'They're not of my doing.'

'You have far better taste. Did they make you wear that dress too?'

'What's wrong with my dress?' I look down at it.

'That was my little joke—you look smashing. Very *glam*.' He wobbles his head. 'How did you like that Mr Bloomineck's speech?'

'It was swell,' I say flatly, refusing to laugh at the joke about my dress, which formerly I would have welcomed, it being for once actually funny. I'll have to tell him it's over between us soon. I can't take much more of his attention. I notice that someone has obligingly filled my wine glass. My soup has also appeared and I know I should eat it along with a roll or two, but my appetite has gone.

'Was it you and Tilly who got Modigliani's this event?' I ask, taking up the spoon.

'I recommended Luigi and Tilly's mum was satisfied. Mitchell was glad to have someone known to me, and the Devanthy family have such a sound reputation—'

'And Mitchell respects you so very much, of course.'

'He may not always show it but, yes, yes he does actually.'

The fact that he's not wounded by my comment annoys me—annoys me more than I can believe. He leans in to say something and his closeness makes me flinch. Before I know what's happening I'm saying though clenched teeth in an aggressive whisper:

'Look Egremont, there's no easy way to say this but I don't want to see you anymore.'

'Why? What have I done?'

'Nothing—everything. Oh, the truth? I can't bear you.' Okay, that was too much but it had to be said. I see he's taking me seriously. Jesus, I feel horrible but at the same time relieved, so incredibly relieved.

'Maybe we could have a coffee and say goodbye in private, sometime later?'

'I'd appreciate it if tonight you left me alone.'

'You don't want to talk about it?'

'I need to concentrate on my speech and you're distracting me.'

'I'll be quiet. Or I could listen. Do you want to try it out on me?' Damn, perhaps he didn't take me seriously.

'I just need to go over it—in my head, to myself.' 'You'll be fine,' he says, turning back to his salad self-consciously. He eyes Ben and Tilly, no doubt to see if they saw all that just took place between us, but they're not looking our way. That really went unnoticed?

Watching Egremont eat (I can't help myself) I can feel cupid's arrow finally reversing its way out of my chest. All longing and desire and respect have evaporated. My heart is beating fast, not only with fear at my approaching speech but with embarrassment at what I've felt for him. It's as if I've been wearing beer goggles and now somehow they've been swiped off revealing that my prince is in fact a frog—my Mr Darcy, a Mr Collins. And his conversation—I can't stomach any more of it.

I look around the dining room and see that all the doors are now manned with meat-head bouncers (not one appears to have an unbroken nose). They seem to be in hot communication with each other via their state-of-the-art headsets. It seems only Pru has the antiquated walkie-talkie. The doors around the room fly open and in they come, the footballers and WAGs followed by dolly-birds with bags of stuff, presumably the stuff to be auctioned. There are also bouncers carrying black briefcases. Odd. Excited chatter ripples through the room as the celebs take their seats at a safe distance from us. To my astonishment the briefcases are being opened on the tables and their full of cash! Well, that explains why there's so much 'muscle' in attendance. There are lots of 'wow's and low whistles at the sight of the money. I look again as a spotlight illuminates an open briefcase. It's full of red bundles—they're all £50 notes!

Our mains begin to arrive distracting me from ogling the oodles of moolah. Mitchell and Pru also return. Both are looking flustered, but pleased with themselves as they sit down for their meal. I look down at my dinner. This I will eat (I didn't eat all of the soup).

'Thanks,' I say as Luigi refills my glass.

'How's yours?' asks Egremont nodding at my dinner. 'It's fine,' I say dismissively. I cut into the bird and wish it didn't smell so gamy. I take a bite and force myself to chew. Egremont asks another question. I don't hear what it is thanks to the rising noise in the room, and I don't ask him to repeat it. I know I'm being cruel but I need to make him shut up.

Activity around Mitchell diverts our attention. He's being given a mic. In minutes Mitchell's voice squeaks into life over the large loudspeakers. The lighting suddenly dims and the spotlight comes on again this time illuminating a model holding up a red shirt near one of the roped off tables with cash on it. Another spotlight shines on a footballer. I recognise him from the news. He's the really controversial guy who, when he's not crying or taking a dive, is getting a red card for ankle-biting. I nearly drop my wine when one of the WAGs shouts 'ONE GRAND' in a bid for the red shirt.

Within minutes it's trebled! The women are obviously competing with each other, and by the happy smiles on the guys' faces, it's all okay with them. I feel a gentle hand on my shoulder. It's Luigi.

'Perhaps-a zis-a will steady your nerves-a.' He exchanges my dinner plate for a glass of brandy. 'Ben told-a me you were nervous and-a why.'

I thank him, taking the tumbler with gratitude. I know it will calm me. For sure the wine isn't doing its job—I feel on the border of hysteria.

The auction continues apace with the auctioning off of red strip then blue, but it's not Liverpool and Everton but Arsenal and Chelsea kit mostly. The glamour girls—all legs and false boobs—are walking around holding up the signed merchandise. The male reps are nearly falling backwards off their chairs as they strain to follow the near-naked buttocks weaving between tables.

Flashing lights from an electronic board I never noticed before tell the room they've raised thirty-two grand so far. I'm gob-smacked. Pru Devanthy certainly knows her business. No wonder her daughter's so bloody smug.

Yet another Chelsea footballer stands up with a glamour girl. She holds up a team-signed football that won some cup. The bidding starts at two grand. She begins circulating the tables with the prized ball in her over-manicured hands. Seriously, her nails look like eagle's talons—if she grips it too hard she'll puncture the thing.

I need the loo again.

As I pass a table of footballers they erupt in bawdy laughter. I give a paranoid side-glance but see they're relishing a 'shot competition' and ignoring me. Shot glasses of clear liquid are being downed in sync by the whole group of them, and—Oh. My. God. Mitchell's in the middle of it! Mr Won't-leave-the-room-without-a-bottle-of-evian-stuck-to-his-hand is downing what look like tequilas (salt and limes are in the mix). He—Mitchell—slaps the talon-nail girl on her barely covered arse as she passes by with the raised football in hands. She takes it with more than good grace—far from saying 'prick' under her breath she looks like she's loving it. Urrgh.

Whether I've left via a different door I'm not sure, but now I can't remember where the loos are and I find myself lost in a myriad of corridors. I see a cluster of white shirts beyond some potted ferns. It looks like the waiters. They're smoking! Although he has his back to me I can see Luigi among them—also puffing on a ciggie. I'll ask him where the loos are, and may even scrounge a fag. As I approach I'm taken aback by hearing the thickest Scouse drawl from Luigi's mouth. He can't see me yet, the ferns are too thick and he has his back to me, but it's him speaking—no mistake. And the other waiters too—not one has an Italian accent. Fakes! I hang back. Another waiter speaks:

'I can't believe that's all he paid.' He shakes his head and looks at the floor.

Luigi speaks: 'Mitchell's a tight fuck. He doesn't even pay minimum wage. Fucking Eggers said he'd come good though. Dozy bastard. Should have known not to take his word on it. And not so much as a tip for any of us. No kiss me arse nor nothing. Tight prick. Feel like fleecing his wallet. An' all that money they're raising in there. God, wouldn't you like a piece of it?'

'It's a sound night though boss. Wall-to-wall fanny and fame out there.'

'They're a shower of tossers and tight as he is,' says 'Luigi' stubbing out his cigarette in the plant.

I turn around and retrace my steps. Thankfully I see a sign for the ladies around the next corner.

Back in the dining hall, the noise level has reached a new high. The room is full of excited cheering and hoots. I hear Mitchell saying, 'Ladies and gentlemen we've just gone through the four hundred and fifty grand ceiling.' I look at the electronic board flashing with the six figure number. I blink and look at it again. I can't believe what I'm seeing: £450,000!

I walk back to the table with my head reeling, not least from the booze. I see another famous footballer—a very married one—playing tonsil-tennis with a glamour girl who's having a rest from strutting around the room with merchandise. What's the guess he—or they—are staying the night? Next to him, looking bored, is a Spanish Liverpool player. I've seen him before. He does a lot of charity work. Think he played for Barcelona once. He's drinking what looks like espresso coffee. That's what I could use.

When I sit down I see that I've hardly touched the

brandy Luigi gave me. Phew, I won't be as far gone as I thought. I smile again at rumbling 'Luigi's' disguise. How stupid Egremont is to have believed it was real all this time. What a chump they must think he is too. 'They're from Naples.' Try Norris Green.

I take out my notes again and squint at the type. Shit, I can't read it. I put the paper down. It doesn't matter. I know what I've got to say. There are more squeals of delight as someone gets a signed ball for thirty grand. Jesus, the WAGs and footballers are buying each other's stuff. But it's just pocket money to them. I drink more brandy.

The chesty models hold some signed posters up. Other people in the room bid. The lights come up again. Is it being wrapped up? Mitchell, still at the other table, gets to his feet unsteadily. He thanks everyone for their contributions and then he starts shouting 'Over five hundred fucking grand. That's what we've raised here tonight. Five hundred bags o' lovely fucking sand. Oh, sorry, you'll have to edit out my French,' he says to the cameraman, laughing. Someone whispers something in his ear. Mitchell looks around as if something's wrong and then he announces my name.

My name! Shit! I'm not ready.

Before I can say, 'Just give me a minute, you jumpy little fuck', I'm standing up with a mic in my hand and a camera pointing at me. A camera pointing at me! The cameraman indicates a red light and puts his thumb up. It must be running. I say 'hello' into the mic and a horrible piercing sound goes around the room. Mitchell, after taking his seat at our table again, tells me to pull the mic away from my mouth. I do and my second 'hello' comes out fine and clear.

To my relief, as the room becomes quiet, calm engulfs me. Mitchell nods for me to begin and—and I don't believe what I'm seeing—he's just mouthed, 'You're a fucking loser' at me. There's no mistaking it. And he's doing it again! With a shake of my head, I mouth back, 'Okay baby, you got it.'

Here goes, and I'm going to get straight to the point:

'Until recently I was in telesales, and, well enough said about that.' Pause for laughter. Oh, there is none. Continue quickly. 'But it was thanks to Mitchell *Aaarrison*'—I do his cockney accent. This gets a ripple of laughter—'I was given a chance to get up off my arse and have a go at face-to-face sales. But alas, after the briefest assistance, the brittle crutch that was Mitchell's lame support was summarily taken away and I was left—'

'Show us ya tits, love.' I look around in amazement to see who made the comment. 'Come on, love.' It's the ankle-biter! Laughter follows from his table and he's pelted with bread rolls from his mates, all convulsed with laughter now. The cameraman turns on them.

Before I can think better of it I find myself wading in: 'You're lucky you can kick a ball, mate. If you had to live in the real world, you'd probably be on the dole or stacking shelves.' As the words come out of my mouth, I don't regret them. Instead, I feel indignant wrath rising, which could be something to do with the howls of laughter I'm getting from ankle-biter's buddies, not to mention the infamous fouler himself grinning at me like a cretin. He blows me a kiss.

'I'd like to see you bag five hundred grand for some of your shirts,' he shouts, sticking his middle finger up at me.

I feel the red mist descend.

'You raised over five hundred grand between you, but it's not even a day's 'work' to *one* of you. How obscene is that when there are kids living around the stadiums without even a pitch to practice on or a club to go to at the weekend? Nice work for your community I don't think. Ha! *Community*, there's a dirty word for people like you who drive from your gated mansions in armoured vehicles to and from the clubs. Jesus, we look on like so many lepers as you pass by. Why? LOOK AT THE STATE OF YOU. It wasn't like that before the creation of the so-called Premier League. You were obliged to put something back then before that greedy FIFA demon was spawned. There's a little kid in my road who would love to play for Liverpool but he doesn't stand a chance. His school doesn't even have a field let alone a team. The only thing he can do is kick a ball around the street in the latest designer-kit.'

'Can't he find the park?' shouts a voice thick with sarcasm.

'Too many dangerous dogs on the prowl. Haven't you read the papers? Oh no, silly me, you're probably illiterate.'

'Can someone get that fucking demented cow off the mic?' says the ankle-biter swiping the air in dismissal of me.

'She's right. We make too much money. And dew act like pigs most of you.'

I gasp in delight. The ex-Barcelona player is standing up for me. Literally. He's getting up from his seat.

'Take it easy, Miss,' Herbert Bloomingdale calls out. 'These gentlemen have done you proud tonight.' He applauds the table of buffoons.

'Oh shut up,' I hiss. 'And what would you know, eulogising about fucking ink-toner for crying out loud. God, how I hate all that positive-thinking rot. You either like your job or you don't. End of. Privileged to be working for Harrison's? Do me a favour. If you saw—'

I see the Spanish player leaving. Damn. I should have kept with that rant. Shit, I'm getting confused. Mitchell is grabbing the mic. They're all jeering and laughing at me.

'Yeah, laugh like hyenas. You—'

Mitchell is strong-arming me out of the hall. And now I'm yelling:

'You shower of meat-heads with your bitch wives squandering the match-thrown booty. Thinking they're Queen Shit when they're just so much shit.'

'Well that wasn't what we planned,' says Mitchell calmly as the dining room door closes on us. I look at him confused. Why isn't he yelling at me? Behind him is a bouncer staring at me menacingly, looking like a bull considering whether to charge.

I turn back to Mitchell. 'I know,' I say feeling drowsy all of a sudden. 'But why did you call me a loser?'

'I can take care of her, Mr Harrison,' says the bouncer. 'It's okay, she can have a coffee and sober up in my room,' he says steadying me.

I don't protest. I'd rather be in Mitchell's hands right now than that gorilla's. 'Come on, time to cool off,' he says pulling me toward him. I don't care for the bouncer's expression now. He's leering grotesquely at me and Mitchell. I turn to Mitchell and see he's mirroring the gorilla. Oh no! I know what's about to happen. I try to break free of

Mitchell but he tightens his grip around my waist and forces me to walk. The bouncer races ahead to get the lift for us. I go to scream but I'm shoved into the lift which takes my breath away. When I focus again, I see the bouncer waving at me as the lift door shuts.

# 21

I PULL MY HEAD AWAY FROM the pillow, which is not easy to do as my head feels like it's filled with lead. Twinkling lights outside the window and a panoramic view of the city skyline tell me I'm not at home. Where am I then? I try to focus my thoughts. The Annual Dinner. My speech. Mitchell's room—I'm still in Mitchell's room? I look to my right with a feeling of dread. My chest heaves with relief when I see there's no one next to me.

'Eve, open the door,' says a familiar voice from outside. I climb off the bed and turn a light on—I'm naked. Please don't tell me Mitchell did this. Please tell me he didn't undress me. Or worse? Did we? I walk to the door and look through the spyhole. It's Ben. 'Wait a minute.' I look around for something to cover myself with. I find a robe in the bathroom.

I open the door to Ben. He walks past me.

'So this is the penthouse suite,' he says, hands in pockets. He gives a whistle of appreciation as he looks around.

'Didn't expect Regency.' He inspects an oversized chest of drawers.

'It's palatial,' I add awe-stuck, looking at the gilded mirrors, antique cabinets and gold-leaf wallpaper.

'Looks authentic too.'

'I don't remember how I got here.'

'Mitchell put you in here. He wasn't long though, so I don't think there was any funny business. He told everyone you were—let me get this right—sleeping it off.'

'Where is he now?'

'Mitchell? He's downstairs. He's just started his speech, and judging by the number of pages he's holding, it's going to be a long one. He'll probably spend the first half hour apologising for you.' He laughs.

'Oh God, my speech. It turned into a rant.'

'It was pretty funny.'

'Funny—was it?'

'Put it this way, the footballers gave as good as they got. I wouldn't worry. Everyone is loaded down there anyhow. Shouldn't imagine they'll remember too much in the morning.'

'But the cameras. It'll be on TV.'

'You won't be aired, I can promise you that.'

'It was Channel 9. You'd know then,' I say vaguely, and then the memories begin to return. I sit down on the bed and bury my face in my hands. 'What made me do that?'

'A bottle of wine and two tumblers of brandy on an empty stomach I'd guess.' He sits beside me. 'I thought you were terrific if it's any consolation.' He prises one of my hands from my face.

'Shouldn't you be downstairs with Tilly?'

'She's left. Eggers took her and her mother home. Pru was appalled by the bawdy antics.'

'Why did you stay?'

'To make sure you were okay.' 'Me?'

'Yes, you.' He kisses me gently on the mouth.

I pull back. 'You shouldn't have done that.' I touch my lips. The sensation of his kiss lingers. It feels nice—so nice.

'She's not my fiancée. We broke up.' He puts an arm around my shoulders and pulls me to him. 'It was long overdue,' he whispers in my ear, kissing me there and pushing me back onto the pillow. He undoes the cord of my robe and I don't stop him.

'We would never have made it as man and wife,' Ben mumbles into my neck. 'She's too—'

'Needy?' I whisper closing my eyes and smiling at the cliché.

'Something like that.' He kisses me more intensely.

I attempt to embrace him fully, but he resists. 'I'll be back in a moment,' he says, getting up.

He leaves for the bathroom, removing his shirt as he goes. I slip the robe off. The satin sheets feel wonderful against my skin. Everything is dreamy and soft and wonderful.

I have to stifle a whimper of surprise when I see him coming towards me wearing nothing but a condom that doesn't quite seem to fit his erect penis.

'It's a little on the small side.' He's looking down, obviously referring to the condom. 'It'll serve our purpose though.' He gets in beside me.

Minutes later I'm looking at Ben lying on his back panting. It's all I can do not to say 'Is that it?' My increasingly throbbing head is becoming a more pressing matter, however—as is the realisation that I need to get the hell out of this room.

'What's up?' he asks, turning his head toward me.

'It's a sudden headache.'

'I have something for that.' He reaches over the side of the bed. As he fiddles with (I'm guessing) the pockets of his trousers, I gather he's also easing the condom off with his other hand. I look away.

'They'll put you right.' I turn back. He hands me two tablets and gets a glass of water from the bedside table.

I swiftly gulp the pills and greedily drink the water. He jumps out of bed and starts to get dressed.

'Yeah we should go,' I say, attempting to get up.

'You don't need to go immediately. What's the rush? I promise Mitchell will be hours, if he makes it back at all. Just rest a minute. I'll let myself out.'

I watch him leave and feel my eyes get heavy again.

# 22

I BLINK AWAKE AND INSTINCTIVELY DON'T move. It's daylight and I'm still in Mitchell's room. Heavy snoring makes me freeze. Whose is it? I turn and see Mitchell, fully dressed, on the other side of the bed. Gingerly I pull back the sheet. I spot my clothes and after deftly easing off the bed I tiptoe over to pick them up as quickly as I can. In a few silent seconds I'm dressed. I spot my clutch bag on the table. Result! I see something on the floor. I pick it up.
'Whatcha got there?'

I nearly drop the thing in fright.

I take a look at it. 'I think it's your room key.' I place it on a small table.

'You know you're fired?'

'I quit. That was my swan song last night.'

'Your hysterical speech?' He rubs his head and sits up. 'What time is it?' He looks at this watch. 'Two o'clock!' he explodes. 'Jesus shitting Christ, it can't be. Fuck, where's my phone?'

'Here.' I grab it from the table where my bag was and hand it to him.

'Close the door on your way out,' he says angrily staring at his phone and frowning like he can't think who to call. He looks at me. 'I'll have the car picked up today, so make sure you stay in.'

'Right, okay.' I look around to make sure I've got everything.

'What the fuck are you waiting for?'

'Nothing,' I say with loathing and yank open the door.

\* \* \*

As I pull up outside my house in a taxi, I'm irritated to see half the road is sat on next door's wall. I'll have to run the gauntlet of 'dirty stop-out' as I pass them in full evening regalia. And sure enough that's the first thing they greet me with. I put my key in the door to let myself in and close it on hoots of laughter from my impromptu audience.

I head straight upstairs, fending off Mum's questions as best I can. When I see myself in the bathroom mirror I understand what all the laughter was about—I look like I've been dragged through a wet hedge. I quickly slap cream on my panda eyes and Scouse brows and reach for a brush.

When I come back down in my jeans, she's waiting at the foot of the stairs.

'So tell me all about it.' She nods expectantly. 'I bet it was one heck of an after-party. Did you meet anyone famous?'

'Some footballers. Well, I saw them there. Was there anything on the TV?'

'No, I was so disappointed. But I expect there will be tonight. I'll put some coffee on and you can tell me all about it. Do you want a sandwich? Lunch, well dinner now, will be a while.'

'No thanks. I had a big breakfast.'

'Really—and can I ask who with?' She looks at me mischievously.

'There were a bunch of us.' I go into the sitting room. As she goes to make coffee, I sit down with a sigh. It's going to be a long morning of telling lies. I won't tell her about work yet. I'll have to get something else fixed up first. Damn, the car! I'll say it's getting a service. She won't suspect anything.

An hour later, she's stopped asking questions, and although she's disappointed that I haven't become a WAG, she's satisfied that I had a 'good night out' and everything is fine.

'That can't be Mitchell,' I say seeing a yellow Porsche pulling up outside.

'What love?' asks my mother distractedly, still reading the paper.

I jump up and go to the window. I see Mitchell getting out of his car. Tommy and his pals are already meerkating at the Porsche. They're all wearing black tracksuits and matching puff caps with a chequered band. It makes them look like diminutive special police. Must be the latest fashion, I think distractedly.

'What is it?' asks Mum, lowering her paper.

'It's Mitchell. He's about to call here.'

'Your boss!' She throws the paper aside and comes to the window. 'He looks angry. Have you done something wrong?'

'The car needs a service. Maybe he's having to pick it up himself.' I watch him approach, chewing on his sucked-in cheek like a maniac. Mum and I nearly jump out of our skins when he bangs on the door fit to bust the lock.

'Good God. There's no need for that,' says Mum looking horrified. I rush out to the door, praying he won't make a scene.

As I open it, I know there's something very wrong.

Mercifully next door and her cronies have gone inside. 'Where is it?' he hisses through gritted teeth.

'Where's what—the keys?' I pick them up from a table by the door. I hand them to him wondering why he's overreacting.

'The fucking money,' he says snatching the keys out of my hand.

'The printing money?' I feel panic rising. 'Sorry, I don't know what you mean.'

'Right. Okay. Now.' He's breathing heavily. He looks around before looking back at me, his face flushed with anger. 'You're not going to make this easy for me, I see.'

'Are you going to bring Mr Harrison in?' asks Mum cheerily from the sitting room.

'I have to go out.' I step outside and pull Mitchell with me.

'That's a boss car mate,' says Tommy coming towards us.
'Fuck off, you little runt,' sneers Mitchell.

Tommy looks at me horrified. His mouth has fallen open a little. I give the briefest shake of my head warning him to back off. He steps away instinctively, but I can see he's not sure what he should do.

'Get the fuck in,' hisses Mitchell yanking open the passenger door and shoving me.

Once I'm in the car, he drives off with a screech, hardly giving me time to close the car door. Tommy and his friends are agog.

I look at Mitchell. I'm desperate to ask what he means about the money but the words won't come out. 'Slow down!' I yelp as he goes through a red light. I look around praying for a police car.

He turns suddenly into the park and stops outside the closed police station.

'Right, I'll say it again—slowly, so that you can't mishear me. Where. Is. The. Fucking. Money?'

'What money?' I ask in a whimper.

'The five hundred grand you took from my safe.'

'Five hundred grand?' I splutter. 'Mitchell, I haven't taken any money from your safe. I didn't even know you had a safe.'

'I know you'll have all sorts of compromising pictures of us on your phone, so I won't even ask to see them.'

'Mitchell, I haven't got any pictures. Jesus, you can see my phone—anything you want.'

'They'll be downloaded and ready to go, hidden away by now. But let me make myself clear—no naked selfies will protect you. My wife will be relieved I wasn't with a whore for a change.'

'Wait a minute. Someone's stolen the charity money? Is that what this is about?'

'Not someone—YOU.'

'I didn't steal any money, Mitchell.'

'You've been hatching this since I put you on the road. Eggers and Tilly's mob must have told you just about everything without realising they were dealing with a convicted criminal.'

'I'm not!'

'Oh yes, you fucking are. They call you "young offenders", but that just means little thief—in your case.'

I feel the colour draining from my face. 'I was fifteen years old. My dad had just died. I was—'

'Your dad—funny you should mention him. Dear old crooked Dad. I read all about his sticky-fingered past today.'

'Don't you dare judge my father.'

'Why?' he spits. 'It's all over the fucking internet what that thieving bastard did. He didn't crack safes but it's the same fucking difference.'

'He was wrongly convicted.'

'Yeah, whatever. What I know for sure is that you're a fucking little tea-leaf and you've done it again. But I'll tell you something—you're a lucky little tea-leaf because I'm giving you the chance to give it back. And you will give it back because you're a dumb little amateur tea-leaf who thinks she can take on someone like me. But you can't sweetheart—not without getting yourself hurt, or'—he looks at me with narrowed eyes, his lips white with tension—'or worse.'

'Mitchell, I don't have it. On my life, I don't know what you're on about—honestly.'

He puts both hands on the steering wheel and drops his head. He speaks into his lap: 'I'll give you till tonight. If you're not back at my room by nine with *all* the money then I'll be at your house with the police at nine fifteen.'

'But I don't have it,' I say, nearly choking with fright. He looks at me. 'That's why you stopped making sales—you had other things on your mind.'

'I generated a lot of business,' I say distractedly.

'You were a fucking liability. I was carrying you.'

'What do you mean you were carrying me?'

'How do you think you got those first orders?'

'Jessop's?' I'm trying to think back.

'Yeah. I set them up. You couldn't sell tea to China, which is why you spent most of your fucking time dozing in car parks.'

'I worked my arse off for Harrison's.' He gets out his phone, taps it then shoves it in front of my face and I see a map. 'That there'—he points to one of the dots—'is your car sitting idle outside ya mum's house. I've seen it there *soooo* many times when it should have been sitting in the car park of a trading estate while you were out canvassing. I know you've been anywhere but where you were supposed to be.'

'You track the cars?'

'Yes, I track the cars. Most of the time, I see them heading for their correct destinations and they're on the move pretty frequently. Your dot moved very little, I had a little fun pretending I didn't know where you were and sending you back to where you should have been, but now the fun is over and you need to respect that. You took me for a fool. It's time to take me seriously.

I go to undo my seatbelt but see I didn't put it on. Reaching for the door handle I turn and repeat that I didn't steal the money.

'I should have known what you were up to when you snuck back in with the key.'

'I was leaving, not coming in.'

'*Liar!*'

'Haven't you checked the CCTV? It was probably one of the hotel staff,' I say as my ability to think straight returns.

'I'm sure you know only too fucking well that my floor doesn't have that shit on it. Didn't see you coming, though, did I?'

'Shut up, Mitchell. For Godssake shut up. *I didn't take any money*,' I scream. The noise of it deafens my own ears.

'Actress,' he growls through clenched teeth.

'I'm happy to go to the police with you. We can go now. You can come to my house—anything you want.'

'I was thinking of having the filth raid your hovel but you'd know not to have nothin' there.'

Tears sting my eyes.

'You must have watched me put the money away. Jesus, I was hammered.'

'You were drunk!' I suddenly understand what might have happened. 'Maybe you never made it to the room with the money. It could be with the footballers, or the committee, or whoever else was organising last night. Have you checked with anyone else?—Tilly? Her mother? Or—'

He looks at me with murderous eyes.

'I put that fucking money in my safe. You were lying in the bed with your nose not two feet away from me. I probably said the number out loud because I thought you had passed out. Maybe you and your bitch-friend Adam did it together. You're a better actress than he is, that's for sure.'

'Mitchell, I'm telling you, I didn't take—'

'Only you could have taken that money. Now get out of my car and be back at my hotel, at my room, before nine tonight with that money. I'm going there now. And don't think of running away because make no mistake I will find you and you will get hurt.'

I get out of the car without saying any more. As I watch him speed away, I remember Ben. He was in that room.

*Tilly's mob must have told you just about everything.* Mitchell's words ring in my ears. Told me what, that Mitchell would keep the charity money in his hotel-room safe? Then Ben would know that too.

No. No. No. I'm barking up the wrong tree. The money wouldn't have been there when he came in. And anyway, Ben—he's a rich kid. He wouldn't—*couldn't*—have done it, unless he's some frickin' cat burglar. And what about Luigi—or whatever his scouse fucking name is—what did he say? 'Not so much as a tip. No kiss me arse nor nothing. Tight prick. Feel like picking his wallet.' A hundred people could have done it.

I'll have to go to the police myself. But I'll call Adam first. No! It would mean admitting I was in Mitchell's bedroom all night and until two the next day. But oh, it wasn't Mitchell, married psycho boss whom Adam knows I hate that I had sex with. Noooooooo, I did that with *engaged Ch-Gue-fuckin-vara*, who Adam hates possibly more than Mitchell. Wouldn't Adam just love that! He'd be Full of sympathy I DON'T THINK. Come to think of it, I don't fancy telling the police all this either. Won't they *lock* me up?

As I walk home I feel a flicker of hope. Mitchell might be bluffing about the police. He'd have gone to them already if he was going to, wouldn't he? He won't want any scandal. It would be all over the newspapers that he was sleeping with someone else and cheating on his wife whose company he runs. God, his reputation would be shot. But that still doesn't mean he won't hurt me. Oh God.

## 23

WITH RELIEF I HEAR MUM CLOSING the front door. She's gone to work. I'd expected her to come up to my room and try to coax me into getting up again. But she's accepted I'm ill. What am I saying? I *am* ill. But I'm alive! I didn't go to Mitchell's hotel and he didn't come to find me last night.

I haven't told Mum about the stolen money and losing my job. Her mood didn't invite a confession. Confession—interesting choice of words. Is that not the language of a guilty person? Ha! But if Mitchell doesn't find, or doesn't suspect, someone else, and sometime soon, I'm going to be—well …

My head hurts.

Yet I feel calm. I throw off the quilt and get up.

After going to the bathroom (where I had to look away from the mirror because I couldn't bear the frightened look on my face) I go downstairs. I can hear rowing next door. 'Ya lying little fucker,' becomes audible as I put my ear to the wall.

'I'm not lying Mum, honest,' pleads Tommy.

I go to the window in the front room and see little Tommy running out of the house—God he's a waif of a child. He's hurrying down the street but looking back, presumably to see if he's being pursued by his mother. He's safe; she's rowing with his brother now. I switch on the TV to drown out the noise.

The Jeremy Kyle Show comes on. I go into the kitchen. I know I should eat something but my stomach—I just couldn't. My eye is suddenly drawn as if with magnetic force to the wine rack and I think the unthinkable. Should I?

Having a drink would give me the clarity I need to think about what I'm going to do next. But it's the morning. Surely I can't—

It's being poured and I feel relief.

I take the drink into the living room. The situation is weird—horrible in some ways, but it's also thrilling. I take a sip. The wine fires down my throat (it's Australian Shiraz, silly per cent proof). 'Up yours, Mitchell, ya cockney twat.' I raise the glass to the ceiling.

I take a seat and watch the events unfold on the Jeremy Kyle 'show'. The fascinatingly ugly warring sides are waiting to hear 'who's the daddy' of some toddler who's back stage enjoying a momentary respite from the fighting. Jeremy Kyle's got an envelope in his hands which will confirm the poor bastard's parentage. I look at Jeremy's demonic phizog. It's a Tarantino devil face.

The vicious 'rellies' all but drool with inarticulate anger at the dumbstruck dead-beat who doesn't give a shit if he's the daddy and doesn't need to. I take another drink and hear the same kind of rowing coming from next door. They're not low enough for the Jeremy Kyle Show. They're Scousers too—not making a show of yourself is in the DNA.

I press the off button. I hope one day all those kids he publicly humiliates grow up to sue the cunt. He's the biggest child abuser of the lot—masquerading as a fixer, but all he's really doing is creating more misery in people's lives for mass entertainment and his own wealth. He's violating the wisest of the ancient codes: least said soonest mended. AND HE KNOWS IT. They all know it. He makes me ashamed to be English.

The phone rings. I freeze. It's Mum. She knows. Shut up. She doesn't know anything. The answer machine clicks into action. An automated message comes on saying my mother has won something. Could anyone really fall for a call that begins 'Congratulations'?

Sales. I guess I'm done with sales. No bad thing, except that I have a very bad feeling and I can't quite put my finger on it. Oh yes, it's because I'm about to be sent down for theft (I'm using the prison lingo already), and for an impressive amount. The judge and jury won't be lenient either because I've robbed (supposedly) charity money. The football clubs too will doubtless throw their weight behind this—that is if Mitchell doesn't get there first and make me brown bread.

That's why he isn't going to the police. He can't make himself a suspect in my murder!

I finish the glass of wine and feel another wave of panic seize my body. I was seriously going to put the glass in the sink but now I *need* another one. I've got to figure out what I'm going to do. Will I go and see Mitchell's wife? No. I'll go and see Mitchell. I'll cry, plead, grovel at his feet until he believes me.

I pour brandy this time. Brandy is the drink of crisis, and I'm in a crisis. Isn't it the drink that steels the nerves? It will fill my feeble body with courage and give me the determination to sort this out. I get the appropriate glass: a crystal tumbler from Mum's mahogany cabinet. It will add dignity to my undignified act. The glass is satisfyingly heavy in my hand. Ah, wait, this tumbler isn't a brandy glass. They're round with a stem. Still, I prefer this one. I like its weightiness. I pour a decent measure, one befitting the degree of impending catastrophe. No, no, no, NOT that. I'm going to rid/absolve myself of this problem today.

Returning to the sitting room I have a lighter step. I consider the TV again but hold back. No more Jeremy Kyle or other rot. Besides, I have schemes to plot and riddles to solve.

I've never been good at riddles though. They're like those puzzles they give you in maths when they ask *if it takes one man four miles to walk with three apples how many men does it take to walk three miles with four apples?* My head implodes before I've even got to the end of the sentence. I drink some brandy. It goes down surprisingly well.

The voices have stopped next door. I go to the window. She's across the road sitting on the neighbour's wall shrieking with laughter. There's about eight of them out there. They're always laughing when outside.

I hear the faint but distinctive ringtone of my phone ringing upstairs. I drink some more brandy and ignore it. No, it could be good news. Perhaps it's all over. I quickly put my drink down and run upstairs.

Before I discover it's a voice message from Mitchell, I turn the air blue with curses when I trip over one of Mum's QVC packages in the hallway and bang my face on the side of the door. I try to ignore the pain as I listen to Mitchell's message: 'You in? I'm coming to yours now. You better be by the time I get there.'

I break out in sweat—cold sweat. Or is it blood from the fall? I go to the mirror. It's sweat, but there is a red mark developing on my face.

'Mitchell's coming here,' I say to my reflection like it's going to tell me what I should do. I turn away. I can't speak to him, especially when I'm like this—half cut and half dressed. I run downstairs and put the lower bolt on the front door. What now? 'Go to bed and lock yourself in,' a voice tells me. Following my own advice, I grab the brandy bottle and the glass and head upstairs to lock myself in my room. It isn't long before there's aggressive banging on the door. My heart feels like it's going to burst out of my chest. It stops, but I know it won't be for long. And sure enough the banging starts up again. I picture the families over the road staring with wide-eyed interest at the suit with a Porsche trying to gain entrance to our house.

I down the drink and stifle a cough. I lie back and close my eyes. God, I don't know when I've felt so tired …

# 24

As I rouse from sleep I hear banging and someone yelling. I sit up and feel the urge to vomit. I get off the bed and go to open the door. But it refuses to budge. It takes a few more futile attempts before I remember it's locked.

I unlock the door and pad along the landing. I hear Mum's voice outside. She's trying to get in the front door. Oh God, that's right—I bolted it on the inside.

'Sorry, Mum. Just a minute,' I shout and run downstairs praying I won't vomit.

I wrestle with the bolt, and when I finally open the door I see many faces staring at me with curiosity. Tommy, and his brother and, of course, their mother are among the onlookers. Mum says something off the cuff, as if it's a joke, and ushers me inside, closing the door on our audience.

For a moment, we stand looking at each other in the cluttered hall.

'You stink of alcohol. What's the matter with you?' She pushes past me. I look around at the numerous parcels piled up in the hall. For some reason they're calling me.

'Come in here, Eve,' she says sharply.

I close my eyes for a few seconds. The relief it gives is tremendous and I wish I could keep them closed for a lot longer. I open them and join Mum in the kitchen.

'Why was the bolt on the door?' she asks, offloading her shopping bags. Looks like new towels. Like we didn't have enough.

'Well?' she snaps, throwing her coat on the back of a chair. I stare at her. 'What the hell has got into you? Why have you been drinking?'

'I feel sick. I am going to be sick,' I manage to say before turning and heading for upstairs.

When I come out of the bathroom I'm ready for the interrogation and her angry face, but when I look at her, she's so full of frightened concern that it makes me burst into tears.

'Oh love, what is it? What's wrong?' she says gently and puts her arms around me.

'At the dinner on Saturday—Harrison's dinner, they raised a lot of money for charity.' My voice starts to falter.
'Yes and what happened?' She searches my face as if she'll find some answers.

'The money was stolen. Someone took it from Mitchell's room—from the—from his safe. It was over five hundred thousand pounds.'

'Oh my God.' She clamps a hand on her mouth. She removes it suddenly. 'And why is that worrying you so much?'

'Mitchell's accused me of stealing it.'

'Good god, Eve. How could he think—suspect it was you?'

'I was in his room that night,'

'How much money was it you said?' Her face is contorting with panic.

'Five hundred grand.'

'*Five hundred thousand pounds*?' She gasps, looking at me in horror. 'Oh God, Eve, what have you done?'

'Nothing, I haven't done anything. I didn't take any money.' Am I hearing her right?

'But you were in his room. I'm guessing that you slept with him. You didn't come home. But you *hate* that man. Why else would you go to his room if you didn't intend to steal that money?'

I look at her, the breath leaving my body as the colour drains from her face.

'You have to give it back. You must give it back. He has a wife. He won't want the scandal.' She begins to pace the hall like Columbo working out who done it. My heart quickens with indignity—and my hackles are rising in protest.

'Well *are* you going to give it back?' she asks, staring at me like a deranged analyst.

'I'm getting sick of saying this,' I growl. 'For the last time, I didn't take that fucking money.'

Blinding light flashes and my face smarts. It takes me a moment to realise that she's slapped me. I stare at her with my mouth wide open.

She leans against the banister crying. 'Eve please don't do this. I won't be able to save you this time,' she sobs. My hands clamp my face involuntarily. I know what's coming and there's nothing I can say to stop her thinking what she's thinking.

'I didn't take the money,' I moan into my palms.

'I wondered why you weren't bothering with work. That's why you were with Egremont. What an idiot I am. You wanted him to tell you where the money would be.' She looks at me intently. 'You can't get away with this, you must know that.'

'Away with what? I haven't done anything.'

'Is it in the genes?' she says sounding crazy—she's suddenly cheerful. 'Your father was a thief and his daughter's a chip off the old block? Is that what I'm seeing now? You know, I really thought it was out of your system.'

I look at her—stunned. 'Dad was guilty of those embezzlements?'

'Of course he bloody was.' She massages her temples.

'But—was his suicide because he couldn't deal with the shame—his own guilt?'

'He did that because he couldn't face anything—God knows. It certainly didn't help us. I had to face it all alone—clean up his mess. I'm still cleaning it up with *you*. Oh God, Eve, you have to—'

My face starts to spasm as she goes on. I swear it'll be her who's slapped next.

I'll leave—tonight—find my own place. Can I stay with anyone? Adam?

NO.

I'll find a bed and breakfast till I can get somewhere. In fact, I don't have to stay in Liverpool. I can go anywhere. I could even go abroad! France or Germany—Spain.

But would it be seen as a sign of guilt if I disappear?

'I'm not going to stand for any more of this. I'm moving out—now.' I frantically open my wardrobe doors and pull out a dufflebag.

'You'll do no such thing,' she screams. 'You won't be like him—a coward. You'll face what you've done, and you'll give that money back. In fact, I'm going to find it myself. Is it in that bag your holding? I bet it is. Give it to me.' She attempts to pull the bag off me.

I try to snatch it away but she's got hold of it too well. But damn she's not having it. She yanks it again with force and it comes out of my grip. She reels back and begins to turn around. Then she yelps as she stumbles over a box. I look on fixed to the spot as she spirals toward the stairwell. When I can move, I'm too late and can only stand and watch her bouncing off the wall and stairs all the way to be bottom.

Tommy's freckled face is peeping through the letterbox by the time I reach my mother. 'Ring a fucking ambulance,' he excitedly instructs his mother. He grins at me nervously baring pointy little cat teeth just coming through.

I look at my unconscious mother and contemplate the lucklessness of being sent to prison for matricide as well as grand theft when the only crimes I've committed are skiving off work and stealing money when I was fifteen, something I've never repeated.

# 25

Handing over the five-pound fare, the cabby looks at me with concern. My hands are shaking so bad I drop some of the coins on the pavement. 'Don't worry, girl,' he says with a sympathetic nod and drives off before I can give him the rest of the money.

On my walk to the hospital entrance I'm faced with a mob of patients smoking despite the fact that there's a huge poster draped across the glass frontage announcing A SMOKE FREE ZONE.

A guy in a manky dressing gown steps aside for me to pass. He's attached to a drip, which he's obviously wheeled out himself. And he's not alone in that. I have to pull my gaze away from one man who has evidently unplugged himself from some contraption. There's a row of multi-coloured valves clamped to one side of his neck and he's sucking on his cigarette as if his life depends on that instead.

I can't believe what I'm seeing. There's a group standing around some red-haired women. They're having some kind of can party. Her friends look as if they're homeless. Good God. She's obviously a druggie whose mates are doing their visiting *al fresco*. I notice that bottles are being furtively distributed among them by a man whose nose is covered in scars, (like the lion in The Lion & Albert monologue). I walk near them. A girl—she can't be more than seventeen—snatches a quart bottle of brandy from his Lidl bag. I watch with a feeling of *deja vu* as she gulps it down thirstily. I'm transfixed by the violent muscle contractions of her throat. I look from one to the other. Of course! It's the drunks who used to stink out the bus shelter. I half expect one of them to raise a can of Special Brew at me. 'Wharra you fuckin luckun at?' one of them snarls. I'm struck by the colour of his face, so yellow it's almost green.

His liver must have packed in.

I jolt my head away and hurry through the revolving door, marvelling at the chatty doctors and nurses who are walking to and fro amidst this Bedlam scene without a glance. Mum's in Ward D. She's broken a leg and fractured several bones. I left an abusive message on Mitchell's phone blaming him for what's happened and telling him he can go to the police or go fuck himself, it's all the same to me.

I see the sign for Ward D and follow the arrow.

As I approach Ward D, I see Mitchell pacing up and down outside. Before I can go in another direction, he's seen me.

'Still no money, Eve.' He stops me with a hand on my arm. 'I'll admit you've got some guts. But I'm getting tired now. Perhaps you've spent a bit. I'll waive that. But you'll have to give me what you've got because I'm telling you—'

'Save your breath, dickhead.' I practically spit in his face. I stand still right in front of him. I can see he's surprised by my confidence. 'I'll tell you for the last time, I didn't take your money. While you're busy harassing me, someone's busy spending five hundred thou of your easily made gains.'

'Like I believe that,' he scoffs, but for the first time I see doubt in his face.

'You're an idiot for being so indiscreet about where you were keeping it.'

'Shut up,' he says confusedly. What—only now is he seeing what he's let someone else get away with?

'You're going to let me go now?' I look at his hand on my arm.

He releases me with a shove. 'You think your mother's in a bad way,' he hisses. 'If you've taken that money, you won't need a hospital, you'll need a morgue, that I can promise you.'

I watch him walk away. My heart's thumping like crazy. What now?

I can hardly look at my mother's sleeping face when I enter the ward. She has eyes like aubergines. Am I to blame for this? I am! Will she forgive me? She might even be scared of me. One's own mother scared of her daughter! It's horrible—obscene.

'Is that you, Eve?' she croaks giving me a jolt.

'It is, Mum.' I'm barely able to get the words out.

'Do I look a fright?' she asks, opening her black swollen eyes.

'You do,' I say, surprised that a relieved smile is crossing my face. She reaches out a hand and takes mine in hers.

'This isn't your fault, Eve. I'm sorry for what I said to you. It was unforgiveable.'

'I really didn't take any money, Mum, honestly.'

She nods. 'I know, but Mitchell thinks you did and I'm scared for you.'

'Did he come in here—just now?'

'He did. He's convinced you've got it.'

'Not anymore.' I nod towards the corridor. 'He looks like he's beginning to consider the idea that it could be someone else.'

'I don't know, Eve,' she says tiredly, closing her eyes. 'Just rest Mum. I'll do the talking.' She shakes her head slowly.

'Don't stay at home, Eve. Ring Auntie Vie. She'd love to see you. Don't tell her where I am though. She'll come here and I don't want her followed—or involved.'

'Don't worry, I'll stay somewhere else.' I'm lying. There's not much more Mitchell can do. He'll be having me followed in any case. 'When do you think they'll let you come home?'

'In a few days, I hope. Just stay with Vie till then.'

When I leave the hospital I get a text from Laetitia asking if everything's okay. I call her.

'Hey, what's up kiddo? I was going to ring you tonight to find out what the hell happened at the dinner. You're the talk of the office.'

'Do you want to come for a drink—at my house? I could order take-in and tell you all about it. Oh, sorry, I'm being hasty. I should tell you—can you speak right now?'

'Sure, kiddo.'

'The charity money from that dinner has gone missing and Mitchell thinks, or did think, I took it. You may not want to be associated with me right now.'

'I'll be there kiddo. You're still at your mum's address?'

# 26

'What do you think?' I ask, refilling Laetitia's glass with Chardonnay.

I've told her everything except I didn't tell her I actually 'did it' with Ben. I just said that we talked and then he left me and the next thing I woke up next to Mitchell.

'It must have been this Ben person.' She nods her head in deep thought. 'It has to be him.'

'But Mitchell was drunk out of his mind. Anybody could have taken it. He probably didn't make it to the room with the money, or someone helped him in and then they took it.'

'Possibly, but Ben sounds dodgy. I'm not buying that he let the mother and fiancé leave without him.'

'He works for Channel 9 remember, and they were televising the night. Not him, okay, but reason enough to stay. And how would Ben have got his hands on it? I remember him leaving the room.' But as soon as the words have come out, I realise I didn't see him actually go out the door, or I don't remember him leaving.

'He could have got back in the room, taken a spare key without you seeing. That's a suite of rooms—he could have hidden anywhere while you were asleep. He'd have known what state Mitchell was in. Probably Mitchell passed out with the money on the floor, or it was on the bed with him, something like that.'

'No! I would have woken up or Mitchell would have.'

'You!' she laughs. 'By all accounts I don't think so.' I can't argue with her. 'You'll have to tell Mitchell that Ben was in his room. I can't believe you haven't already.'

'I don't know.'

'Sweetie, if you don't tell Mitchell, and tell him tonight, I will. You can't keep this to yourself, kiddo. Mitchell could be a dangerous man.'

'Then that's not fair to Ben.'

She sucks air through her teeth and drinks more wine. 'Get Ben on the phone now. I'll speak to him.'

'I don't have his number.'

'Get it from Egremont. Come on—do it now.' Feeling that I have no choice I phone Egremont. He picks up almost immediately.

'Egremont—hi. It's Eve.'

'Eve! Hello. How are you? Sorry, I was going to call. I just wanted to let the dust settle. Has your hangover gone yet?' He attempts a laugh.

'The reason I'm phoning is—it's just that—I need Ben's number. Do you have his number?'

'Yes, I do. Just a minute, I'll get it for you.' The disappointment in Egremont's voice is palpable but I don't care. Moments later he's giving me Ben's number.

'Thanks, appreciate that.'

'Can I see you?'

'No, sorry. It's over. Bye.' I hang up. Laetitia pulls a face at me telling I shouldn't have been so abrupt. 'Do you want me to call Ben *now*?' I ask her, fighting back annoyance at her unnecessary scruple over Egremont's feelings.

'Yep. No time like the present.'

I dial Ben's number. 'He's not answering.'

'Give it time.' Laetitia is about to say something else when Ben's voice says 'Yes?'

'Ben, it's Eve. Can you talk?'

'Yes, of course,' he says matter-of-factly.

'Is Tilly with you?'

'No.'

'I don't know how to tell you this.' I look at Laetitia. She nods for me to carry on. 'The night you came to Mitchell's room—at the dinner. The charity money was stolen and Mitchell is blaming me but—'

'Wo—let me stop you there. What do you mean when *I* came to Mitchell's room?'

'To see me.'

'I was never in Mitchell's room.'

'Ben, you know you were—with me—and five hundred grand went missing from the safe.'

'My dear girl, you seem to have got yourself into a bit of a scrape. I think you're mixing things up by involving me. You were out of your skull, darling. I dare say you had nothing to do with all this. Mitchell too was rather the worse for tequila and should *not* have been chief treasurer. Really, was Mitchell in charge of all that money raised?

What a thing. Are you calling me from the police station?'

'No, from home.'

'You haven't been arrested?'

'No.'

'Then all may yet be well. Now please, do the right thing and leave me out of this. Tilly and I are engaged again and all is right with the world—with my world anyway, and as much as I'd like to help you, I can't.'

The phone goes dead. I stare at Laetitia who's frowning and looking worried.

'He denies coming to the room,' I say in a daze putting down the receiver.

'Then it was him. He took the money, kiddo. Though God only knows how you prove it.'

'His engagement's on again. He doesn't want to jeopardise that. That's why he's denying being with me in Mitchell's room.'

'Yes, I suppose a girl like that would call it off if he admitted to sleeping with you. And if he does work for Chanel 9 then it isn't likely he'd be a thief. Plus, maybe he thinks you're trying to frame him.'

'*Me*, frame him?'

'Oh, I'm not sure what to think, kiddo.'

I sit down deflated. 'His voice was so, I don't know, so slick and unconcerned. He couldn't give a stuff about it all.'

'That's rich kids for you, kiddo.' She shrugs and reaches for the bottle.

'But thanks for coming round, and trying to help. I really appreciate it. I take it you haven't seen Mitchell?' She shakes her head.

'You look like you haven't slept kiddo.' She runs a finger under my eye gently.

'I haven't much.'

'Well why don't you get your head down? I'll stay with you if you like, if you've got a bed.'

'You don't have to.'

'The cats have got enough food. Be glad to, and I can sleep in this.' She looks down at her pink velour tracksuit.

'I'll clear the boxes out of the spare room.'

'I'll do that. You just get upstairs.'

'You're a good friend, Laetitia, thank you. And I'm sorry for the times I—'

'Get to bed, kiddo.' I kiss her on the cheek and say goodnight.

# 27

Mum and I freeze at the sound of a knock on the door. The curtain in the bay window is half closed so we can't sneak to see who it is. I take a deep breath, get up and go to the door. I force a smile when I see it's Next Door.

'I don't mean to bother you, love, but is everything okay? I was going to come before but. Well is everything okay?' I look at Tommy's mother and struggle to answer. "R'Tommy told me how that bloke with the Porsche spoke to you—and to him. And I saw myself how he shoved you in his car. I thought you were being kidnapped! And he's been back. Listen, you've got nothing to worry about. I know people—we in the street—know people who can sort him out, if he's real trouble.' I go to speak but falter. 'My name's Michelle by the way.' I laugh at her intuition.

'Thanks Michelle, but'—I sigh not knowing what to say. 'You just give me a knock if you need help, babe. You understand me?' I nod that I do. 'How's your mum?'

'I'm fine, thanks Michelle,' shouts Mum. 'We'll have a cuppa when I can get around better.' Michelle cranes her neck to look past me.

'Alright babe, and you tell this gorgeous daughter of yours that she's got support. We stick together round here. Make sure she knows it.'

'I will!'

'Okay, girl, I'll let you go, but you know where I am—right?'

'Right, and thanks.' I pat her on the shoulder and close the door with an awful sense of guilt.

'Well, that was unexpected.'

'I know. Mum, I feel terrible about how I've treated her.'

'You haven't treated her in any way. She doesn't know your thoughts.'

'Are you sure? She knows all about Mitchell and that I'm in trouble. These walls are thinner than we know.' Before she can answer there's another knock at the door.

'Can you get that—please, Mum? My nerves have gone.' The look she throws me shows concern but it's tinged with irritation probably because she's going to have to struggle up out of the sofa to answer the damn door on her crutches, and no doubt it's another neighbour thinking they're Mafia material.

I listen as a woman whose formal voice I don't recognise introduces herself. I freeze. This is it.

'Go through,' Mum says. 'She's in the sitting room.'

My heart races in anticipation. It's finally come—my interview with the police. So he's moved things on. I brace myself for the interrogation. Will I be believed?

'Hello Evelyn. I'm Becky Harrison.'

'You're not the—Sorry, Becky Harrison, *Mitchell's* wife?'

'I want to talk to you about the charity night.'

'Yes, of course.'

'May I sit down?'

'Yes,' I say getting up, though not sure why I'm on my feet.

'Can I get you a drink? A cup of tea or coffee?' says Mum.

'I don't want to put you to any trouble, especially with your leg. You must find it difficult to get around.'

'It's no trouble at all. Well, not much.'

'I'd love a cup of tea then, thanks—no sugar and a little milk.' The gentleness of her voice makes me relax a little. She sits down in Mum's usual place and puts her handbag by her feet.

'I'll make a pot,' says Mum leaving us.

'I know you didn't take the money, Eve.' She looks at me, smiling.

'You do?'

'Yes.'

'Has it been found?'

'No,' she says with a sigh.

'Do they know who did take it then?'

'I suspect—in fact I'm almost positive—it was my husband.' A gasp by the door makes us both look over. Mum's standing with her hand clamped to her mouth.

'Actually, do you have something a bit stronger than tea?' Becky asks, looking between Mum and me.

'Of course,' says Mum sounding like she's no idea what she's saying. But then she gathers herself and says firmly, 'Shall I open a bottle of wine?'

'I'd prefer brandy—if you have some.'

'We have brandy,' says Mum hesitantly. 'Would you like me to put some in your tea?'

'No tea for me just now.'

'Here, I'll do it. You'll struggle, Mum. Sit with Becky.' I take Mum's arm and lead her back to the sofa.

'You and I will have some wine, Eve. Open that Chardonnay in the fridge.'

I go into the kitchen with mixed feelings. Mitchell take the money? No, impossible. It can't be true. He genuinely thinks that I have it. Can she be in her right mind? I hear Mum asking Becky to help pull the table into the centre for our drinks.

When I'm seated again, drink in hand, Mum and I look at Becky in desperate anticipation.

'So what's going on?' asks Mum after Becky has had a sip of her brandy. I feel pity for her when I notice her hand shaking around the glass.

'My marriage is a farce. I knew it was a mistake but my father insisted, so I went along with it because—well the facts don't matter now.' She gulps down the rest of the brandy and I indicate the bottle to see if she wants more. She pours herself another glass with a much steadier hand. 'Mitchell conned my father into believing he—that's Mitchell—loved me. Oh and he was going to "cure me" of my drinking "problem"—' She makes air quotes with her free hand—'My father insisted that I marry him in the end.' I struggle not to urge her to get to the point.

'And a dying father gets his wish. You see he wouldn't leave his fortune in my care. Noooo—he wouldn't trust the family money to me. So—'she starts laughing weirdly—'he puts it into the hands of a crook.' She nods with exaggerated significance at me, then at Mum.

'Becky, what can you tell us about the stolen charity money?' asks Mums patiently.

'Mitchell's mad you know,' she says as if she hasn't heard the question.

'Do you have proof he took the money?' I ask impatiently. 'I know he did it. Of course, *proving* it is a problem. What *can* you prove?' She looks at us with a dumb expression of hopelessness. Mum and I instantly look at each other with alarm.

'Well what do you know? Can you tell us about that?' asks Mum, voicing my thoughts.

Becky reaches for the brandy and I get up and grab it. 'Don't have any more—please—at least not until you've told us something we can use.'

She looks at me with one eye closed and her mouth pulled down like a comedy drunk.

'Becky, please tell us why you think Mitchell has the—'

'*Know*—why I know,' she snaps.

'How do you know Mitchell took the money?' I'm forcing my voice to stay calm.

'Because he's gay.'

'Are you suggesting gay people are prone to theft?' asks Mum stupidly with a pained expression. I roll my eyes in despair.

'Don't be ridiculous,' snorts Becky. It's my turn to have a drink. 'When he told me he'd spent the night with you, Eve, I saw it all. He was *framing* you because believe you me, he certainly didn't want sex with you.'

'I thought he was going to rape me.'

'All for show.' She gazes into her empty glass.

'Gay or not gay, I don't believe Mitchell has the money because he truly thinks I have it.'

'I've had enough run-ins with spurned lovers to know what I'm talking about. My husband is gay, a modern-day Ronnie Kray, but one into station-ray.' She laughs at her rap pun, and Mum shoots me a concerned look. 'Not sure when it happened, the gangster part, but happen it did.'

'But he really thinks I stole from him that night. No one could act being that convinced it's me.'

Becky looks at me with narrowed eyes like she's considering what I've said. 'Honestly, I don't think he does have that money. He was drunk out of his mind too. Anything could have happened to it.'

She gives an empty laugh to this. 'So it didn't quite go to plan. Well you are in trouble because it'll probably be one of those thug bouncers who took it. He's bought drugs he can't afford or they just plain robbed him.' She sighs deeply looking utterly deflated. I hand her back the bottle.

'Of course, I can't believe I didn't think of it before, those hideous bouncers.' Becky nods at my words looking as sick as I feel.

'Your only hope of being left alone is if Mitchell finds out which one it was, but that isn't likely to happen.'

'But why would Mitchel need to steal money for drugs and risk everything? He's so wealthy.' Mum nods frantically as if I've said something irrefutable.

'The hotel is remortgaged to the hilt and haemorrhaging

money. We, no, *I'm*, probably going to lose it, along with Harrison's. He's borrowed so much money against the businesses that we won't recover.'

'He has also gambled incessantly both with my money and his life. It's why he hasn't gone to the police—his affairs wouldn't hold up to their scrutiny; he'd be hauled in for fraudulent accounts, tax evasion, money laundering and God knows what else. Also, he's been accused of theft before in similar circumstances—charity money that he was in charge of going missing. The money miraculously reappeared and he was off the hook. It was me that made him give it back.'

'Have you told all this to the police?' asks Mum.

'It wouldn't be any use. Mitchell made sure they wrote me off a long time ago. He told the police I'd hidden that charity money as a trick. I didn't do myself any favours when questioned. Now they have me down as a fantasist, paranoiac. But I'm more afraid of what Mitchell would do to me if I did tell the police. He's become unhinged.'

'Is he dangerous?' I ask, suddenly feeling timid.

'He's without conscience and now he's desperate. He knows some horrific people too. God knows what they're capable of. She downs her brandy and picks up her bag. She lets her head droop. I think she's crying.

'Won't you have some coffee?' asks Mum.

'Coffee?' She laughs bitterly and wipes her eyes. 'No. I'm going home.'

'I'll call a taxi for you.' I get up.

'My driver's outside.' She pushes herself off the sofa.

'Thank you, Becky.'

'What are you thanking me for?' She stands up unsteadily and looks at me with her mouth twitching nervously. Her expression is dreadful. I suddenly realise she's scared.

'I'm thanking you for being brave in coming here. It couldn't have been easy. And now I can go to the police. I won't mention your name. *You* may not be able to have him and his cohorts investigated but I can.'

She blinks into the distance as if trying to think. 'I'm afraid what would happen if you did that, Eve. The police couldn't protect you from that world he's fallen into.'

The spark of hope fades. 'Sorry I can't help more,' she says edging past me.

'Eve will walk you to your car,' says Mum heavily.

After I've deposited her in the car, the driver shaking his head at me as if it's my fault she's in a state, I'm shocked to see Adam walking up the road. He waves to me. I wave back, brightening.

'Long time no see,' he says when we meet. 'How are you?'

'Not good. Do you know what Mitchell's accusing me of?'

'Yeah, Laetitia called me and told me what's happened. I had to come and see you.'

'Will you come in? Mum and I just opened a bottle of Chardy, and you won't believe what I've got to tell you about Mitchell, though God knows what I'm going to do with the information.'

'I'm all ears, girl.' He looks uneasy.

When I've finished telling Adam Becky's story, he says, 'I fucking knew it.'

'At least we can now rule out Ben.'

'Ben. Yes, Ben. I wanted to ask you about him going to see you in Mitchell's room. Laetitia said you just talked for a bit and that he only came to check on you. Is that right—he stayed for a short time and then left?'

I hesitate.

'Then he was in that room for longer?' He's getting worked up about it.

'Yeah, Ben was with me for part of the time—in Mitchell's suite, but I can't remember for how long.' God, I can hardly look at Adam as I'm saying this.

'Try to remember. Did he go into other rooms?'

I hesitate again and I'm fully incriminating myself now.

'Well, he told me they'd split up!' I protest. 'You slept with him? In Mitchell's bed?'

'I wasn't clear-headed. I was—' 'So you did?'

'Yes.'

'And you were drunk, seriously drunk?'

'Yes.' I'm becoming tearful and frustrated by the way he's accusing me.

'Would you like to stay for tea, Adam?' asks Mum putting her head round the door.

'Sorry, I've got to get off.' He runs a hand through his hair and throws me a terrible look.

'We can't persuade you to stay?' asks Mum smiling but looking concerned.

'No, I've got to go.' He rushes out without another word.

'What was his hurry?' she asks. 'He just got here.'

'To get away from me, I think.'

# 28

Three days later I'm woken up by my mother's screams.

'Eve! Eve! Eve, come in here, *now*.'

When I get to her room, she's sitting on the edge of her bed watching the news. 'What is it?' I ask blinking the sleep out of my eyes.

'Mitchell's dead.' She points at the screen. 'He threw himself off the balcony of his hotel—or was pushed. They don't know.'

'Mitchell Harrison's dead?' Am I really awake?

'That's his hotel.' She flaps her hand at the TV. I look at the screen and see it's the Harrison Plaza sure enough. The stupid revolving H at the top giving it away. But the entire building is covered somehow in a picture of Mitchell with writing all over it—all over his photograph

'Someone put that poster over his hotel. They don't know who. It's a shroud poster—they're illegal, or that one is. Oh Eve, what does it all mean?'

I read out the writing emblazoned over the hotel: *'Mitchell Harrison stole the Five Hundred Grand.'*

'Can you believe this, Eve?' I shake my head in disbelief. A reporter comes into view holding a larger-than-life microphone with a big number 9 on it. I sit on the bed next to Mum.

'Mitchell Harrison's dramatic and mysterious, indeed gruesome death emerges from a background of intrigue amidst allegations of involvement in serious fraud when five hundred thousand pounds was discovered missing from his hotel room after a charity gala event that he organised. Rumour and speculation is putting Mitchell Harrison at the centre of claims that he is connected with known criminal gangs and may have stolen the money to pay off substantial drugs debts. In an effort to solve this case the net may need to be cast far and wide in the search for the person or persons responsible for his death or involved in the events surrounding what may turn out to be his suicide.'

Mum leans her head on my shoulder. I know she's crying. I put my arm around her and let the tears of relief fall from my own eyes.

# 29

M Y PHONE CHIMES TO SIGNAL an incoming message. It's from Adam. Adam!

'WHAT U UP TO LATER?'

There were the familiar capital letters. I'm tempted not to reply after the way he left me but I text back, 'Not much.' He must be dying to gossip about Mitchell and Postergate (that's what they're calling it).

It's been a couple of days since Mitchell's death and I haven't moved from the house. Mitchell and the stolen charity money now dominate the national news as well as local newspapers and channels. There seems to be no end of ex-lovers the police are trying to track down, and half the gay community of Liverpool and London are currently on TV or in the papers talking about how bad Mitchell was. Oh, and Harrison's has gone bust. It's shut down. Laetitia phoned and made a joke about our scouting the agencies together, which I suppose I'll have to do soon enough.

I get another text message from Adam:

'CAN U MEET ME IN THE EVERYMAN AT 2:30?'

'OK,' I reply. I switch off the TV and run upstairs with a growing smile. Friends with Adam again! Time to get myself spruced up. Shoot, it's nearly two o'clock now.

\* \* \*

I'm disappointed to see that Adam is sitting with *that* actress friend, Anna (the one who played Jill), when I enter the Everyman bar. Her beautiful ebony black hair is gathered in a ponytail. It makes me notice how fine her eyebrows are. No denying they make a handsome couple.

When I approach she immediately gets to her feet. 'Don't leave on my account,' I say automatically, but she's clearly busy and laughs off the suggestion.

'I'll see you Saturday night,' she says to Adam after kissing him. 'Nice to meet you again, Eve,' she chirrups before skipping away.

'And you,' I lie, my fake smile giving me jaw-ache. 'Here, sit down,' says Adam with a nod to the vacant space left by Anna next to him. I sit opposite him instead. A brief raising of his eyebrows and the way he pulls his mouth show the gesture stings him a little.

'You've got a big night out planned?'

'Sorry?'

'She said "See you Saturday".'

'It's some party. I just say yes to everything. It makes life easier.'

I look at him with fatigue. Why he feels the need to lie is maddening. Do I look like I can't cope with the fact that he has a life and a girl? 'Who'd have thought the next time I saw you Mitchell would be dead and Harrison's gone bust?' I'm trying not to think about the last time we parted.

'You must be relieved, Evie.' 'Yes, that I am.'

'And no police or anyone came to your house or anything?'

'No.' I look at him. 'You can rest easy—I'm not a suspect.'

'That wasn't the reason I was asking. I just wanted to know if you're being left in peace finally.'

'I am.'

'Then let's talk about something else.' He lifts up his chin at me.

'You don't want to talk about Mitchell?' 'No, I don't. I'm sick of hearing his name.'

'Well, I can understand that, but what's the occasion for this drink?'

'Well, let's get one first.' He gets up. 'Now what choo having, babe?'

'Wine—anything.' I realise I've missed his old way of speaking to me.

'Be back in a mo.' He sounds excited about something. Perhaps he's landed a major role.

As soon as he's back and our glasses are filled I tell him to spill the beans. I know he has some news. 'You have something to celebrate, Adam. I can tell.'

'Okay, I'll tell you. I've landed a few good parts. One of them is in *Casualty*.'

'Really?' He nods.

'That's excellent. Congrats.' I pick up my glass and toast him.

He waves a hand dismissively.

'Well, it makes me warm to hear of such success. You deserve it. You're a fine actor, Adam. Have you got your super-cheesy soft-focus picture ready for the theatre walls? Everyone who appears in *Casualty* has one.' I smile challengingly.

'Fuck off,' he says laughing.

After we've been quiet for some moments I break the silence. 'I came to my senses about Egremont by the way. Everything you said was right. It just took me a little while to see it for myself.'

'Seriously, it's all over—no messing about?'

'No messing about; it's quite finished.'

'Thank God for that.' We become quiet again. It feels uncomfortable.

'I've come to my senses about a lot of things.'

'Oh?'

'I was an absurd *bitter little person*. I hated Tilly mostly because I wanted to be her. I wanted her house, her father, her life, even the sister. That will disappoint you, I know, but it was the truth.'

'No. I can understand that.' My smile thanks him for his sympathy.

'Hey,' I say, forcing a brighter smile, 'what happened about your plans to write your own play?'

'Oh, I've done that.'

'You have?'

'Yep.'

'*And?*'

'It's doing the rounds.'

'What, it's on at a theatre now?'

'*No*, it's with agents.'

'Oh, sorry, of course. What's it about?'

'You'll see soon enough. I don't want to talk about it.'

'Okay, I'll shut up. Of course you'll be successful.'

'Now you can shut up,' he says, surveying the room like he's looking for someone. Was he suddenly thinking of her now? God, talking about his writing has made him switch back to *his* world. Perhaps she helped him to write the thing. Perhaps they're a writing team. Would they soon be shacked up in a poky garret, sharing cigarettes while bashing out their latest kitchen-sink masterpiece? Well, I won't stay long. It's enough that he's made friends with me.

'I'll have to be getting back soon, Adam.' I finish my wine. He looks back at me, distracted. He didn't hear what I said. 'I'll go now,' I say again and get up.

'Why? Stay!'

'You're clearly waiting for someone. It's okay, I'm not offended. I'm glad you brought me out.'

'*Brought you out?*' he sounds like the words offend.

'I get that when your other friends enter it's my cue to leave.'

'Come again?' He pours two more glasses of wine.

'You always kept me away from your friends, except for that night at the club, but then you couldn't avoid that and then I never got to hang out with you after all.'

'What?' he laughs.

'Don't do that.'

'Don't do *what*?'

'Look all surprised at what I've just said. Have the decency to understand me. I'll spell it out for you—you never introduce me to your friends because you think I'm odd. You told me that the night at the club. You said I was odd.'

'Evelyn! I don't understand you. Well, wait, I see now possibly what you mean, but you've got it all wrong, babe.'

'How *wrong*?'

'Well, first off, the reason that I've never introduced you to any of my friends is because it's always been "the lads". They're not like the thesps an' all that pretentious bollocks. It's just the lads I went to school with. I thought you realised that—it's just like our sort of little club. Don't tell me—' He breaks off and starts to laugh in amazement. 'You've been silently resenting not being asked to join us? Not being asked out for pool, footie and weed?'

'All right, stop laughing. I hadn't thought of that.'

'I'm not laughing. Well, only with incredulity. Look, if you went out with "the girls" you wouldn't think of inviting me along.'

'If there *were* girls to go out with, no, I suppose not.'

'I can just see it now, you sitting home alone thinking I'm in me flat an it's all like *Friends*, girl-boy-boy-girl right round the living room, all sipping beers and joking.'

'Something like that—all right then. But, girlfriends. Why is it that you've never told me about *any* of your girlfriends?'

'What girlfriends?'

'Oh, get lost.'

'No, really, *WHAT GIRLFRIENDS*?'

'What about you and Jill—Anna. Please don't tell me there's nothing between you.'

'*Anna*—the adzuki bean freak—the girl who lives on quinoa grain and tempeh cutlets? Not me.'

'I didn't understand half of that sentence.'

'Oh, music to mine ears. I was listing the weird food she lives on and never shuts up about. Terrible food is a topic of conversation with her. Can you imagine?'

I recall Egremont raving on about linguine con aragosta, alla insalata di campo and the like and throw him a sympathetic smile.

'But you are going out with her, it's obvious. And you must be pretty far gone in your relationship if you must say yes to everything she organises for you both.'

'No. Just what she organises—for everyone.'

'But you'll go to the party with her on Saturday.'

'Saturday?' he says with irritation seeming not to recollect.

'She said see you at the party. Look, it doesn't matter. Forget it.' I drink more wine wondering where this is going.

'I don't have a permanent girlfriend. I'm basically single.'

'Does Anna know about your single status?'

'It's beginning to sink in.' A dark smile crosses his face. 'Sounds like you're being dishonest with her, or not being fair.'

'Babe, don't worry about Anna. She knows the score. What am I saying? She practically dictated the score. And if by any remote chance she did think we were *together* in that locked sense then she's a slut because'—he smiles in a lighter way—'let's just say she's enjoying her freedom all the same. Seriously, I'm not being an arsehole or anything to her. She's not like us.'

I don't press him. I think I know what he's getting at. 'You know, Adam, you've changed. You've lost your angry head.'

'Comes of doing a job that makes me happy. You should try it.'

I look at him with narrowed eyes.

'I could help you try it.' He leans forward slightly.

'That's something else you've stopped doing—you've stopped swearing. My God, what happened, Adam? Did you finally grow up?'

'Grow up—will ya listen to it! Oh, Eve—come 'ere.'

I get up and go over to his outstretched arms. What the hell, I could use a hug. He pulls me onto his knee. I encircle his neck. Our faces are brought close. I hold his gaze—the sensation is more pleasant than strange. In fact it's delightful, but the memory of the last time I saw him intrudes and breaks the spell.

'What—what is it? Why are you looking at me like that?'

'I'm remembering the last time I saw you.'

'Ah,' he says looking a little ashamed. Then he adds (in a snooty accent), 'A good memory is unpardonable on such occasions.' I smile at the Austen reference, but it doesn't get him off the hook.

'Seriously Adam, your natural impulse was to back away from me when I needed you and that hurt.'

'Except I didn't back away. I went to save you.'

'Oh?'

'I was responsible for that shroud poster wrapped round the Plaza.'

'Liar!' I pull away from him—disgusted. I try to get off his lap but he holds me tight.

'I didn't expect what happened but I'm not sorry and you won't be.'

'You were with Mitchell'—I lower my voice to a whisper—'when he jumped?'

'Not when he jumped—no.'

'When were you with him—why were you with him?'

'I was trying to get him off your back. He intended to pocket the money and blame it on you, but someone else got their first. Yet he was convinced it was you and worse he was beginning to tell people it was you. I knew that poster would stop any heavies going after you. That poster would firmly place suspicion back on him.'

'You did that poster!' I feel panic rising in me again.

'And it worked. I just didn't anticipate the fatal outcome.'

'But am I really in the clear? The money hasn't been found. Perhaps they'll come after me still.'

'It has been found.'

'The money—all five hundred grand?'

'All of it.'

'Oh thank God! Oh, Adam—really? Then it's all over—but who took it?'

'It was Ben.'

'No! So he's been arrested?'

'No, he's quite free.'

'He still has the money?' I'm getting seriously confused.

'No he doesn't still have the money.'

'But the police have it, right?' He shakes his head. 'Then who does have it?'

'I do.'

## 30

EVEN THOUGH HE'S SHOUTING my name and everyone's looking I can't stop running. I don't want to hear anymore. No more about that money. No more fear of the police. No more sick drunken Becky. No more suspicious mother and her allegations, accusations—only now I won't have innocence on my side if I listen to Adam. 'Will you fucking stop, Eve.'

'I don't want to hear it. I don't want to know what you've done.'

'But I did it for you. Well, actually, taking it from Ben was the result of serendipity but—'

I turn and fly at him.

'Seren-fucking-dipity?' I yell in his face. 'You've stolen nearly five hundred grand and you think you're going to get away with it because of luck. That and using me as an excuse?' I put my face even closer to his. 'People like us don't get five hundred grand scot free. Not now. Not ever. Don't you fucking get that?'

'You're catching a bus with me. Come on, don't argue.' I want to scream but instead I close my eyes and count.

When I open them I nod. 'Good,' he says with relief.

The bus is full and we have to sit apart. My head is reeling and none of my thoughts are articulate. The bus turns into the Albert Dock. The place is heaving with busloads of school kids and tourists spilling in and out of the cafes and museums. Becoming increasingly windblown, we walk along cobble stones past the boats until we're staring at the choppy dirty waters of the Mersey.

'I took that money to get you off the hook.' I look at him.

'And then you got greedy?'

'Things changed. Mitchell was dead by the time I got home with it. Look, will you hear me out? Can I tell you what happened? All of it?'

'Yes. Tell me.'

'As soon as I knew you were in trouble—after Laetitia told me—I went straight to the bastard's hotel. The first thing I saw was Mitchell's yellow Porsche. Actually, I heard it. The noise from the alarm was deafening. It was all smashed up. The hotel staff were outside gawping at it with their hands over their ears. You could tell it wasn't an accident and that someone had taken a golf club to it or something.'

'God,' I say in a whisper.

'I took the lift to the top floor. Mitchell was in. I knew something was wrong, really wrong when he opened the door. He was sweating like a smackhead on giro day. He kept saying, "Tell me you've got my money. Tell me that bitch gave you my money." It was obvious he really thought you had it. It didn't matter what I said about your innocence, he wouldn't believe me.'

'You did that for me?'

'Let me get this out. I need to tell you.'

'Okay.'

'He exploded when he found out I didn't have his money but before he could do anything, his phone rang. He looked at the screen and started hyperventilating. He took the call in the bathroom but I could hear everything. He was telling some bloke that he didn't have the money yet, but he would get it. I could tell the guy on the line was threatening him. Mitchell started whimpering like a dog begging this bloke not to do whatever it was. Then he—cowardly snivelling fuck—said your name. He told this fucking gangster prick to get it from you. That's when I saw red and left.'

I stare at Adam amazed. 'And when did you think of the shroud poster?'

'That came to me almost instantly, when I was walking out of the hotel. I saw one opposite advertising a new gym. The Drogar Theatre had had some done. I knew they'd have the contact. They're actually illegal, these ones, but anyway, it doesn't matter. I got it done.'

'But the money—how come you have the money? No, wait. What made you think Ben took it?'

'Two things. I knew Mitchell didn't have it because he genuinely thought you did. The other person in that room that night was Ben, but you had said he was only there for a short time. It wasn't till you fessed up that you'd slept with him there that I saw what must have happened. That changed everything.'

'You ran out on me that day because the penny had dropped?'

'The penny? It was a brick.'

'So what made you so sure it was Ben?'

'Don't take this wrong, Eve—I knew he wasn't into you enough to sleep with you just for the hell of it. He's the kind of guy who risks nothing he doesn't have to. Laetitia also did some asking around her TV friends, of which she does have some, and it turns out he's seriously into Tilly, and he's faithful. Apparently, she isn't and he's something of a dupe, but that's another story. Anyway, her father thinks he's a no-mark, which of course he is. Ben needed the money so he could marry her.'

'How did you manage to steal it from him?'

'There was filming up by the Old Church near Covent Garden, one of those period dramas. I'd been doing some work as an extra. Ben was there off and on with Channel 9 doing camera pieces. Actually, from what I could tell he was little more than the tea boy—but anyway. When I went, he was there again. I kept in the background. He was bragging about his apartment and invited a few of them over. You'd have thought Leonardo DiCaprio was among them he was so chuffed when they agreed to go round. I couldn't believe my luck. I followed to see where he lived. I was planning to go back later and break in but there was such a crowd and he never even looked at me.'

'You went in there and then?'

'I did. He took everyone out onto the balcony to see the views. It was quite a sight—them all dressed in ruffs and wigs. I went straight to his bedroom and started opening wardrobes. It was sitting there in a zip bag—not even hidden like five hundred grand is small change. That's how much of a spoilt rich twat he is.'

'He'll think it could have been any one of them.' I don't believe it, but I'm seriously wondering if Adam really could get away with this.

'Exactly. Eve, he tried to pin that on you. I also saw he had a bag full of benzos.'

'Benzos?'

'Benzodiazapine. It's for treating insomnia. It's a sleeping pill, a tranquilizer.'

My look is asking how he knows all this.

'It's what me ma had in her bedside drawer. I could just about read before they took me off her. Anyway, the point is, that's what he'd have put in your drink when he saw the alcohol you'd drunk hadn't done its job. Why else would you have gone back to sleep in Mitchell's suite?'

'For my headache, he gave me aspirin. And he was putting a drink in my hand all night.' It's starting to dawn on me finally.

'Neither Mitchell nor Ben succeeded though. But we can.'

'How can you know that?'

'Think of the people chasing after him. There isn't one person who won't think the underworld sucked up that money. The police will be chasing dead ends for years or they won't even bother.'

'Mitchell didn't go to the police about me,' I say, looking at the choppy river.

'Exactly,' says Adam more hopefully. 'We could use that money, Evie. You could get yourself on a media course and develop your documentary skills. You could do your piece on the parks and the schools—help kids like Tommy. You know where the money came from. It's money that needs to be given back, but in some meaningful way.'

Turning away from the sea I look at him. Disguising a sigh, I say, 'We could open our own Academy with sports facilities to rival those of Eton. I'll commission Tilly to bedeck the walls with inspiring art. Why, she may even give a few sculpture classes to our lumpen little proles. You know, with all that money, we'll not only give the underprivileged kids something to do at the weekends, we'll take them skiing to Passo delle Radici or wherever they like. With our *five hundred grand* there won't be a horizon too distant for our urchins to reach.'

Adam smiles and shakes his head. 'Art teacher Tilly aside, all that you just said isn't an impossible dream.' I groan with frustration. 'The money can't do all that at once, but we can rally people and raise money over time—create our own kind of charity. That Spanish footballer—the one who liked your speech—'

I look at him in astonishment.

'I know it all darling.' He winks at me. 'We'll get him on side. There must be hundreds, thousands of decent guys, and for that matter, sportswomen like him. You can pitch to the schools to get them involved too—put your sales expertise to some good use finally. Me too, I'll muck in.'

'What we have in our hands is a stone. What we need to do is make it roll.' He plays out an action that looks like someone ten-pin bowling.

'Adam, you're dreaming. It's wrong and you have to give the money back. I don't have any more words.'

He looks away. When he turns back to speak I can see he's struggling to find a new angle.

'What are you so scared of, Eve? I thought you had more balls than this.'

'Balls?' Then I hit him with it: 'My father committed suicide because he stole and got found out. I don't want you to end up like my father.'

'I read about your father and I'm sorry. But that was different. Very different. You know it was. Stop blindly confusing the two. One was a crime—end of. This is an opportunity.' I smirk at the hollow sound of his last words.

'Okay, not put well, but ... Look, have faith in me, Evie—that's all I'm really asking.' He takes my hand. His mouth is straining with consternation. His eyes are pleading with me to agree, and suddenly I can't think of a single objection. There's something in his look, in that little speech, which convinces me of his truth. He nods and breathes with relief when he sees he's got through.

'Life certainly wouldn't be dull,' I say welling up with emotion.

'It won't.' He puts his arms around me. 'And don't worry about anyone finding out about the money. It's forgotten. No one will miss it now and we'll be discreet.'

'It's hard to believe I could actually do something I'd enjoy.'

'It's never been easier to make a noise in the media. You'll be an award-winning docu-journo in no time.' I frown at this. He carries on. 'Champion the scallywags,

Evie. Get their playing fields back. Campaign against the smashed-in bus shelters, boarded-up houses and any other piece of urban ugliness that offends you, and hook up with everyone else who wants to put boats back on the park lakes and live in a decent place.'

'Boats on the lakes? I think that was your axe to grind.'

'Ah, maybe it was. Perhaps we'll have to fight that cause together.' He smiles and we both start laughing. 'But you see what I'm getting at?'

'I do, Adam, and indubitably, I begin to think this not-so-diabolical scheme could work.'

He nods in firm agreement and cuddles me close. 'And if you marry me someday, which of course you will—.'

'Don't talk about marriage. The idea makes me cringe.'

'Not now then, but one day, then we'll have to have Laetitia as bridesmaid.'

'If only to see what she turns up in?'

'Oh yeah'—he hugs me tighter—'that I wouldn't miss.'